Julius Stinde, L. Dora Schmitz

The Buchholz Family

sketches of Berlin life

Julius Stinde, L. Dora Schmitz

The Buchholz Family
sketches of Berlin life

ISBN/EAN: 9783742894083

Manufactured in Europe, USA, Canada, Australia, Japa

Cover: Foto ©Andreas Hilbeck / pixelio.de

Manufactured and distributed by brebook publishing software
(www.brebook.com)

Julius Stinde, L. Dora Schmitz

The Buchholz Family

THE
BUCHHOLZ FAMILY.

SKETCHES OF BERLIN LIFE.

By Julius Stinde.

Translated from the Forty-ninth German Edition.

In Two Parts. Each, 12mo, $1.25.

"We cannot recall another work, fictitious or other, in which the middle class is viewed from the inside. The author does not as an outsider satirize the class he describes ; he merely laughs at such follies or absurdities of individual members of it as, in life, their friends would see and smile over."—*The Nation.*

"The author's hilarity is always cheerful and elevating, and for unadulterated humor, for quiet, unobtrusive fun, commend us to this famous book."—*Hartford Post.*

"Not Berlin alone, but the great Chancellor himself, have expressed their delight over the Buchholz family. All those quiet, innocent household festivals which delight honest Germans are pleasantly described. Herr Stinde's pen is of the quiet, pleasant kind, and never coarse, and he is the best representative of true German humor we have yet seen."—*New York Times.*

THE

BUCHHOLZ FAMILY

SECOND PART

SKETCHES OF BERLIN LIFE

BY

JULIUS STINDE

TRANSLATED, FROM THE (FORTY-SECOND) EDITION OF THE GERMAN ORIGINAL

BY

L. DORA SCHMITZ

NEW YORK
CHARLES SCRIBNER'S SONS
1887
[*Authorized Translation*]

CONTENTS.

THE BUCHHOLZ FAMILY.

PART II.

EDUCATIONAL PLANS.

As long as my daughter Emmi was still unmarried, I did believe that she might become happy with the man who, according to my idea, Providence had selected for her. But now I think the contrary, and can only suppose that human life develops as many varieties as the balsams we sow in flower-pots. We fancy that only well-developed, rosy-red blossoms will come up; but when they do appear, some of the flowers are of a most ordinary shade of violet, others are red, but single; whereas not more than two or three show blossoms of the kind described in the catalogue. Some do not come up at all, or if they do, the buds drop off before opening.

Or is it that good fortune is not big enough for every one to have a slice, such as I and my Carl have had? Why` is it that we are happy and content? Because Carl would most assuredly have had the highest respect for his mother-in-law, had it not been that she died before our marriage. I could swear that Carl would have acted very differently towards her from what Dr. Wrenzchen does towards me. I cannot, indeed, complain that he is wanting in polite speeches and phrases, but the more pleasant his manner, the more suspicious he appears to me; for, according to what cultured people say, those who excuse, accuse

themselves. If he meant all he said, he would at once
have packed off that cook of his, when she was not
only rude, but insolent to me. A mother-in-law has as
much right in the kitchen of her newly-married daughter as the daughter herself, especially when the young
wife is inexperienced and is about to give her first
party; for although there may be no question about
treating the guests to a surprise, they ought at all
events to be made to feel some degree of respect for
the household arrangements. Therefore when a cook
hinders a mother-in-law in this duty, planting herself
in front of the hearth, and, by making use of uncul-
tivated language, forces the mother of her mistress to
concentrate herself backwards out of the room, then, I
say, it is the sacred duty of the son-in-law at once to
fetch in the police, and to have the wretched creature
locked up with all possible speed. Now as the doctor
did not have this done, I know well enough what to
think of his polite speeches and complacent remarks;
these may be said to be the brazen shield of the arch-
fiend, by means of which he wishes to thrust me off,
that I may not have an opportunity of telling him the
truth to his face. But he will find all that useless;
opportunities cannot be thrust aside for ever. When
once they do come, they come with the certainty of
the multiplication table. And then we shall see!

I had at first resolved never again to cross the threshold on the other side of which I had been so shamefully treated without provocation. On second
thoughts, however, it struck me: before Frau Buchholz submits to be chased away by a fury in the
kitchen, things would need to be very different. One
does not so readily give up one's innate privileges. Of
course, when I go to the house I take no more notice
of that cook than if she were mere air; not a look do I

give her, not a "good-day," not even a condescending smile ; I pass her by as if enshrouded in icy disdain, like a wet bathing-sheet. And she—in her thick-skinnedness—takes absolutely no notice of all this.

Emmi is always immensely pleased when I look in of an afternoon to coffee. Dr. Wrenzchen is at that time out on his rounds, and we can chat away undisturbed about things that men can't in the least understand. What astonishes me is that the girl has so quickly adapted herself to her position as a doctor's wife. She writes down the names of all the people upon whom he has to call, and takes great interest in his different patients; at times even she does not hesitate to make a bowl of strong beef-tea when the case is urgent, and a spoonful of soup is more needed than a spoonful of medicine. It is only on Thursdays, when the doctor goes to his Medical Society—where he plays *skat* till midnight—that Emmi feels lonely and forsaken. "Child," said I, "this is a misery that unfortunately you may have to endure to your dying day; but still you may consider yourself lucky, for there are husbands far more inconsiderate than yours, in fact, who have but three senses, like bears—those of eating, grumbling, and sleeping. You ought never from the first to have tolerated those Thursday-evening goings-out. I am afraid now that it may be too late to educate him."

"If only I were not so utterly alone," said Emmi, " you cannot think how wearisome the hours are when I have to wait for him."—"Do you stay up for him?"—"No, Franz will not have that!"—"So he sends you to bed, does he?"—" He thinks it better for me."—" And all your worry about his not coming home counts for nothing, I suppose? Or can you go to sleep with an easy mind, while he turns night into day with his beer-drinking chums? I couldn't!" "Mamma, what is it you have against Franz?"—"I? Nothing whatever, except these Thursday evenings and the cook." "Oh, don't bring up that old dispute, mamma; the girl has had her scolding and will not forget herself again. As to Franz, he bargained for these Thursday evenings from the very outset, and I agreed."—"If you are happy as things are, it is not for me to interfere; you must know best what your nerves can stand. But what is the use of my talking my tongue sore, if you will neither see nor listen."

Emmi was silent; she then asked: "What harm is there in his spending one evening in the week with his friends? I cannot have him gilded over and rolled up in wadding."—"Is that a tone in which to speak to me, Emmi?"—"Mamma, you must remember I am a married woman now, and do not need to account to any one but my husband for what I do. You know I love you dearly, but I do not like to be treated as if I were still a school-girl."—"And can you not understand that I am acting only for your good?" I exclaimed, "do you think I do not notice that you are not as happy as you ought to be? Do you mean to say you look forward to your Thursday evenings?"

Emmi shook her head almost imperceptibly; but I saw it. After a time she said cheerily: "I mean to get a little dog; it will be a companion for me."

Just as I was about to make a reply, a visitor was announced. It was little Frau Lehmann, the lawyer's wife, with whom Emmi had become rather intimate; and I must confess I like her very much myself, although she is rather inclined to be scraggy. She looks nothing by the side of my Emmi, for Emmi has developed beyond all expectation—her full round arms give her quite a stately appearance; still, little Frau

Lehmann is very bright, and when once she gets over her shyness before strangers, looks very neat and pleasing. Still she never was what we call pretty.

When Frau Lehmann heard of Emmi's wish to have a dog, she said: "I advise you not; a young dog snaps at everything, and lays hold of the newest things first. We used to have one, but in less than a week it had ruined two pairs of embroidered slippers, and a rug that had been given to us; and then if the creature was left alone of a night in the passage, it evidently got home-sick, for it howled in the most piteous way. My husband had to get out of bed and give it a beating to make it change its tune."—"The poor creature!" exclaimed Emmi.—"If a dog howls or makes a noise, it has to be taught better," I put in; "for what men require, that they must have. Did you get the animal to behave better?" I asked.—"We had a good deal of fun with it afterwards," Frau Lehmann answered; "but when our first child was born, we got rid of it. It is not good to let children and dogs play together, dogs are apt to have diseases. You can ask your husband about this, Frau Wrenzchen, he will know."—"It could surely not be dangerous," said Emmi curtly, as if not pleased with the conversation. "I think you had better give up the idea of having a dog," said I, in a soothing tone, "your husband will surely only be too glad to remain at home, once in a way, to please you; or you could come to us when you feel wearied alone—you know you will always be received with open arms in your old home." Emmi seemed to be thinking the matter over, so I considered it well not to say more at present, and therefore turned to Frau Lehmann with the question: "Does your husband go out much of an evening?"—"It depends," she replied, "he has his club and meetings,

which he cannot do without."—"Have you to wait up
for him?"—"I used to be silly enough to do that, and
would keep looking at the clock every five minutes,
and ended by having a cry when it got very late; but
now I find no time for watching and waiting. The
children are up and about early of a morning, and
they are my little world, and give me occupation
enough. And moreover a man must at times have
an opportunity of discussing other matters than domestic worries and nursery affairs, so, of course, he
goes out of an evening sometimes."

"When I was young, men did not go out to restaurants as often as they do nowadays," was my reply;
"but these places are got up in such a luxurious way
now, so utterly beyond the means of the middle
classes, that men get perfectly spoiled, and end in
finding nothing comfortable enough for them in their
own homes, and in the simple arrangements there.
One ought, therefore, to try and prevent their going
out much; and, at all events, when they do go, it
ought to be with their wives."—"And are the children
to be left at home in the nurse's charge?" put in Frau
Lehmann, "I do not agree with you there. One cannot trust these servant-girls for any length of time.
When they know that their master and mistress are
out every evening, they think themselves at liberty to
do as they please, and accept visits from goodness
knows who; they are even quite capable of locking
up the house, and going out for a walk themselves."

"Have you experienced this yourself?" I asked.—
"Oh yes," replied Frau Lehmann, smiling; "one evening when we returned home from a party at an unusually
early hour, my husband actually caught a cockroach
in the kitchen!"—"A cockroach!" I exclaimed, in
surprise.—"Yes, indeed! that's the nickname given

to the fusilier guards from the barracks in the Chaussée Strasse."—"I could tell you a pretty story myself from that quarter," I blustered out.—"You, Mamma?" said Emmi.—"I? . . . Oh, no . . . certainly not."—I felt that I had turned scarlet up to my ears; but I could not and dared not tell Emmi of the affair with the soldier, who, taking me for Jetty, had laid hold of me in the store-room. Were Emmi to tell Dr. Wrenzchen that I had meant thereby to give him an opportunity of proposing to her, he would lose every vestige of respect for me. I recovered myself, therefore, as quickly as possible, and said with forced composure: "What the story was, I do not altogether remember; moreover, it didn't happen to me, but to a friend of mine, and wasn't very interesting after all."—Dark spots in a human life are indeed like rust stains on a fireplace, they are for ever eating their way through. Frau Lehmann, who, thank God, was in a talkative mood, started the conversation again by saying: "And what airs they do give themselves! you would hardly believe it possible."

"You need scarcely tell me that, dear Frau Lehmann," I replied quickly; "for if any one has had experience with servants, it's *me*. They are becoming more high and mighty every year, and would not think of wearing any dress that did not come from Gerson's establishment. And one knows well enough where they get the money from! They make out that visitors give them gratuities; but if they don't find these sufficient, they take to pilfering. Last year asparagus was ridiculously cheap; but when I sent our servant marketing for me, the bundle always cost a halfpenny more than when I bought it myself, and I can assure you the stalks were none the thicker. If one did not forcibly close one's eyes to what goes on, one would never be without the police in one's house."

"I find my servant honest enough," said Frau Leh-mann; "and I should be very well satisfied with her, were she not so wretchedly *difficile* about her eating. My husband is very fond of meat cooked with veg-etables—mutton with savoy or turnips when they are young, for instance."—"My husband won't touch them; I may once in a way venture to give him Tel-tow turnips, but he does not much care about them," was my remark.—"Or beef stewed with white beans, with a little vinegar," added Frau Lehmann; "but our servant won't touch these dishes, she says she has never been accustomed to such eating in her own home, and yet her father is only a common labourer in Rixdorf!"—"The truth is, that they are all aiming at something beyond their own station in life," I replied, corroborating Frau Lehmann's statement; "and when a girl nowadays accepts a place as a servant, she comes as if she were doing one a favour, and then laments to herself that she did not become a pianoforte-player or something of the kind. My washerwoman has a daughter who is being taught the piano, and while the young lady is drumming away at a *Reverie*, the mother has washed three shirts. And yet these people can hardly get a wink of sleep for the hunger that plagues them."—"It's a mercy there's not a conservatoire in Rixdorf yet," said Frau Lehmann, "else my servant might probably be musically in-clined as well. As it is, I have had to forbid all novel reading. Just fancy, she had actually been subscrib-ing for some novel brought round by a hawker, and for which she had to pay forty pfennigs a week—that is more than twenty marks a year!"—"Why, that's more than princes and barons give for books," I exclaimed, horrified.—" And you can have no idea how abominable the book was; in the very first chapter lime is thrown into a foundling's eyes to burn it blind, and this is followed by murder and assassination, and every conceivable atrocity. My husband says such reading has a most injurious effect upon the morality of the people."—" And yet she can't eat meat and vegetables cooked together," I added.—" Is your servant a reader, Emmi?" I asked, for she seemed to have be n listening with but little interest, her thoughts perhaps occupied with other matters. " There must be some trouble in her mind," thought I, " like a splinter in one's finger, that at last begins to inflame and fester."—" I cannot say that I need complain about mine," she replied, evasively. " As long as the girl prepares our food as Franz likes it, and does her work, I have no reason to find fault."—" Of course not," I replied, somewhat annoyed, " yours is the beau-idéal of every perfection. Do not be vexed at our discussing so ordinary a subject; the question about servants was not introduced into the world by you, nor are you likely to put an end to it."—" I can't think how we got on to the subject," said little Frau Lehmann, rather disconcerted.—" It began with the dog," I replied, " and so Emmi is herself to blame."

Frau Lehmann, who must have noticed Emmi's abrupt manner, now rose and said, " Do not be vexed, my sweet, dearest Frau Wrenzchen;" and with this she laid her hand on Emmi's head, drew the little pouting face to her, and gently stroked the fair, golden hair and cheeks of my youngest child, who did indeed at the moment look a little pale. Emmi replied, " Well, I can't say I take very much pleasure in inquisitions held against servant-girls!"—Frau Lehmann smiled, and said jocosely, " Next time, then, we'll discuss the weather; or, better still, I'll bring my boy with me, the young jackanapes—he'll give us enough to talk about. My advice to you is to get a canary, like mine, it keeps the whole house cheery; but I hope one day before that you will pop in upon us in a friendly way." Thereupon "good-byes" were said and Frau Lehmann went.

" What is the matter with you, Emmi?" said I, when the lady had gone.—"She is so taken up with her own children," replied Emmi, peevishly; "and then, why need you have told her about the dog?"—"You did not tell me not to mention it!"—"You might have known that I shouldn't like it. What have other people got to do with my feeling lonely at home sometimes?"

"Your husband must positively be made to sacrifice his Thursdays to you," I replied, with decision; "and in any case you can arrange to spend the evenings with us when he goes out for his own amusement!"

"Without Franz?"

"If he leaves you to yourself, you can surely leave him once in a way!"

" No, Mamma, I will not do that."

"I mean without any rudeness on your part, of course," I continued. "I shall send you both an invitation for next Thursday, to potatoes-in-their-skins and herrings, which I know he is so fond of. The following Thursday the Lehmanns might invite you, and so on, till we get him out of his irregular ways. He must be gently and imperceptibly chained to the family. If this proves unsuccessful you must try the plan of leaving home yourself one evening."

She shook her head thoughtfully.—"Think over what I have said," I added. "If he does not give in now, he never will ; and the little bit of happiness you ought to get out of your lives will be off before you know where you are. Think it over." I then brought my visit to a close.

That same evening I told Carl that I had invited Dr. Wrenzchen and Emmi to spend next Thursday evening with us. "Do not be surprised, however," said I, "if I have the herrings placed on the table undivided."—"Why such a new-fangled idea ?" asked Carl, somewhat puzzled. "It is a delicate piece of domestic diplomacy, Carl," was my reply, "by leaving the herrings whole, Dr. Wrenzchen will be unable to pick out all the middle cuts for himself, as he did last time ; he will have to eat the head and tail bits, like the rest of us."—"But supposing he likes the middle cuts best ? You are generally disposed to give your fellow-creatures what they like best, Wilhelmine."— "I do, Carl, gladly, as you know ; but in the present case it is a matter of education. He's not nearly old enough to have nothing but middle cuts."

THE PRESS FESTIVAL.

MANY changes have occurred in favour of literature since it has risen to the rank of a profession. This, as we know, it formerly was not ; for only on the rarest occasions was anything produced. Literature was generally taken up as a secondary occupation. In fact, it is now no longer considered a disgrace to belong to it ; indeed, we find the Press itself declaring that it has become the seventh great power. I must, however, confess that I have never yet met an editor with a crown on his head, or with a purple robe on in place of a great-coat. It would certainly create a sensation were one of them to promenade *Unter den Linden*, or to go to Kranzler's for a cup of coffee, in any such attire. Still, if one happens to come into personal contact with an editor he makes a very liberal impression, and seems opposed to all domineering principles, except as regards what his own paper may have to say. Apart from the steam-press he is like any other mortal, and his spare time is devoted to amusement.

Hence a Press Ball was announced ; and as a fête is always grander the larger the number of people that attend it, tickets for non-professional persons were also issued. The seventh great power might to a certain extent be said to be giving its court ball ; hence not to attend the festival might be said to be an act of opposition. Besides I had only seen the Winter Garden, with its tropical plants, during a concert, and had never yet seen the adjoining rooms. I was therefore anxious to see what sort of appearance the place would present on a festive occasion ; and I must say my expectations proved far too moderate when I found myself face to face with the reality. It was superb. Up above were the electric lights and wreaths of roses, music on both sides, and on the exquisite parquet floor a large gathering of dancers, who might forthwith be termed a very graceful company—that is to say, the ladies more especially ; the outsides of the gentlemen being distinguished only by the difference in their white neckties ; which were of various shapes, of various materials, and in various positions. Intellect, which is regarded as man's special ornament, is not so much in request at a ball as good dancing ; hence a nimble-legged sub-lieutenant may eclipse even a member of the Ministerial Council, whose dignity seems to have run into his knee-joints. The ladies, on the other hand, looked angelic in their elegant toilettes, and they formed an æsthetic contrast to the gentlemen of the party.

These were my first thoughts as I entered the festive rooms with Uncle Fritz. Carl would not come, much as I urged him; he made out that he stood a long way off from the literary circles. "Carl," said I to him, "do you not every morning read your newspaper?— can you exist without it? Well, then, have you no wish to meet the gentlemen who provide you daily with your mental food, face to face? You can put your subscription-ticket in your button-hole if you like, to show that you belong to the Press as a reading member."

However, it was impossible to persuade him; so, being anxious myself to attend the Press Festival, I asked Uncle Fritz to accompany me. He agreed at once, saying that as I belonged to the profession, he might surely venture to go. He expected, moreover, he said, to enjoy himself very much, if only I did not bully him as I did Carl. The answer he deserved for that remark I kept to myself at the time, for fear of frightening him from going with me; and then, too, the poor fellow has still that secret love-trouble of his to bear.

One day, when an opportunity occurred, I said to him that I could not imagine anything more thankless than when the object of one's affection remained at such an unapproachable distance. His reply to this was: "You are wrong, Wilhelmine, epistolary love has its bright side too." This showed me how determined he is not to give up Erica. But my idea is that the grandmother won't give her to him.

My Carl had another reason for declining to attend the Press Festival. His friend Moderow had a cask of

some special brew which he meant to open that same
evening, and they were all going to meet to enjoy it—
old Bergfeldt, Schramke, Steinkohlen-Müller, and in
addition to their usual party Dr. Paber too, perhaps.
So I said : "Well, then, you may go ; for if there's a
doctor among you, you will probably not come to any
harm. But be sure not to be the last to leave, and
take care not to get under the wheels in coming home."
Betti was to spend the evening at the Police-lieutenant's, where Mila's birthday was to be celebrated; and
so Uncle Fritz was my only escort to the circle, with
which I was partially acquainted as a reader, but
which I had never before met *vis-à-vis.*

When we arrived the dancing had already begun. I
felt somewhat overpowered at the sight of such a large
gathering of people, all strange faces to me ; for, of
course, I could not know how renowned they might be.

Luckily I caught sight of Herr Kleines, who looked
like a mock attaché to an embassy, and I went up to
him. "Do you know the corypheuses?" I asked.—
"All of them," he replied.—"Then point some of them
out to me," said I. He answered that most of them
were exactly like their photographs. That was not
enough for me. When he found that I was not going
to let him off, he gave me his arm and steered me
through the crowd.

He did apparently know a number of the notabilities,
but it struck me that they did not seem to recognise
him. He asked me whether I had got my autograph
album. When I said no, he led me to a Turco-Arabian
tent, made of real Persian carpets, where stood a gentleman who handed every lady a little book in which
the notabilities had entered some intellectual remarks,
in order that they might remain unmolested during
the Festival, and thus able to devote themselves wholly

to the pleasures of the evening. For, indeed, it would be irksome to any notability to have to prove himself a man of intellect throughout the evening. One member of the Committee had undertaken to distribute a literary and poetical souvenir, which was all the more troublesome, as, every time he presented a copy, he had to show the person how it had to be opened. The lid had in fact to be pushed aside to get at the contents, which were both novel and surprising. Those persons who tried to open the case in the usual way, at once destroyed the book, which again was a surprise. If all books were made in this fashion, the book trade would take an unexpected rise; and hence the novelty deserves all praise, for, of course, the object of the Press is to encourage progressive development.

The dresses of the ladies, which I could examine more leisurely when I began to feel more at my ease, were simply magnificent. There were velvets in red, in blue, in black, all embroidered with gold, and brocaded silks in the most marvellous patterns edged with the reallest of laces and flowers. Pearls and diamonds were as numerous as the unnumbered stars of the Milky Way. In a word, the dancers there were all Capitalists.

Herr Kleines declared that many of them had quantities of paste about them; but I'm not likely to believe such calumny. What lady would venture to face the penetrating gaze of the Press in imitation jewelry?

As was but natural, I met Dr. Stinde, who seemed pleased to see me again. We sat down a little to the side, under the branches of an orange-tree, to which real oranges had been attached by wire in a very cunning way; this reminded us of Italy. "It is less dan-

gerous here than on Vesuvius," said I by way of
opening the conversation, which Dr. Stinde immediately took up, and we both revelled in the most delightful of recollections. When any eminent persons
passed by he told me who they were, what they had
accomplished with their pen, and in what department
they had distinguished themselves. This, I need
hardly say, was instructive. "Is that anyone particular?" I asked, upon catching sight of a gentleman
with very expressive eye-glasses on a boldly-curved
nose.—"Why, don't you know Paul Lindau?"—"I
had imagined him very different," I replied; "he is
much more interesting in looks than in his books.
And I should never have imagined him with that expression of suffering round about his mouth."—"That
he probably owes to his critics."—"Do they venture
to attack so uncommon an author?"—"Critics never
hesitate to attack anything; but it was Lindau who
showed them how the thing was done."—"I do not
quite understand?"—"Well, dear Frau Buchholz,"
said Dr. Stinde after a time, "poets are very much
like the birds in a forest; they all sing in their own
way as best they can; and just as every bird cannot
be a nightingale, every poet cannot be a Schiller or a
Goethe. What does it matter that their songs are
not all masterpieces? Well, Lindau appeared on the
scenes one day, and laid hold first of one singer and
then of another, mercilessly plucked out their feathers,
and left them to hop off stark-naked, amidst the
laughter of the rest of the world."—"That is positive
cruelty to animals," I exclaimed, horrified.—"It is
only poets that are treated in that way," continued
Dr. Stinde, "in order that the public may admire the
smartness of critics. And as no one sees the tears
wept by the despised poet, and no one is troubled by

his secret sorrow, Lindau's little jokes were eagerly welcomed by the public."—"And is this the kind of joking that the others learned from him?"—"Yes; and, in fact, they have proved themselves good pupils. Some have devoted themselves exclusively to becoming literary sharks."—"Without further ado?"—"The less ado the better. When Lindau himself began to ponder and to create—when he, too, like the other birds of the forest, started a song of his own, they made a set at him and plucked the brightest feathers out of his body; and however much it hurt him he had to put on an air of pleased indifference, for he did not wish to commit himself. Now, perhaps, you can account for the melancholy expression round about his mouth. You must have noticed that any vexation first becomes evident by the person letting the corners of his mouth drop."—"That's just what my Betti does at times," I added, in support of his remark. And as a Press Ball is the most appropriate scene for discussing literature, I added: "Our Betti has talent, but she has not yet quite got into the way of writing poetry. If I knew of any one in the profession who could give her some hints, she might accomplish something. Any plucking out of feathers that Lindau might attempt, he would have to settle with me!"—"I do not for a moment doubt that," replied Dr. Stinde, laughing; "a few minutes ago I met a gentleman who is a member of the National German Rhyming Society, who may possibly be the kind of man you want."—"He would only need to teach Betti the elementary rules, and, perhaps, afterwards touch up her verses. I should think this is all that is necessary in art and literature?"—"For a lady quite sufficient," said Dr. Stinde, "what may otherwise be wanting her talents will effect."—"You certainly have hit the nail on the head there, Doctor," said I, and then asked him whether it would be likely that we could find the gentleman now.

We set out on the hunt for him, and found him leaning against the trunk of a palm tree, his head with its cluster of fair curls, resting thoughtfully upon . his right arm, the hand artistically touching his cheek. His left hand was holding a red velvet note-book. His necktie was not white, but light-green in colour. In fact, I had always pictured a living poet somewhat like this man. Dr. Stinde introduced us ·to each other—"Feodor Wichmann-Leuenfels—Frau Wilhelmine Buchholz."—"I am very pleased," said I.—"You were no doubt just writing some poetry," added Dr. Stinde, pointing to the little note-book.—"You have guessed rightly," replied Herr Feodor Wichmann-Leuenfels, "and I think I have succeeded in penning some excellent lines. Will you judge for yourself?"— "Not just now," said Dr. Stinde evasively, "but if you would read your poems to Frau Buchholz, at her own house . . . ."—"That is just what I was about to ask," I broke in, interrupting the Doctor, and gave the young man our address, with the request that he would call upon us. When he had accepted the invitation Dr. Stinde drew me away forcibly. "Are you not an admirer of poetry?" I asked.—"All in its own good time and place," was his answer; "I like poetry best when I can read it quietly to myself. If I find a single grain among the chaff in a book of poems, I am but too delighted, for I know that all the inferior portions will be forgotten, and that which is of value will live. When time has purified it, the people will store it up in their treasure house, that is, in their hearts."—"Do you think the people have an understanding for such things?"—"No," he replied, "but

they have feeling. So-called understanding may be
said to be the patent with which critics cause so much
mischief. It is not understanding that creates works
of art, but feeling; it is to feeling that we owe all
that is best in us. And thus, when understanding
casts its supposed infallible judgment upon the inexplicable charm of poetry, it always seems to me as if
some one were trying to measure the scent of flowers
by the yard. No philosopeer has yet solved what the
beautiful really is."—"But surely there can be nothing simpler than that," I exclaimed; "the beautiful is
everything that is beautiful; a blind man might even
feel that with his stick."—"You must surely have
studied Hartmann's philosophy of the unknown," said
Dr. Stinde.—"What makes you think that? and how
can you suppose that a practical woman like me can
find time for study? Still I admit I have an appreciation for what is beautiful, for I always prefer it to
what is ugly."

"I will introduce you to a gentleman of the profession who is quite of your opinion," said Dr. Stinde;
"here he is coming towards us. Herr Ludwig Pietsch.
. . . . Frau Buchholz would be happy——" "Ah! I
shall be charmed," said the gentleman, and gallantly
gave me his arm. I, however, could not get out a
word, I was so overpowered at the thought that I was
walking beside Ludwig Pietsch; one word from him
in the *Vossische,* and next day I might be standing before the world in spotless glory; or, it might happen
that he mentioned some one else, then one's choicest
dress might as well have been thrown to the cats.
The majesty of the great power overawed me, as he
graciously began to address me and let his eye rest
upon me. However, his manner as an accomplished
gentleman presently gave me courage, and with a be-

seeching glance up at him, I said : "Pray do not examine it too closely, Herr Pietsch, I have only got my second best dress on to-day; when one reaches a certain age——"—"Now you are jesting," said he, kindly cutting short my last words, "with your charms you put many of the youngest in the shade."—"If the Press says so I suppose it must be true," I replied, embarrassed. He then drew my attention to the wonderful tones of colour which the electric light brought out upon some of the ladies' dresses, and explained the whole animated scene to me, after which we had to part, however unwillingly, for the lectures were about to begin, and many other ladies were no doubt hoping to be taken notice of by him.—On Tuesday, sure enough, I found my name in the morning paper, and the paper-boys had to carry me—among the list of distinguished visitors and recognisable to all my most intimate acquaintances — through all Berlin, bringing radiant joy into cottages and palaces.

The ideal part of the festival then began. The stage—as I learned from a contributor to an archæological paper—was arranged exactly according to an antique model, except as regards the curtain, the bed-screen and a Bechstein piano. A lady of the dramatic profession recited something. She had a copy of the poem fastened in front of her fan, as the ancient Greeks had no prompter, but she spoke as if from her very soul. Unfortunately I could not follow a word she said, as the acoustics of the Winter Garden are rather indistinct, and I was rather far back in the area, but I was deeply moved by the tone of her voice. And, indeed, it does not much matter about the words if only the hearer is affected, and particularly at a Press ball.

The considerate committee had arranged a break in

the proceedings for supper, in order that the musicians, too, might have some refreshment. There was one thing that did not please me, in fact, that had long displeased me, namely, that the men-servants should be running to and fro in tail-coats, like the gentleman-dancers; of course the servants' coats differ in so far as they show a greasy-kind of shininess. At such festivals the attendant spirits ought to be clothed in a suitable livery, or have white aprons tied on in front of them, as has become the custom in some of our more fashionable restaurants. Uncle Fritz thinks that any such arrangement would affect the value of left-off tail-coats, and that this would exercise an unwarrantable reaction upon the national wealth. From a domestic economy point of view he may be right; but I hold to my opinion as regards the outward look of things at a festival.

I was much pleased in making the acquaintance of a lady colleague, that is, of Frau Vely, the authoress of very charming novels. "My dear Frau Vely," said I to her, "how do you come by all your knowledge of life? our human existence seems to have scarcely a secret from you?"—"Dear Frau Buchholz," she answered frankly, "I write with Leonhardi's blue-black ink, it does not put drags on to the wings of the mind." I determined to procure some of that ink the very next day, not being one of those who overlook a good piece of advice; for it often happens that a great deal depends upon mere trifles. We conversed for some time, and quite agreed that the festival was incomparable.

That it was indeed, for although the oranges gradually disappeared from the orange trees, where human hands could reach without actual climbing, still the notabilities remained. Celebrities were to be seen on

all sides, celebrities whose portraits even we in the
Landsberger Strasse do not manage to see, and
towards the end of the evening I had almost thrown
off the uneasy feeling that had oppressed me on first
entering. I even took the liberty of introducing
myself to Ernst von Wildenbruch, and recommended
him to try Leonhardi's ink, telling him that anything
written with that ink could not fail to win the approval of the Press.—"My dear Madam," he replied,
" I have used nothing but that ink for years, my *Chris-
topher Marlowe* was written with it from beginning to
end."—"Then I do not comprehend the critics," I exclaimed is astonishment.—"You are not alone there,
dear Frau Buchholz."—"Do you know what," said I,
" I would advise you to give your tragedies very
cheerful endings, the Press has always something to
say in favour of what provokes laughter."—"One tear
which a poet calls forth will drown any number of
vexatious utterances that appear in print: tears form
the dew that produces new buds."—"And so you work
on heedless of what they say?"—"Yes, precisely so,
dear Madam."—"Even when you know that they will
at once be down upon you again? That is truly cour-
ageous."—"Poetry is my second home, I have sworn
it the same fidelity as my German Fatherland."

Unfortunately, just at that moment there seemed to
be a general break up, and although I would have
liked, above all things, to have had some further exchange of thoughts with other of the notabilities, I
was obliged to set off homewards with Uncle Fritz.
He had enjoyed himself too, and thought the show of
ladies magnificent.—"Well, you see," said I, "how
unnecessary it is for you to look abroad, when you
can have a far greater an I a better choice at home."—
" Unfortunately, the married ones were the nicest," he

replied.—"What sort of principles are these?" was
my remark.—"Come now, Wilhelmine, that's enough,"
he answered abruptly, and began whistling a valse.—
"How very different Ludwig Pietsch was," thought I
to myself, "and how well informed all the other gentlemen were. But brothers rarely have any sisterly
feeling of tenderness."

My heart was so interlarded with my experiences,
and so full of the many meetings I had had with distinguished persons, that I wanted forthwith to tell
Carl some of the occurrences most worth knowing;
but it was as impossible to rouse him out of his sleep
as it must have been to wake Sleeping Beauty when
she had begun the first quarter of her hundred years'
sleep.—I called out to him, "Carl, here I am back
again." He never stirred or moved. I shook him.
But all in vain. I felt certain of this; they must all
have been drinking some specially poisonous stuff, for
I had never yet seen Carl so etherised.

In what sort of state had he come home? Perhaps robbed of everything he had? No, there lay his
watch on the table, and the glass not broken. But his
purse? It was in his trouser-pocket with his keys,
where he never left it when in his normal state. "He
will have a pretty headache to-morrow by way of
punishment," said I, examining his purse, for it struck
me as unusually bulky. What could be inside? A
very handful of beer-tickets. I must know what this
meant. "Carl, what's the meaning of all these beer-
tickets?" I called out into his ear, raising him up
and shaking him gently as well as I could.—"Mina
. . . . one bit more . . . . to get out of the habit!"
he muttered with some difficulty, and turned with a
jerk out of my hands and fell back among the pillows.
"Whatever makes him call me Mina?" thought I, "it's

quite contrary to his usual way. Well, just a little patience, to-morrow I shall know what they've been doing to him. It's a pity, to be sure, that he'll not be able to enjoy my account of the Press festival; that can be appreciated only by a clear head and an interest in the ideal."

With the thought whether Ludwig Pietsch would remember me, I put out my light.

DOMESTIC ART.

WE paid a visit to the exhibition of cheap furniture that was being held in the glass building of the late Hygienic Exhibition, and as the prices asked for some of the articles, of really good workmanship, were astonishingly low, we purchased a wardrobe to replace the large clothes-press which had been standing in the passage. The lower drawers of the old one would never open properly if one wanted anything out in a hurry, and then too the thing was worm-eaten. Carl approved of the investment, for the new wardrobe is divided in the middle, and he can now have his realm all to himself, and no longer needs to grumble that his clothes are hung on the back pegs, and that when he wants some particular coat he is sure to lay hold of the wrong one.

When, however, the new wardrobe was put up, we found that it was smaller than the old piece of furniture, and hence that it did not cover the same space of wall. Now the piece of wall covered by the old press had never been papered, for I remember we bought a remnant of paper cheap and it proved hardly sufficient to paper the whole passage. We could not get it matched at the time, and thus the wall behind the press was left in its original condition, a bright blue in oil paint. But, of course, not a trace of this was seen when the old cupboard stood there.

" The whole passage will have to be repapered for the sake of that new piece of furniture," said Carl ; " what shall we have gained by the change ? "

" Don't trouble about that, wait and see how cleverly we shall manage it."

He shook his head as he went off, but did not venture to oppose me by slighting remarks.

I had said " we," meaning not only myself, but Betti and me, for without her help I should not have been able to carry out my idea.

Betti had, in fact, taken to painting lately, for she had no inclination whatever to become a governess, and yet did not wish to be without some regular occupation. And what was the use of her trying to pass a hard examination, simply to keep children tidy and to teach them a little spelling? Uncle Fritz too dissuaded her, by maintaining that "children are horrid, they can do nothing but cry or sleep ; the pleasantest moments in family life are when the children are asleep." —My reply to this was : "You will talk very differently some day, my boy."—Whereupon he answered, "I have certainly had to put up with noise enough from our club-poets, but I shall never get accustomed to infants' music unless I invest in a pair of india-rubber ears."

" Children's voices are like angels' voices," said I, " but, of course, they need be one's own children. Your vocal society, 'The Whooping-Cough,' no doubt makes a pretty hullabaloo ; I wonder the neighbours tolerate such uproar."—"They gain something by it, at all events ; they would scarcely know what a mouse was like if they hadn't preserved one in a glass case."

Betti had always shown a taste for art. Even as a child she would cut out figures from the fashion papers, colour them neatly, and then gum them into an exercise book. And painting has become such a favourite occupation with ladies, that the most eminent artists give them lessons nowadays. And then to think what prices are now given for paintings! Menzel, a short time ago, got £4500 for one picture, and, as Betti says, he has not even used the most expensive colours. Such demands we, of course, should never make, although naturally one would like to cover one's expenses.

Betti, to be sure, is only at the first stage yet, and paints upon articles of wood ; still I must say she has been very diligent. She has painted three clothes-brushes—one for me, one for her father, and one for Dr. Wrenzchen—all three in flowers. They might have been bought at a shop, they are so artistically finished. If only the varnishing did not come so expensive. Betti tried to do it herself at first, but she never succeeded altogether, and could not manage to get a smooth surface properly. Smaller articles, such as plates, paper-knives, pocket-books, and little boxes, are very useful for giving away as presents ; among our friends and acquaintances there are birthdays enough to make it difficult to overtake them all with any show of respectability.

So on the day in question I said to Betti : "There is now a chance for you to give a proof of your talent, and we will mightily surprise your father. What I want you to do is to paint in the pattern of the wall-paper where there is no paper on the wall, and to make it look exactly like the rest of the wall. He will be astonished when he finds that he can't distinguish between the deception and the reality, unless he examines it very carefully."

Betti, it is true, did think this would be too difficult for her, as she had never yet tried wall painting, a branch which was to be taken up later, under Gussow, when she had finished with painting on wood, and had passed through a course of landscape painting, which is very carefully taught by the society of Lady Artists; still she said she was willing to try. From the outset I had looked forward to the moment when I should be able to say to Carl : " Now, then, what do you say to that ? And to think that the expense would not be worth speaking about ! Simply an instance of domestic art."

We took a couple of old cream jars and went to fetch the paint. It was not easy to find the right shades, but I hurried home and ripped a piece of paper off the wall from below the place where the press had stood. This I gave to the young man in the colour-shop, and it enabled him to understand exactly what we wanted, and he mixed the colours accordingly. When Betti saw this she was most anxious to set to work, a proof that she has the talent. The young man also selected the brushes, a large one for the grounding, and several smaller ones for working out the details. That same evening Betti sketched out the pattern, and on the following morning, as soon as Carl had gone to the office, we set about the work. That is to say, Betti undertook the artistic part, and I stood by to assist her with good advice. However, as she declared she could do nothing if I kept watching her, I went off to the kitchen. We were going to have pigeons for dinner, which Carl likes very much if they are carefully prepared, and cooked briskly, with a little onion and parsley root ; so I had enough to do. Cooks rather dislike preparing this dish, as it gives some trouble, and, moreover, they are apt to tell lies about it, by declaring that there were no pigeons of the kind to be had at the market.

However, before the last bird had passed through my hands, my motherly interest in Betti's artistic work induced me to go and see how things were progressing with the fresco painting. I found Betti in a not very amiable state of mind, for when I appeared in the passage she said rather shortly : "What is it you want?"—I noticed at once that something was amiss, for when Betti's voice has a snappish sound she is not given to be amiable, and so I said with the utmost gentleness : "Well, have you succeeded in accomplishing anything, my child?"

Betti came down off the kitchen steps, upon which she had been standing while pasting up the pattern she had sketched, and then examined the work from a perspective distance.

"Do you think it will do?" she asked.

What could I say? If I said "No," she was quite capable of replying : "Well then, take the colours and brushes and do it yourself." If I said "Yes," then the painting would, of course, remain as it was, and Carl would have every reason to find fault, for the result of Betti's work was really not much of anything.

So after having examined her work from different points of view, and with some show of artistic appreciation, I said : "Betti, the pattern seems remarkably like, but the colours do not quite correspond. Do you not yourself think that the colours are a few shades too light?"

"It *is* all too light," replied Betti, "yet how can this possibly be the case when the young man mixed the colours himself so carefully according to your pattern? Can it be the light, mamma? You know

artists always complain that unless the light is right
it spoils their best paintings."—I was about to agree
to this possibility when a most unwelcome thought
dawned upon me, and proved to be right. The fact
was, I had taken, as a pattern, a piece of the wall-
paper that had always been covered by the old clothes-
press, and which, therefore, had retained its original
and lighter colour.

"Now, mamma," said Betti in a tone of vexation,
"why do you interfere with things when you know
that you know nothing whatever about painting?"—
"No, no, my dear," I replied, "you cannot say that
of me ; have I not climbed nine flights of stairs in the
Vatican to see the genuine Raphaels and the other celebrities in oil?"—"The whole Vatican would be of
no use to us here, mamma," interposed Betti ; "I shall
have to go and get the proper colours."—So she strip-
ped off a piece of the darkened wall-paper and flew
off to the shop, for she too was anxious to have
finished before noon, and I was meanwhile left to my
own thoughts. It seemed clear to me now that Art is
by no means so very easy, and demands a goodly
amount of genius as well.

When Betti returned she said : "Mamma, the work
cannot be done in the way we imagined. First of all,
a background has to be washed in, and when it is dry
the pattern has to be painted upon it."

"Who told you so?"—"The young man in the shop
explained this to me ; he has been in the Academy
himself, it seems."

"Has he studied under Gussow then, that he pre-
tends to know so much?"—"I did not ask him that,
but he did say that selling colours brought in more
money than art."

"He told you that, probably by way of excusing

himself. Think what an amount it would represent
for Menzel to have sold £4500 worth of oil colours
and floor varnish ! He would need to have been selling the stuffs day and night. No, one cannot believe
offhand what such a person says, and need know exactly what he means."

While we were conversing in this way Betti had
painted in the background with the large brush.
There was some paint over, so I used it in trying my
hand at painting a wooden box, and did not find it
very troublesome. " Betti," I exclaimed in glee, " we
shall never again, after this, need to have painters in
the house, we can do everything ourselves, and save a
pretty penny."

When Carl came in to dinner, of course we could
not conceal the painting that had been begun. He
looked at it, shook his head, and said : " Wilhelmine,
I am afraid the difference will be noticed. You had
better give up the painting and have the whole passage repapered."

" And throw money out of the window," I exclaimed.
" No, Carl, I'll not have that ; and it's no encourage-
ment to art to find fault with things at the very outset,
in a hasty way. Wait a little, and then pronounce
your judgment. To-morrow you will have a very
different piece of work to criticise ! " This proved to
be true, but unluckily the work turned out very different from what I had anticipated.

What the reason was I do not know, but when Betti
on the following morning painted in the pattern, the
wall looked stranger than ever. " Betti," said I, " you
have not got quite the right knack yet, I think. What
do you say to painting the whole wall one colour ?
Papa, it is true, prefers it being papered, but that's
because he hasn't confidence in us ; he is sure to be

quite satisfied when the passage is once done, and looks lovely."

We sent the girl Doris to the colour-shop with a pot sufficiently large to hold paint enough for the four walls, and I told her to bring another good-sized brush for grounding, as I meant to help in the work myself. We had decided in favour of sky-blue, having got the idea from the old unpapered patch on the wall, and because everything old-fashioned is again the fashion now.

We were anything but idle. Betti, mounted on the kitchen steps, undertook to see to the upper regions, while I, on my knees on the floor, attended to the lower parts. When we got to the end of our paint Doris was despatched for more. It was a regular hurry-scurry.

"The only thing wanting now are visitors," said Betti jocosely, for she was enjoying the painting as much as I was.—"That would be a pretty mess!" I exclaimed. "Betti, we must be quick and see that we are not interrupted, that the work is finished at once, before papa comes in."

Haste, however, is both exhausting and mischievous. In her hurry Betti knocked the pot of paint off the steps, and the good blue paint splashed over the floor.

There is nothing more horrid than upset oil paint. We wiped it up. But it always seemed to come out again. Nothing we could do would remove it altogether. By way of consolation I said to Betti : "The floor would in any case have required a coat of varnish. Doris will have to fetch some more paint soon, and so she may as well bring back some brown varnish for the floor at the same time."

"And a nice bright red for the border at the top and bottom of the wall," added Betti.

"Will one cupful be enough?"—"Let her take the large office jar," suggested Betti, and off Doris went.

Betti was right. A border did seem necessary to give our work an artistic finish. She hoped, as I myself did, that when once the red lines were drawn in, the unevenness of the painting would not be so conspicuous. Betti again mounted the ladder, and, as she had the ruler in one hand and her brush in the other, Doris had to stand below to hold up the paint pot.

After a time Doris ventured to remark: "Miss Betti, you really mustn't let the paint drop so, my jacket and my whole face are covered with paint." This was true enough, I must admit.

"And this jacket I put on to-day for the first time," Doris continued in a grumbling tone.—"Well, well," said I, "if the paint won't wash out you shall have a new one." With this I turned to my work again. A few powerful strokes with the brush and I could exclaim : "I've finished ! "

But before I had got so far Betti had been muttering : "Mamma, I can't get the border to do, it keeps running down into the other colours. I feel quite desperate."

I must confess I had not expected very much from the border myself, and yet I have never in my life been so deceived about anything. Sure enough there was the red trickling down in long stripes into the blue, for all the world like the choicest of fringes. We tried to drive the red lines upwards with the blue brush, but this seemed only to make matters worse.

"We shall have to do it all over again to-morrow, from the very beginning," said Betti dolefully.

"All this mess over again ! " I exclaimed ; "just look how you have splattered yourself with paint, Betti, and look at Doris ! "

"Sausage-making, which we used to do at home, is nothing to this!" exclaimed Doris.

I used up the remaining blue, by giving a final touch to the wall, Doris cleared away the pots and brushes, and then Betti and I went off to change our dresses. I could never have believed that oil-paint could have splashed so much, some had settled on the very back of my neck. And how difficult it is to get it out of one's finger-nails! It is perfectly astonishing what a speck of paint accomplishes when it gets on to the wrong place! What would the towels be like? Things no longer looked very promising.

We had scarcely finished dressing, and tidied things up as far as we could in the hurry, when Carl and Uncle Fritz came in. I recognised their voices in their exclamations at our handiwork.

"Don't let us go out to them," I whispered to Betti, "let them quietly recover from their first impression, for the first is always the strongest."

Then they came in. Carl, as I could at once see, was not in the best of humours, but Uncle Fritz's eyes actually beamed with delight, and mischievous jokes were flickering round about his mouth.

"Wilhelmine, did I not tell you . . .?" Carl began, in a reproachful tone. Uncle Fritz, however, interrupted him with a laugh: "No, Carl, old fellow, now don't prove yourself a barbarian in art, there's not another such landing as yours to be found in the wide world. Were you to exhibit it at the Cantian's Platz, you would assuredly get the large gold medal."

"I beg you not to make any such insulting remarks," said I; "when people have done their best, there's no need to cast ridicule upon them."

"You no doubt took the blue grotto in Capri as your model, Wilhelmine," continued Uncle Fritz, pay-

ing no heed to my remark. " If only you were to tie
a boat to the wardrobe, the thing would be perfect ! "

" You needn't excite yourself," I replied, " our main
object was economy, and that is quite beyond your
comprehension as a bachelor."

" Economy! " exclaimed Carl, " what have you spent
upon all this m . . . m . . . manœuvre?" (he struggled to find a mild expression, the dear, good fellow).

" The work itself is our affair, and thus will not cost
a farthing ; the rest of the things I have had put down
to our account."

Carl called Doris, intending to send her to the
colour-shop for the bill. Doris came at once, as she
heard herself called sharply. When she entered Uncle
Fritz simply gave a roar of delight. The girl hadn't
had time to wash off all the red paint, and would have
presented an alarming appearance to any one who did
not know what she had been about. Even Carl said,
" Doris, you cannot possibly go out like that ; the
neighbors would think you had committed a murder."

I was uncommonly glad that Doris could not go
out, and that I had time, by carefully leading the conversation, to get Carl off the subject of the bill. For
as appeared afterwards, we had managed to squander
such a considerable amount of paint, that the landing
might as well have been repapered, and without taking
at all a cheap paper, as had, of course, to be done in
the end. I did not tell Carl about Doris's ruined
bodice and dress, which she insisted upon having
made good to her, till the whole affair had been almost
forgotten, and I had solemnly promised Carl never
again to try domestic art upon doors or walls, but to
employ skilled workmen, who earned their livelihood
by the work. I had never imagined that economy,

under certain circumstances, could lead to such an outlay of money.

Betti has again taken to painting wooden articles, although Uncle Fritz declares she has a prodigious talent for painting human beings—as he had seen in the case of Doris. Of course such ill-natured remarks were met with cool disdain by us, and who knows but what the landing might not have been made very beautiful if we had been able to follow out our inspirations uninterruptedly? The old masters took centuries to attain their excellence, and we had scarcely two days at our disposal. But Uncle Fritz has not the slightest idea of all this.

How long Betti means to continue painting on wood, must soon be decided, for I already perceive that we shall here have a case of the supply outdoing the demand. Besides, what can be done with all the things? It shall be my endeavour to win her over to literature, although she does not expect to learn much from Wichmann-Leuenfels.

A REGATTA.

It was high time the regatta came off, for the everlasting talk about rowing had spoilt our pleasant Sundays for three weeks previously. Nothing can be more homely than a family gathering on a Sunday; business is left behind locked office doors, ladies put on their latest newest dresses, and the gentlemen do honour to the day by wearing the cleanest of linen and good cloth coats. In the kitchen, too, somewhat more trouble is taken than upon ordinary week-days, and the cookery book, although not generally used on week-days, is indispensable on a Sunday; for it is pleasant to surprise one's guests with some extra good kind of dish. A family party of this kind on a Sunday really seems to have something sunshiny about it.

Dr. Wrenzchen, my son-in-law, of course agreed to join us at dinner on Sundays, for this would enable them to dispense with cooking at their house, and their servant could go out. That girl of theirs is spoilt in a most inconceivable way. Uncle Fritz has for years been a regular Sunday visitor at our house. He sometimes brings a friend with him, to which we have no objection, and when Betti invites one of her companions we are only too glad; for well-dressed young people are a good set-off to the table.

But mere eating does not make a happy party; there must be pleasant talk, and this we generally had, for Dr. Wrenzchen collects anecdotes throughout the week to provoke laughter, and Uncle Fritz is far from having got to the end of his cheery talk.

But since the crews began to practise, and the day of the regatta is drawing near, Uncle Fritz had not a thought for anything but boating. His vocal society was not enough diversion for him, and he had become a member of the rowing club as soon as that was started. His language got full of foreign expressions, and he assumed a manner that made one suppose that aquatic sports must have a deteriorating effect upon a man's culture. I had often to pull him up for this. Then, too, Dr. Wrenzchen was not at all so enthusiastic about rowing as Uncle Fritz, and persistently refused to become a paying member of the club. This almost invariably led to a dispute between them. Uncle Fritz, moreover, continued to chaff the Doctor about the candlesticks which his colleagues had presented to him as a wedding present, declaring them to be only electro-plate, which Dr. Wrenzchen denied. Their talk, however, had never been as unpleasant as it had lately become, and yet we had to cook for them with the same good-will, and to make the usual Sunday additions.

Thus it was really the highest time that the regatta came off and put an end to these everlasting disputes. For when once humanity has measured its strength, we at last have peace; and this holds good of a regular war, as well as of a horse or a boat race. The boating men seem to spare themselves no trouble, for they had a man over from London for the express purpose of making them give up their beer drinking and potato eating. Meat is the only thing they are allowed to eat, and smoking is altogether forbidden, for it is said to weaken the physical strength as much as young vegetables and late hours. On the other hand they have to get out from under their blankets early of a morning, and row till they get corns in their hands, and are nothing but muscle and sinew. This kind of medical treatment is called training. I should like to know how much there would be left of Herr Kleines if he were trained? I should think nothing but a skeleton and the eyeglass he has lately taken to wearing, perhaps also a spark of the wit, which even Uncle Fritz cannot deny that he possesses.

The long-expected day arrived at last, but with atrocious weather; for days beforehand it had poured in torrents, and on the Sunday morning it came down in the same drenching way. But as the crews were to row whatever happened, as some of the men came from distant cities, we decided to drive out to Grünau in the afternoon, notwithstanding the weather. If people only make up their minds, they can enjoy themselves even in the rain. However, we were fortunate, for upon reaching the Görlitz station at half-past two, the sky showed several patches of blue. It might, therefore, clear up after all.

What crowds of human beings there were at the station! A barrel of herrings is nothing to it. Of space there was nothing to speak of; a dense mass of people were pushing their way into the vestibule, and as dense a mass was pushing its way out. However, all the people got their tickets and also places in the train, for as soon as one train steamed off another was immediately drawn up. Maybach must have been doing a brisk business. When he made up his accounts that night he must assuredly have thought that these boating men put a good bit of money into circulation. The cabmen had their share in the profits, and the tramcars and waggonettes too. There seemed to be a regular migration of the people to this end of the city, a district they otherwise rarely came to see.

The more the sky brightened the merrier the people became, and we were a cheery party in our carriage also, although it contained far more than the prescribed number; however, as Dr. Wrenzchen took his wife on his knee, and Carl squeezed himself into as small a space as possible, we did very well, especially as it was not long before we reached Grünau.

We had ten minutes' walk through a fir-wood after leaving the station. Afar off we could hear the sound of music; we also saw a triumphal arch that had been erected and prettily decorated in honour of the Crown Prince; shortly after that we came to the stairs that led up to the platform, where Uncle Fritz had secured seats for us. I went up without expecting to see very much, and was therefore immensely surprised at the view upon reaching the top.

What a sight! The river Spree is very broad at
Grünau, and looks like a beautiful large lake; the
shores rise up gently and form a narrow strip of
meadow land by the side of the water, and this strip
of land is bounded by a wood of oaks and pine trees.
Further up the river to the right stand the Müggel
Hills, like a miniature mountain landscape, and to the
left, in the distance, the church tower of Köpernick
peeps out pleasantly from amid green trees. The
Langen Lake, as the river is called at this point, had
been decorated in a festive style; in the middle of the
water lay an endless row of large and small sailing
boats, covered from top to bottom with innumerable
flags and streamers that fluttered gaily in the wind.
I would never have believed that so many flags were
to have been had, and such brightly coloured ones
too. And then the numbers of steamboats that were
every moment bringing new batches of people; and
the hundreds and hundreds of little boats with ladies
and gentlemen in them, and the merry bit of bunting
waving at the end. It was only on the water that
there was so much stir. The platform held thousands,
and along the shores other thousands were standing,
while some sensible folk had set up booths where the
multitude could get refreshments.

I could not look long enough at this busy life out
here in the midst of the open country, on the wood-
encircled lake and its shores; and I fancy every one
who was there must have been quite as enchanted as
I was.

Close to our platform was the Crown Prince's pavilion, made of some red material and gold fringe,
and decorated with festoons of oak; it stood exactly
opposite the goal where the race was to be decided.
Of a sudden loud hurrahs were to be heard. The

Crown Prince had arrived. He entered the pavilion accompanied by Prince Wilhelm and Prince Heinrich; every one rose from their seats, and from all sides, from the banks and from the boats as well as the large ships, joyous shouts of welcome arose. The band struck up *Heil Dir im Siegerkranz,* and just as the Crown Prince was bowing pleasantly in acknowledgment, the sun broke through the clouds, shedding its brilliant light over the whole scene of varied colour; the water glittered, the flags fluttered gaily, and wood and meadows looked as fresh as May. We had the brightest of weathers on the green banks of the Spree, regular Hohenzollern weather!

Then the races began. The firing of a gun was the signal that the crews had started far off down the river beyond the Bammel-ecke, where likewise thousands had taken up their stand; at the same moment a red balloon was hoisted to the top of a high flagstaff, and looked exactly like a monstrous poppy in the green surroundings of nature. Nothing could, of course, yet be seen of the boats, but soon they were to be seen coming round the corner. Those who had field-glasses turned them to the point where they had appeared far off. "Who is in front?" was asked right and left. "Is it the Berlin men?"—"The Magdeburg crew seem to be even with them!"—"Where are the Stettiners?"—"Rather far behind."—"The Berlin men are in front!"—"Now they are coming to the curve, then we shall know!"—"Bravo, the Berlin men are ahead."—The boats were coming up, the crew with the large red star on their backs were in front, the light blue Stettiners not far behind. Now we shall see! How they dipped their oars, quicker and quicker, and with increasing force every moment. The boats skimmed along the water like

razors. Then the front boat flew past the goal! It
was the red-starred crew of the Berlin Rowing Club!
They had won!

I was so excited that I could scarcely join in the
universal shouts that welcomed them, but Dr. Wrenzchen shouted enough for two, and smirked away
enough for three; he is always as happy as a little
king about anything that confers honour upon Berlin!
The crews then rested upon their oars. How they
panted! It must be regular horse-work to come in
first. They then saluted the Crown Prince and rowed
back.

The shouts of delight were, however, suddenly
somewhat damped by the appearance of a cloud, from
which fell a shower of peculiarly large drops of rain.
Umbrellas were put up, and in a second the whole
gay and festive scene had vanished. This was only
for a minute, however, for to judge from the laughter
and merriment beneath the roof of umbrellas most
people seemed to have adapted themselves to the inevitable, and were having their fun; and, indeed, ill
humour will not make small misfortunes one jot the
better. It was only those who had on new velvet
dresses that did not join heartily in the merriment;
they would certainly have to send their garments to
Spindler to be steamed and done up, and would thus
lose their fresh look. At any fête where it is likely
to rain, simple dresses are, therefore, generally to be
preferred.

I was absorbed in thought under my umbrella, when
Carl whispered to me, " Did you see them ? "—" Who ?"
I asked.—" The Bergfeldts."—" Is it possible ? " I exclaimed.—" Emil is over there with his betrothed and
his future mother-in-law ; Bergfeldt and his wife are
in front of us, down there in the most expensive seats."

—" Of course she must be here, things couldn't go on
without her ! " I replied, annoyed at her presumption,
" otherwise she might have been content with other
seats."—" They are having champagne," added Carl.
—This cost me a laugh.—" They ought rather to keep
their money and pay their brewer," said I ; " she
understands as little about champagne as a peasant
about cucumber salad. We might ourselves have had
champagne, Carl, only we don't care to be so pretentious. However, if you were to offer me a cup of
coffee, I should most gladly accept it. It would be
uncomfortable to me to sit down there, in such a
bumptious kind of way like some persons."

The rain continued pouring for some time, but when
some one in a loud voice called out, " Umbrellas
down," they were all clapped to at once, for a com-
mand properly given is always obeyed, and not a
single *en tous cas* would have been tolerated. It was
clearing up again also, and the sun was shining over
on the Müggel Hills. Before very long we should
have the sun again ourselves.

" We shall have the best of weathers yet," said I to
Betti, who, however, paid no heed to my remark, and
kept looking, in a melancholy kind of way, across the
water. I watched her a little, and then said to her
anxiously : " Child, are you crying ? "—" Oh, no," she
replied, " it was but a drop of rain," and she dried her
eyes. " If those Bergfeldts are the cause of her
trouble," I thought, " it really is disgraceful of the
family."

In trying to discover what she was looking at, I saw
a young man I knew very well talking to several
others, some little way below in front of us. It was
Herr Max and his friends ; but although I tried with
Carl's opera-glass to find Felix Schmidt among them,

I did not succeed. I knew then what the drop of rain meant : tender recollections had changed into a tear, which in its turn flowed away into nothing, like the unexpressed hope which we had both cherished in our hearts—my silent child and I.

Our attention, however, had again to be turned to the regatta, for one of the most important races was about to take place, namely, for the Emperor's prize. This was a challenge cup, held for the year by the club that won it, and which had then to be competed for anew. Last year the Berlin Rowing Club won it, and now the Berlin Rowing Society, a Bremen and a Frankfort crew were going to try for it. Not any of the other crews succeeded in getting it, however, and after the Frankfurters had twice run into the Bremen boat, they were not allowed to join in the third start. The Berlin Rowing Club won the Emperor's challenge cup again, so it will remain in Berlin, where, indeed, it really belongs. The Crown Prince had the crew of the winning boat introduced to him, and talked a good deal to them, and we were not far off. The Prince is reported to have said that he takes the greatest interest in rowing, and that the Club might always depend upon him attending their sports if his presence was desired. That was truly splendid of him.

The Berlin victories had already induced Dr. Wrenzchen to change his opinion about boating, and when he heard what the Prince had said, he forthwith buried the hatchet which he had hitherto always swung at Uncle Fritz's head when they got on to the subject of rowing. "Well, old boy, what do you say now ?" Uncle Fritz asked him.—"They are a set of confounded fellows, those boating men of yours," said the doctor playfully.—I ventured to remark that I found his language very unsuitable, and added :

" Dear Doctor, on a day of such honour to Berlin as this you might pay more heed to the choice of your words, or has the breeze from the water already had a bad effect upon you ? What are our neighbours likely to think of us ? "—" Dear little mother-in-law, it's only external," said he in reply, and went off with Uncle Fritz to have a glass in honour of their reconciliation.

When they returned the Doctor had actually become a paying member of the Club, which, in my opinion, he ought not to have done in that offhand way without Emmi's approval. It was for him to consider that it would give rise to other outlays of money which might be spent in a more useful way, for instance, in purchasing sufficient crawfish to go round when next he gives a dinner party.

Between the parts we descended from our platform and sat down at one of the many tables which the proprietor of the Restaurant had set up among the trees. Carl treated us to the promised cups of coffee, with which, I think, we were more content than other folks with their champagne. Emmi as well as Betti agreed with me in this, for neither of them care about champagne, and I myself never liked it even when a girl. When the weather is chilly, with rain every now and again, all sensible people prefer something hot, except those, of course, who are pretentious and make a dead set at their health by drinking what's cold. That is certainly not my way. Uncle Fritz took us to see the prizes, which were tastefully arranged upon a table under the oak trees ; gold and silver goblets, a challenge shield in silver, and other valuable articles either for decorating mediæval German rooms or for quenching thirst. All were beautiful and artistic. While my daughters were examining the different things, and Uncle Fritz was explaining the meaning of the ornamentations, I suddenly perceived Herr Max close to us, and in the twinkling of an eye I had laid hold of him. He did not seem prepared for this, as I divined from his embarrassed look, but I did not give him time to recover himself, and said at once : " It is fortunate that we have met, for I must have a word with you. Please give me your arm."—He did so, and before he had time to utter a word we were out of the girls' sight in among the pine trees, where the Grünau Society for Improvements in the Neighbourhood have laid out a number of roundabout pathways, which, however, are not patronised by straight-forward-going people.

I began by saying : " I have much to complain of, Herr Max, and may at once tell you that it concerns your friend Felix's behaviour towards me and mine. You are his friend, I believe ? "—" Most certainly," he replied.—" Well, then, I am right in addressing myself to you ; as a true friend you will not withhold from him anything I may say."—He was about to answer, but I continued : " Please do not interrupt me, it is my turn now, one after the other. You may claim the same right afterwards. Why did your friend not accept the invitation to my daughter's wedding, although I wrote him a special note ? Why did he not even take the trouble to send me an excuse ? What reason had we given him for treating us with such want of consideration ? I think he had no cause for thinking us inhospitable. And you yourself have not acted very much better. What can you say in his justification ? "

He stood before me, his eyes fixed upon the gravel path, as if his answer were to be found there. Then raising his kindly blue eyes, which seemed to have a sorrowful look about them, he said in a low voice, " Nothing ! "

" Is that all ?" I asked.—" I cannot and dare not say more," he replied.

" You were frank, and showed confidence in me at Tegel. You seemed happy in your friend's happiness then. Are you as honestly fond of him to-day as you were then ?"—" Undoubtedly," he said firmly, and his face brightened up.

" Then let me know the mystery."—He again became silent, but after a little said : " The time has not yet come for me to speak, but you may rest assured that you shall know all when I need no longer be silent, and I trust, then, that all will turn out for the best."—" There is nothing very definite in all that," said I ; " can you not be a little more intelligible ? " He made no reply, but asked : " May I send him your kind remembrances ? some such message would, I know, be very welcome to him."—" So he is not in town ?"—" No, Felix has left Berlin for a time."— " Why ? "—" To gain experience in his business."— " Well, you may send him my kind remembrances, for that matter, but, if we were to meet, I do not know that I should have any very pleasant words for him ; and I cannot say that you with your mysterious talk are any more to my liking."—" I am sorry to have aroused your displeasure, but I will gladly bear with it for my friend's sake."—" I do not say I have anything very much against you, but still there's a smell of burning, and in spite of your friendship for him, you can't deceive me. I trust to your keeping your promise when the time comes."—" I shall consider it my duty, however hard a one it may be."

As I found that there was nothing sensible to be got out of him, we turned back. As we passed the stand where the carriages were all drawn up, I saw Emil Bergfeldt standing beside a grand turn-out. As soon as he saw me he commenced fussing about with the horses, as if the position of some strap had to be altered, then he examined the off-horse like a professional horse dealer, although his knowledge of horseflesh could have been learned only from the sausages he had in his own home.

Just then the coachman brought him a glass of grog, which he had evidently ordered on the sly, for he flushed up when he saw that I had noticed him ; he tried to wave the coachman off ; however, mistaking what Emil meant, the man came up the closer in handing him the glass. "I wonder whether he often has a glass like that in secret?" thought I, "or is it only to-day on account of the damp?" I determined to talk the matter over with Augusta Weigelt.

The regatta had meanwhile been continued, and the Berlin men came off first in everything. If Berlin were one day to become a maritime city, its boating men might render the same services at a sea-fight on the wet element, as our lancers do on dry land—they are such plucky fellows. In a sculling race a Breslau man came off first, and on reaching the goal he got as much cheering as the Berlin men had previously. For, of course, every one must have his due.

I am quite willing to admit that, in spite of the Bergfeldts and Herr Max, I have rarely enjoyed myself so much as at this regatta. "To think of all that this Berlin of ours can accomplish," said I to Carl, "it makes me feel quite proud, although, of course, rowing cannot be said to be appropriate for ladies, if only on account of the dress they wear, it would be too barbarous for us."—Carl replied : "With such sports our young men aren't likely to get effeminate, and the desire to be first in every field won't harm the Germans either."—"But all our young men can't

devote themselves to rowing, surely," I added.—
"That's not necessary," replied Carl, "the good example will have an effect. Let every one try to be
first in his own special department, and to surpass his
competitors in good sound work."—"You are no
doubt right," said I ; "in matters of national economy
you know more than I do."

We returned to Berlin by a special train of superhuman length. The high-road, which runs along by
the railway, was crowded with vehicles. The passengers in the train waved their handkerchiefs to those
travelling on the high-road, and they waved cheerily
back, no matter whether they were the occupants of
grand carriages, waggonettes, milk carts, or any other
sort of trap in family parties. Probably the reason of
this was that all were alike happy—about the weather,
about the Crown Prince, and about the victories. And
the Crown Prince was pleased with his Berlin folk
too, one could easily see that. Prince Heinrich, who
has already sailed right round the earth, can nowhere
in the world have seen such a sight as the Lake in its
festive array, and the banks of the Spree crowded
with such multitudes. We were, in fact, all in a state
of great enthusiasm.

Uncle Fritz remained behind in Grünau to attend
the Club's celebration of the glorious events. Two
days afterwards he appeared on the scenes again, as
hoarse as if his throat had been burned, and he declared that he had a perpetual and wearisome ham-
mering going on in his head. "How is that?" said I
sympathetically.—"From drinking such an endless
amount of good healths, Wilhelmine," he replied ;
"we watered the victories in pretty good style."—
"Fritz," said I, "do you call it a 'good health' when
you are scarcely able to see out of your eyes?"

"Wilhelm, it can't be helped," said he, "and it was perfectly glorious!"

IN THE GREEN GRUNEWALD.

WHAT I am gradually coming to find very curious is, that we make most of our experiences without knowing it at the time, and it is only later we find out whether the occurrence was an experience or not. For instance, we may enjoy a delicious evening out in the country, and pay no heed to the loveliest of draughts playing round about us; however, on the following day, when aching pains in the limbs, a stiff neck, rheumatism, or some other surgical trouble makes its appearance (which may be alleviated by volatile spirit of camphor), then we know at once that we have been sitting in some draught, and are, of course, one experience the richer. Naturally, we resolve never to do this a second time, but on the next occasion it may not be a draught at all that we omitted to consider, but sour milk or icy-cold beer, and in place of having a swollen cheek we are the victims of bacilli of the semi-colon shape. Fortunately, however, these creatures cannot exist in very hot wine, as has been discovered by the Imperial Sanitary Association. And this is a mercy, to be sure; for even though superficially polished French people breed diseases in their un-drained seaport towns, we in Berlin will not require to drink carbolic punch, as Uncle Fritz suggested, when our Government had to send Dr. Koch to France for a time, and the daily papers were so full of cholera that one scarcely dared take them into one's hands.

Hot wine may be said to be a scientific experience,

effective even in the case of mere fright, as I learned
from what happened to the Police-lieutenant's wife.
She got rumblings in her inside simply from reading
the papers, and couldn't find her pulse when she looked
for it, and this put her into an inconceivable state of
mind. For, of course, when the pulse ceases, the last
stage has arrived, and the person will do well to begin
arranging about her funeral. However, a few glasses
of hot wine relieved the symptoms immediately, and in
a quarter of an hour the Police-lieutenant's wife could
feel her pulse all over herself. She said it was ham-
mering away under her toes as well as in her temples.
She was, in fact, saved.—" Frau Buchholz," she said,
" if you had not come in accidentally, who knows but
what the black omnibus might have had to be got
ready for me ? "—" Your case did certainly seem rather
serious," I replied, " but still you were pretty far from
requiring to be screwed down. It was only fright
that had struck your inside."—" I sha'n't read another
newspaper till the fruit season is over," said the Police-
lieutenant's wife.—" You are quite right," said I, " an
overripe pear in one hand and cholera reports in the
other, is more than even the giant Goliath could have
stood."

Hence another experience I had made was that
newspaper reading is not always good for people, and
that there is no better means for stirring up a pulse
than hot wine. However, the wine must be really hot,
even though the temperature be twenty-four degrees
by the stove in summer.

The Police-lieutenant's wife does not belong to that
species of human beings who try to give themselves
an air of importance by showing ingratitude, who, for
instance, when they have been on a visit, afterwards
make out that the beds were bad; or, after having been

at a party, fly off next morning to people who are absolutely indifferent about the matter, and relate that
they cannot understand how persons can presume to
set such dishes upon their table. No, she is not a person of that kind at all ; when she had recovered from
her attack of illness, she invited us to an afternoon
excursion to the Grunewald, we were to have coffee at
Paulsborn, and then proceed by Schildhorn to Pichels-
bergen. She hired a grand carriage for the afternoon,
a most elegant turn-out with a coachman in livery; his
great-coat was laid across the box-seat, the front of the
coat with its bright buttons—like a yard and a half of
the starry heavens—hanging down into the carriage.
We two older ladies sat facing the horses, while Mila,
her daughter, and Betti sat opposite to us. The gentlemen were to meet us towards evening in the Kaiser-
Garten, and so we had the whole of an exquisite afternoon all to ourselves.

It cannot be denied that the Kurfürsten-Damm,
where the houses end, is rather sandy, and that the
particles have developed a high degree of flying power;
however, as I had put on my new potato-peel coloured
dress, with light brown satin trimmings, I looked none
the worse for the sand, whereas the Police-lieutenant's
wife, in her black costume and goodly amount of
fringe, soon looked as if she were dressed in packing
paper. At every light breeze some of the district got
in between our teeth, causing a grating sensation.
However, this we did not mind very much, for we
knew that in Paulsborn a coffee-pot, with its alleviat-
ing contents, was awaiting us.

How long will it be before the Kurfürsten-Damm is
finished, I wonder? Berlin will then extend as far as
Grunewald; the Zoological Gardens will come to be
the centre of the city, the Halen Lake will take the

place of the Gold Fish Pond, and the Grunewald itself
will be another Thiergarten. An inhabitant in this
party of the city will have to use a telescope to see the
Victory Column, it will be such a long way off. When
this large suburb of the future has been properly
developed, Berlin will reach right to the Grunewald.
And develop it will, if we have peace, which is very
advantageous for every branch of business, Carl says
(except, of course, for powder-mills and plaster-band-
age works, where, it is said, there is great grumbling
just now; but Bismarck is not likely to start a war to
please them). The shade and scent of forests, and of
wooded lakes, I have always been immensely fond of,
and all this is to be had in the Grunewald, unsur-
passed in quality. Still I must confess that when
driving through it, comfortably reclining in a carriage, the charms of wooded scenery act even more
powerfully upon me.

In accordance with these circumstances we conversed purely in a somewhat higher range of thought,
more particularly about the want of really cultivated
people. This led us to speak of the Bergfeldts. The
Police-lieutenant's wife thought that Frau Bergfeldt
might certainly have her good points; but that, nevertheless, she would not be seen driving in the same
carriage with her through the Grunewald. " Now, you
see, Betti," said I, " that distinctions are necessary;
this afternoon will be a memorable one to us both,
will it not ? "—Mila thought that the weather was superb, and that only a very few ordinary-looking people
were out driving. The reason, she said, they never
went anywhere of a Sunday was, that there was such
a mixed set of people about. Betti, who has latterly
been reading a good deal about the rights of humanity
and the equality of classes, was about to make some

remark on the subject, when, fortunately, the carriage drew up in front of the forester's house at Paulsborn. We all got out, and Betti had to keep her intended reply to herself; it would, I feel sure, have displeased the Police-lieutenant's wife. I do not at all despise any rank or any grade, and value every one who honestly pushes his way in this world; yet, in spite of all the books on equality, it would never enter my head to give my grocer, milkman, or sweep, a *thé dansant.*

We had our coffee, went over the hunting-lodge that stands so romantically by the lake, and then drove further through the green forest till we reached the Havel; after this the carriage rolled slowly along the high-road, from which we had a charming view across the forest and the water. How beautiful it is out there ! No wonder so many restaurants have sprung up at the foot of this hilly shore. We halted at the Kaiser-Garten, where the gentlemen were to meet us. Of course, neither of them had yet arrived. In one's young days a lover never keeps his lady-love waiting for him; on the contrary, he is sure to be at the appointed place before she is; but when one has become a somewhat well-worn article, gentlemen are in no such hurry. This is what is called a universal experience, and has been made by numbers of persons. Carl, however, I must say, has always been very punctual, except when unavoidably detained, and then, of course, he was not to blame.

I should have been very glad to find the gentlemen there, for pleasant as ladies' society may be, still, an exclusively feminine afternoon does become rather uninteresting in the end. All the more pleasant it was, therefore, when a gentleman came up to our table, and politely bowed to us. At the first moment I did not recognise him, but it proved to be Herr Kleines.

"What a sight you look," I exclaimed; "have you got your younger brother's clothes on?"—"Not a bit of it," replied Herr Kleines, looking with admiration at his closely-fitting garments, "it's chike!"—"It's what?" asked the Police-lieutenant's wife, and with this she turned to me, requesting me to introduce him to her, and yet she must have remembered meeting him on Emmi's wedding-day.—One is not likely soon to forget such an odd creature.—"It's chike!" he repeated, and then added by way of explanation: "the latest Paris fashion."—"Well, no doubt, they are a crazy lot, those French people," I exclaimed, "too scrimp and short in everything."—"With their hair, too, shaved off like felons," chimed in the Police-lieutenant's wife.—"One's hair like this is just tip-top," said Herr Kleines, smiling triumphantly at his own degeneracy, "but then it's not every one that understands it."—"There may be something in it to be understood very likely, but beautiful it certainly is not. But pray sit down, we are glad to see you 'chite' or not."—"It's chike," said Herr Kleines.—"Whether it's chike or chite, it's much the same thing," I replied; "at all events, I've never seen you so odd-looking."

Herr Kleines said he had a friend with him, a highly intellectual young fellow, and asked if he might introduce him to us. The Police-lieutenant's wife bowed condescendingly, and said, "With pleasure;" whereupon Herr Kleines disappeared.—"Well, I never," said Betti, "how can any man be so monkeyish as to imitate the French in such tomfoolery, as Her Kleines does?"—"I think it's very *chic*," Mila remarked.— "The word's chite," said I.—"No, it's chike," said the Police-lieutenant's wife. Luckily, Herr Kleines returned, else, probably, there would in the end have been a regular quarrel about that stupid suit of his.

He introduced his friend Herr Pfeiffer, who made a very pleasant impression. He was a man of middle height, had a beautiful dark beard, and manipulated his eye-glasses most gracefully. I noticed when he took off his hat to us that there were signs of his growing out at his crown; but it seems often to happen, that when young men begin to become dangerously good-looking, their hair commences to fall off ; in this way careful Nature manages to lessen the mischief they may cause in families with young daughters.

We very soon found ourselves conversing pleasantly, as Herr Pfeiffer agreed with us that, in spite of all the new communal schools, there was a dearth of really cultivated people, and that it was only rarely that one met with persons who could appreciate the higher aims of life. He said that on this account he felt himself very isolated, and generally concealed his feelings from the unsympathising world, which, nevertheless, would not leave him to himself. That he sometimes fled to the statues in the Museum, where he felt, fully and truly, what he might have said, had but the statues been the living creatures of wondrous beauty, which they once had been when created by pure Hellenism in the days of Pericles and Anaximander. That, on the other hand, the present age—which he must term heartless—shallow—egoistical—he was inclined to despise. Nay, that he did despise it. All this he said with perfect assurance, and in a bass voice which sounded as if he had been speaking through a funnel.

While we were conversing with Herr Pfeiffer, Herr Kleines went off with Betti and Mila for a stroll through the garden, to show them the curiosities of the place: an uncleanly eagle in a cage (which can perform no tricks whatever, except blinking with its eyes, and eating), the monkeys and rabbits, the racing ring, the donkey-riding, and whatever else the place offered in the way of instruction and amusement. We, on the other hand, were engrossed by the charms of Art, which, of course, is as good to talk about as to look at.

Herr Pfeiffer admitted that I was right in maintaining that antique objects decidedly become more valuable from being buried in the ground. "That they are," he said, "and it is at once evident when they have been; but the great, dull-minded multitude passes them by without interest; the general public can only appreciate operettas, what is low and vulgar, the lightly draped Muse, the equivocal." For his part, he only liked the *Fledermaus* and the *Beggar Student*— with those one might be diverted, and he was. The Police-lieutenant's wife agreed with him in this, and said that she too liked melodies that she could remember, and that when she went to a theatre she had no wish to be bored.

While we were sitting thus, in the best of humours, meandering through the realm of the Ideal, Betti returned, and was alone. "Where are the others?" asked the Police-lieutenant's wife.—"Herr Kleines has taken Mila out in a boat."—"Without my permission?"—"My friend Georg will, I am sure, see her safely ashore again," said Herr Pfeiffer.—"But it is already beginning to get dark, and I consider it improper that my daughter should be out on the water alone with him," replied the Police-lieutenant's wife, annoyed.—"I will vouch for my friend acting honourably," said Herr Pfeiffer confidently, and in a specially deep tone of voice, "I cannot endure anything even hinted at against him."—"There is no need for you to defend him, as no one has yet accused him of anything," interposed the Police-lieutenant's wife. Just as Herr Pfeiffer was about to assume an offended look, my Carl and the Police-lieutenant himself appeared. As soon as the latter had exchanged a few words with us, he inquired where his daughter was.— "She is out on the lake."—"Alone?"—"No, with Herr Kleines."—"Who's Herr Kleines?"—"A chite," said I. —"No, the word's chike," said Betti.—"A young man got up in the latest of Paris fashions, at all events," added the Police-lieutenant's wife.—"That's enough for me," said Carl; "I propose we take a boat and bring them ashore; I, for my part, would not like my daughter to be out on the Havel with him, and night setting in. Water is treacherous."—The three gentlemen speedily hired a boat, and set off in chase of Herr Kleines, as if he had been a pirate whom the avenging arm of the law meant to catch by the collar.

The Police-lieutenant's wife then began to make me reproaches for having introduced Herr Kleines to her. "I did so at your own request, as you may kindly remember," I replied.—"You might have known his character, and have warned me."—"As to warning, I had no reason to think of it."—"Yes, you had, for when a young man dresses in such a style, his only object can be to make love to girls; the very shortness of his hair shows one that there's something of a culprit about him."—"He's doing no more than following the fashion."—"My husband will pretty soon let him know what fashion he's after," she replied, so angrily, that I thought it wiser to make no further remark to her, and so turned to Betti with the question: "Why didn't you go with them?"—"Herr Kleines seemed to me to know nothing about rowing, and I had no inclination to get drowned."—Betti's reply put the Police-lieutenant's wife into a terrible

state of anxiety.—"Where can they be? They ought
to be back now! What can be keeping my husband?"
—We all went down to the shore. There was not a
sign of any boat, for the sky had become overcast,
and it seemed pure madness to be out on the water.

We were staring out into the dark, and the Police-
lieutenant's wife was getting into a state of despera-
tion, when some one was heard calling out, "Oh, there
they are!" And there, in fact, were Mila and Herr
Kleines hurrying towards us through the garden.
"Now then," I exclaimed, "where have you two come
from?"—"We didn't care about being on the water
and so landed at Schildhorn," said Herr Kleines;
"we have walked back from there."—"And your father
off in a boat looking for you, you thoughtless child,"
exclaimed the Police-lieutenant's wife.—"And my Carl
too, and Herr Pfeiffer ditto," I exclaimed; "how are
we to get the gentlemen back?"

There was nothing for it but to wait. But how we
did wait! I think Ulysses' wife, in the olden days,
could not have had a greater longing for her husband
than we had for ours, as well as for Herr Pfeiffer. I
made use of the opportunity for informing Herr
Kleines that he would find it pretty hot work to settle
matters with the Police-lieutenant, whereupon he pretended that he had to catch a train to the West End,
and made off.

At last we heard the splash of oars. "They've been
back long since," we called out as the gentlemen
landed. The Police-lieutenant was the first to leap
ashore. "Where's Herr Kleines?" he called out.—
"I'll stand guarantee for him, as I have more than
once taken the liberty to remark," replied Herr
Pfeiffer.—"I'm much obliged to you," answered the
Police-lieutenant, "but I mean him to speak for him-

self, and it will be some satisfaction to have his address from you."

The carriage was ordered, and we took our seats in it as best we could. Herr Pfeiffer declined to drive with us, probably because he would have had to sit next to the Police-lieutenant; thus he preferred returning through the Grunewald on foot. We were rather a silent party going home, and while we were driving through the forest, I could not help thinking what kind of dance the Police-lieutenant would lead Herr Kleines. "It cannot end very smoothly there," I thought. "I certainly shouldn't have the courage to do anything, but the Police-lieutenants may have the nerves for it."

THE PORTRAIT.

BETTI and I had determined to pay several visits to the Exhibition of Paintings in the Cantian Platz, this autumn; in the first place, because we generally go; secondly, because Betti is working away by herself at painting; and thirdly, because on a first visit it is scarcely possible to comprehend Art in its totality, on account of the crowds. As a rule we never went till we had learned from the newspapers which were the principal pictures; however, since we have become convinced that while one reviewer loses his head over a picture, another will run it down to such an extent that one wonders why the law does not come down upon the artist, we do not care much what they write. And I personally care least of all about what Adolf Rosenberg fabricates in the way of criticisms; for I now know that he changes his opinion as he may do his paper-collars. When (as he has done) he asks a certain somebody to deserve the fame which the critics have bestowed upon him, I cannot but suppose that he, so to say, flings off his articles without a thought ; for surely he cannot intend deliberately to expose the way of critics by saying that they manufacture unmerited celebrity ! That would be proclaiming the whole profession to be a company of swindlers. No, I regard the position of critics as higher than that, they have never appeared to me so utterly mischievous. However, Adolf Rosenberg—who uses the "*Grenzboten*" as a spittoon for his poison—has at all events acted honourably towards his colleagues in placing himself in the pillory (by frankly confessing their worthless proceedings), for being himself a critic by profession, he must know how matters really stand.

The Exhibition is no doubt a practical kind of building, but, as its principal outward charm—as seen from the City line—seems to consist in its being water-tight, it cannot be said to lay claim to actual beauty. Its artistic contents we determined to examine in this way : that both of us were quietly to note the pictures that pleased us best, so that when we came to make our second peregrination round the gallery there might be a mutual exchange of opinion. The plan failed, however, for when we entered the first room we caught sight of the life-size figure of a man in uniform, which stood out from a purple curtain with a rich border of gold, in the most lifelike manner, and with an aristocratic look. "Who is that ?" I asked Betti, forgetting the agreement we had made. She read out of the catalogue : "Friedrich Franz the Second, late Grand Duke of Mecklenburg-Schwerin." —"I could see at once that it must be a prince," I replied. "Who painted it ?"—"Fritz Paulsen," she said, reading on.—"Goodness, how it all seems to rise

up before me!" I exclaimed. "Whatever can he
have thought of me?"—"Why, mamma?"—"Well,
child, when I was in Naples, I asked him whether he
would paint my portrait some day, and it was almost
arranged that he should." "How very nice," Betti
said, interrupting me; "a picture of you for papa's
birthday. . . . . You couldn't give him anything more
beautiful."—"Child," said I, "what are you thinking
about? Haven't I just had a most excellent photograph taken of myself, at Carl Günther's, which you
were all delighted with?"—"And so we are still, but
when I look at you, mamma—well, you seem just
made for oils," said the girl, laughing. "How
precious the picture would be to us all!" she continued in a more serious tone, "when . . . "—"When
I am old and ugly," I added, smiling.—"I did not
mean that," she answered, "but we might not always
be with you, and then, in looking at your portrait, it
would be like having your dear self, life-like before
us. Mamma, you *must* be painted."—"If I were to be
hung on my son-in-law's wall, with a somewhat severe
expression of face, Emmi might possibly be the better
for it; there are proofs that the sight of a picture has
roused a conscience for its own good." After a little
I added: "Papa would grudge the money, I am
afraid."—"It wouldn't be so very ruinous, and, mamma, you could pay for it yourself."—"That would
merely be taking from the debit and placing it in the
credit," said I, putting her off.—"All the little money
I have put by, little by little, I would give towards it,"
urged Betti. "Oh, I am so delighted at the thought
of the picture!"

"We shall have to think the matter well over
again," said I, putting an end to the conversation.
"But come now, Betti, and let us look at the pictures,
as we proposed to do."

While wandering from one long room to another, I
was conscious that my thoughts were not paying
proper heed to the pictures before me, but were more
actively engaged—than I myself wished—with my
future portrait. As often as I caught sight of the
likeness of any lady, I asked myself, why was her portrait painted, and was she justified in having it done?
In a good many cases the portrait had certainly not
been painted for the sake of beauty, more probably
for the sake of a likeness. Several were hung so high
that it was impossible to judge in their case. It then
occurred to me that Ludwig Pietsch had made never-
to-be-forgotten remarks about my personal appearance ; and when I came to think the whole matter
over—my half-binding inquiry of Professor Paulsen in
Naples, Betti's anxious wish, my Carl's surprise on
his birthday, and the fact that I was not growing
younger—made me see that I ought to give in without
more ado. I beckoned to Betti and said, "I am
wavering about giving in to all your wishes."—"Oh,
how good of you!" exclaimed Betti in glee.—"But,
Betti, I haven't sufficient artistic enthusiasm to make
my heart take the decisive leap, I must find some
picture that will disperse this last bit of uncertainty."
—"Let us look for it, mamma, I will help you."

It cannot be denied that a great number of unusual
pictures attracted our attention, and we could scarcely
say enough in admiration of the modern masterpieces. Betti thought that the portraits in black
—as if washed over with liquorice—seemed to be
the most fashionable; but I was not in favour of that
funereal style.—"What do you say to this?" she asked
me, pointing to a portrait representing a tall lady in
an olive-green velvet, and looking as if she would
have a friendly reply for any one that addressed her.

—"Ah, that would be exactly to my liking," said I; "only, I fancy my brown rep would suit me better, and then only about half as large: the smaller frames are sure to be less expensive."—"Well, have you quite decided now, mamma?" asked Betti.—"If you think that papa . . . ."—"That's sure to be all right," she said, rejoicing, putting her arm round me; "you dear, good mother, and so you're really going to be painted!"—"Child, child," said I, "you are crushing me to bits. Now let us see who painted that portrait."—"Here it is in big letters in the corner," she replied, pointing to the name. "Fritz Paulsen!" said I, reading it. It was quite clear to me now; it was the decree of fate.

By the time we left the Exhibition I had made up my mind that Carl should have the surprise on his birthday, for Betti assured me that paintings were not only of lasting value, but that their value increased year by year.—"If they do that, then there can be no loss," I replied; "and we haven't got to feed them. One thing, however, Betti, I have resolved upon, and that is not to read a mortal word about the Exhibition in the papers; for if any critic—after a bad night's rest—were to vent his ill humour upon the portrait we both admired so much, all inclination to have myself painted would then and there die within me." —"But supposing it were pronounced beautiful?"—"That we know ourselves it is. And was it not stated in Meyer's popular, wearisome lecture, that works of art are classic when the judgment of the multitude is everlastingly in favour of them? Well, we two surely belong to the multitude!"

A few days afterwards I drove over to the Dorotheen Strasse, where Professor Paulsen resides. When I rang the door-bell, it was opened by a woman who showed me into an anteroom, and said: "There's some

one with Professor Paulsen at present; who shall I
say is waiting to see him?"—I had thought of taking
the Professor by surprise, and so replied : "Tell him
an acquaintance from Italy has come to call upon
him, he will know who it is."—The woman looked at
me doubtfully, and went slowly towards the door
which led into the studio; but before disappearing,
she gave a glance at the objects of art and the old
china ornaments that stood upon a table in front of
the mirror, and upon an antique cupboard—as if to
inform me that every article had been counted. That
is assuredly the domestic dragon who guards the
treasures, I thought, and I was not far wrong, as I
afterwards learned, for the woman Bachmann, as she
is called, looks after the household affairs with more
than an ordinary sense of duty.

Before very long Professor Paulsen came in. He
recognised me at once, and said that as his visitor had
left he was now quite at my disposal, but asked me to
excuse him for a few minutes; and, in fact, he remained away only a very short time, and then invited
me into his studio.

It was the first time in my life that I had been in a
studio, which I had hitherto pictured to myself as an
empty room, where, in the midst of the utmost confusion, pictures were painted. I must confess my idea
was founded upon a non-acquaintance with artistic
concerns. I found myself in a room that reminded
me of one in the Italian palaces, except that Herr
Paulsen's studio showed a much greater attention to
cleanliness, and was arranged more with a view to
comfort. Parts of the walls were covered with tapes-
try, others were adorned from top to bottom with pictures, as in the Museum. Weapons, too, were arranged
on the wall, and on some shelves were figures, dishes,

jugs, and articles in coloured glass. Then there were a number of antique chairs and couches, tables, cabinets, and rugs; everything good of its kind, and wonderfully in keeping altogether.

"Well, I must say," was my exclamation on recovering from my first amazement, "I had never expected this; it will be a pleasure, truly, to be painted amid such surroundings. I must tell you at once, Professor Paulsen, that I have come with this intention."

We sat down in a comfortable corner. The Professor asked me whether I had had lunch, and would not hear of my declining to partake of some refreshment. The woman Bachmann was ordered to bring me something; a good cup of soup and a little cold meat. While taking our lunch we discussed the portrait; Herr Paulsen was not in favour of my brown rep from an artistic point of view; he thought some decided colour would suit me better. So then I suggested my claret-coloured dress, which he approved of. I was to give him my first sitting the following day, and in order that my Carl might not notice anything, he proposed that I should send my dress to his house, where it would be carefully placed in the old German cabinet. The woman Bachmann, he said, would help me to arrange my dress, as she was accustomed to do this. I asked if Betti might come with me, for it occurred to me that my daughter might gain something by watching him paint, and perhaps get some artistic hints. However, he said he would prefer that she did not come till after the third sitting, when she would be able to judge of the likeness. He would, he said, be very glad to see her then.

This was on Tuesday; on Thursday I sat for the first time. I must say a very peculiar feeling came over me as I looked at the canvas upon which my

portrait was to be painted, and it was strange to
think that it could be done without a copy. In fact I
was to be the copy myself, and might talk and amuse
myself, while the artist, with various kinds of brushes
laid on different colours exactly where they were
necessary to produce the likeness.

I asked Professor Paulsen whether he had always
resided in his present house, whereupon he told me
that the town had purchased the land upon which his
old house had stood, as a Market Hall was to be
erected in that quarter. "My old studio," he continued, "had a hanging garden with a view across a
wood-yard out over the river. Directly adjoining my
garden was the *Logengarten*, with its high elms and
lime-trees, like a small forest. In the spring-time the
blossoms of the lime-trees gave a delicious scent, a
bullfinch used to come and sip water from the saucers
of my flower-pots, pigeons from a neighbouring house
came for bread-crumbs that Bachmann strewed for
them; even the yellow loriot built its nest in the trees
by the water, scarcely a hundred steps from the *Linden*, and nightingales might be heard of an evening. I
could fancy myself quite in the country, everything
was so peaceful round about. The wild vine twined
its way up to the roof, and flowers of all colours
flourished there. I liked my little garden to be full of
bright flowers, like the one I remembered by my
parents' house."—"Nothing grows in our garden,"
said I, "too much shade spoils everything botanical.
How lovely it must have been in your old place, especially to have had nightingales in the middle of Berlin!"—"Unfortunately this never lasted very long.
When the little bird forgot itself and the world, in its
song, some wretched cat would creep up and seize it.'
—"Could not the cat be content with sparrows?'

said I.—"No, no, Miss Puss has rather a liking for nightingales, they sit conveniently low among the shrubbery. When the trees were cut down to make room for building, the singing birds left."—"That served the cats right," I exclaimed. "And soon afterwards everything had to be pulled down—houses, the studio and the hanging garden—and there was an end to all the beauty. It is to be hoped that the Market will prove advantageous to Berlin, from a practical as well as from an architectural point of view."

"I, myself, do anticipate some good results," I replied, "for when one sees these market people late of an evening lying on the ground beside their baskets, and camping out all night in the open air, like the lazzaroni—whatever the weather may be—all sensible persons must feel that it is inhuman for any one to treat their health in such a way. And peasants are human beings, surely! Moreover, I expect that the Market will lead these people to be more particular in their manner of behaviour; at present they are, as a rule, very backward in this respect. Fancy what happened to me last summer when most people were off to some watering-place or other. I went one day myself to buy some young peas, and as those offered me by one of the women were over-ripe, I hesitated, and then said (only what was true), 'I would not dare to set those before my husband, I'm sorry, good-day.' Not a syllable did she give me, but the woman in the next stall calls out rudely: 'Never you mind, Frau Meyer, she only wants to do the fine leddy. A fine leddy, indeed! If she were a fine leddy she'd be anywhere but in Berlin at this time of the year!' Now surely such a thing is not likely to happen in the Market Hall without the police interfering and giving the women a benefiting lock-up in gaol! Or are we to be forced to go to Nordeney on account of these market women ?"

Professor Paulsen then made a pause, and I could rise and go and look at what had been done. Primæval man must have looked something like this, I thought —recognisable and yet not perfect in form. The body was only given in outline, and the chair upon which I had been sitting consisted merely of one daub of colour, whereas the place where my hands were eventually to be, was indicated merely by a smudge with his flesh-coloured brush. After contemplating the work quietly for a little, I said : " I had imagined that painters began at the top, with the hair, and then worked downwards bit by bit."—" It's very likely that some may do this," replied Professor Paulsen ; " I, for my part, prefer to give as definite a sketch as possible of the total impression first, and then to work out the details in so far as I consider them artistically correct and effective in each case."—" I'm very curious what it will look like when finished," I said, and then added : " Is that black under the eyes to remain, and am I really as yellow about the neck ? "

Professor Paulsen seemed not to have heard these last questions, but touched an electric bell, whereupon Bachmann appeared. " May I offer you a little refreshment ? " he said, addressing me. " If you could give me another hour to-day I should accomplish more than at another sitting of double the length of time ; yet I should be sorry to tire you ? "—" Have I been sitting for an hour already ? " I asked in astonishment, for it seemed to me that I had come only a short time ago. In interesting society, however, the hours seem to fly.—" You've been here over two hours," said the woman Bachmann.—" You needn't speak unless you're asked," said Professor Paulsen severely, " it doesn't

matter to you how long I make my hours. Bring
in a bottle of 'Johannisgarten,' also some cake and
fruit, or whatever else you may have in that way."
The old woman went off with a displeased look, but
soon returned with a more conciliatory expression of
face, and placed the things her master had ordered
upon the table. Then she gave a look at the portrait
and said quietly : "It's going to do," and went off. I
felt annoyed at this.

The little refreshment did me good, and the wine
was excellent ; I could not remember to have ever
tasted anything like it, and therefore asked where it
came from. It struck me that if the price were not too
exorbitant, I might tell Carl to get some for his birthday. "This Johannisgarten I get direct from a friend
of mine, Otto Sartorius, the proprietor of a vineyard
in Mussbach in the Rhenish Pfalz," he replied.—
"Does your friend supply other people as well ?"—
"Send him an order and see ; you will be satisfied
with what he sends you, I am sure. Since the French
have taken to manufacture their clarets out of Italian
wines, I prefer the genuine German growths, especially
as the price is pretty much the same as that demanded
for the French fabrications."—"I can quite understand that," I replied ; "really one may learn something new every day of one's life," and with this I
jotted down the address.

After resting a little the painting began again, and
when Professor Paulsen had finished for the day, the
picture had assumed a very different appearance. The
woman Bachmann was right after all : it was going
to do.

She helped me to change my dress in the adjoining
room ; and when I took my leave, Professor Paulsen
told me I might bring Betti next time, for, as I had

sat so extremely well, he would require one sitting the less.

Agreeable as this praise was, I could not conceal from myself the fact that I should be too late for dinner, a thing that otherwise never occurred. So I had to think of excuses to give Carl; but he always notices directly when things are not straightforward, so that I am not at all a good one at inventing stories. Of course I got quickly enough back to our part of the world by the city line, still the time at the other end had been too short for me to concoct a proper excuse out of my own head.

At home I found them waiting for me. Carl, how-ever, when he saw my embarrassment, welcomed me with the words: "Was the bridge drawn up that you couldn't pass? or did you get into a wrong tramcar?" —"No," I answered hotly, "you needn't imagine me so stupid as that. I have been trying to find out where we can get a good and proper sort of wine."—Carl looked at Betti, and Betti looked at him, and both burst out laughing, which made me feel very uncom-fortable. "What are you giggling at?" I asked, a little put out.—"So she's been wine-tasting!" said Carl gaily.—"Yes, that she has!" I exclaimed, an-gered by the ridicule, and threw the address of the wine merchant upon the table. "Here's the address if you want to have it, and you may order the wine for your birthday yourself, it will give me no pleasure now to do it after the way you have met me."—"Wil-helmine, if I had only known——" Carl began by way of excusing himself.—"It's the nature of you men; you are for ever, with your rough hands, destroying the delicate threads of affection that women weave for you. But I'll forgive and forget, if only you send off the order to-day. You may as well order wine for punch at the

same time. Come, don't crumple the address in that
way! And now let us have dinner."

We were pretty silent during dinner. I was sorry
to have drawn such a thunderstorm down upon Carl,
but if I hadn't, he would assuredly have got to the
bottom of the secret about the portrait, and, moreover,
I should have had double trouble in getting him to
order the wine. If Professor Paulsen pays us a visit,
we can't offer him anything less good than what he is
accustomed to.

Carl took his dinner hurriedly, and said "*Gesegnete
Mahlzeit*" before we others had had our second helping. I was about to run out after him, to tell him that
things were not as bad as they seemed, when Betti
began: "Why were you so angry, mamma?"—"I
angry?"—"Well, you seemed so, at least."—"And I
had good reason to be annoyed."—"No, mamma, you
hadn't."—"Indeed!"—"What I mean, is, that when
you were so long in coming home, papa got anxious,
and kept on saying: 'Where can mamma be?' I tried
to make excuses, but you know that when papa is
serious and asks a question point-blank, one has to
tell him the truth."—"Well?"—"So I told him that
he must remember that his birthday was in a day or
two."—"Betti, how could you go and tell tales?"—
"I knew that papa would be content with that, and it
was the truth also. If you had met his jokes in a
cheery way, all would have been well. Really, this
time I do not know who acted most stupidly."—
"Betti! is that the way to speak to me?"—"I did not
mean to be rude, mamma, but I am old enough now
to see that you would have gained more by giving in."
—"It's a new thing to hear such remarks from you,
Betti," said I.—She got up, and said in a low voice:
"I once thought there was some happiness for me in

life—we never spoke about it, mamma—but it has all
passed away now; we have both of us been silent
about it, you and I; what was the use of words? You
know it as well as I. The love I thought of giving to
that one person, I mean now to divide between you
all, as well as I can. Now you know why I have come
to look at things differently from what I did. Forgive
me, mamma, if I hurt you by what I said. I did not
intend to."

She went away and I was left alone with a heavy
heart. Betti had resigned herself to her fate; the
spring of her life was past! It was well that no one
saw how I cried. When I recovered I determined that
henceforth her life should be made as pleasant as it
was in my power to make it. Not an unkind word
should ever cross my lips; and if any one should
worry her again, they'd suffer for it!

Carl had gone to lie down, as was his usual way
after dinner; we had knitted him a large sofa blanket
for these after-dinner naps. I went in to him. When
I opened the door he raised his eyes. "Carl," said I,
"if you don't care about ordering that wine, leave it."
—"What is it, Wilhelmine?" said he, without much
interest.—"You hadn't any appetite to-day, Carl
dear?"—"No, I hadn't."—"Was it my fault?"—"I
didn't say it was."—"Carl, I was a little excited."—
"It seemed to me you were. I would advise you, in
future, not to go in for wine-tasting, you cannot stand
a mixture of things."—"Now, Carl, that's a return
shot at me. Are you angry, Carl?"—"No, I'm not;
for you can't alter your natural disposition. Why
should I be angry?"—"Carl," said I, "you've been a
very jewel all your born days. I confess I was more
violent than need be; but still, have I ever wished my
children a better father than you? The hour will

come when I shall stand justified before you; it is not very far off, believe me. Now this evening you shall have the best of beefsteaks for supper, as you ate no dinner. Will you have it cooked with onions or with egg, Carl dear?"—"With both!"—"And I'll have a glass of genuine Munich beer fetched for you; nobody shall say I haven't a warm heart for you. Now shut your eyes for a little more sleep; when it's time for you to be off to the office, I'll come and wake you."— Before I went I gave him a kiss, which pleased him very much. The angel of reconciliation had descended upon us and held watch by his couch. He was well tucked up, too.

The portrait formed the main object of my existence; I was determined that it should become incomparably good even though I had to sit for three weeks like a brooding hen. It did not take as long as this, however, for it was surprising how the painting developed; and Betti, who accompanied me each time, was greatly astonished, and finally came to the conclusion that she would never attain such facility. "The mixing of the colours is too difficult," she said : "a little of every colour is laid on the palette, and those have all again to be mixed together, yet when the artist puts it on the canvas with his brush, it agrees to a nicety with your likeness. The essence of art lies in the artist's insight into nature."—"I am afraid you are wrong there, Betti," I replied, "other people might have an insight into that. No, in my opinion the essence of art consists in an artist always dipping into the right colours !"

Nothing, therefore, came of my idea that Betti might pick up some hints from watching the artist at work ; on the contrary, after this she gave up her wood-painting entirely, declaring that it was mere dabbling in art, and that she had been meanwhile altogether neglecting her literary studies. And, indeed, according to the certificates that she received at the High School, she possessed *talent* ɩ b and *industry* 2 a. Having these guarantees of her ability, I determined to persuade Herr Feodor Wichmann Leuenfels (who had in due course called upon us) to come more frequently to our house, although Betti herself does not seem to be very much edified with him, and Uncle Fritz, in his plebeian way of speaking, always calls him the patent humbug. Now as Carl, too, is not inclined to believe in professional poets, I stand alone in my sympathy for the upward strivings of this young man of genius. And yet Leuenfels is a remarkable man—one need only see with what confidence he aims his shafts at other writers of verse: I consider myself too good, he would say, to subscribe my name to such trash.

Meanwhile the sittings were coming to an end ; it was astonishing to see how the picture became more and more life-like, until finally it was exactly like the reality. The black below the eyes, and the yellow about the neck had vanished, and now formed a most natural kind of shade; the patch of colour that had originally stood for the chair, assumed the appearance of the embroidery exactly; and the hands, which had given some trouble, were precisely like my own.—I was quite overcome when contemplating the finished picture in its frame of carved gold, and thinking what Carl would feel on his birthday. "Art is a grand thing, after all," I said, "but, Professor Paulsen, I am a little too good-looking in the picture, I think."— "You are wrong," he replied, "the portrait-painter has not merely to copy nature, but has to a certain extent to endeavour to obtain a likeness from the

pleasantest point of view. The expression varies with
the humour a person happens to be in, and I have
painted you, as you look when cheerful, when some
good fortune of your own, or that of some one else has
brightened the expression of your face."—"But have
I not turned out a little too young-looking?"—
"Mamma, how can you say such a thing?" Betti
interposed. "In the picture you are exactly like what
we have always known you, ever since we can remember, our dear, kind mother. You never looked any
different from what you do in the picture."—"If you
are satisfied, I do not need to object, for I'm not un-
human. I did not have my portrait taken from vanity's sake, Professor Paulsen, but because my children
insisted upon it."—"Then you have very sensible children," said he.

The sittings had been a real pleasure to us, so we
were sorry when they came to an end. Betti had
watched the Professor painting, or played on the piano
anything she happened to know by heart. Sometimes
also she amused herself with the dog Peter, a shaggy
kind of creature like a poodle, that would dance round
and round, looking, for all things in the world, like a
furry foot-sack gone mad; one could never make out
which was the head and which the tail. The woman
Bachmann, who was full of praise about the picture,
told me that in the old studio they had a dog called
Paul, and that it might have been a human being
were it not that it had a dog's skin, and that at times
it was cleverer than many a human creature, but that
a malicious old witch had given it poison because the
dog always barked at her. Bachmann said she noticed
the dog was ill at five in the evening, and at twelve at
night it looked up at her again, and wagged its tail
as if it had wanted to say, "Bachmann, it's all over

with me; give a kind message to master from me "—
that was the end. Her master was much grieved
when she went in and told him. But the old wretch
of a woman did not escape punishment; she ended in
getting a couple of months' imprisonment for slander-
ous talk and disturbing the peace of the house.
"Thank God," said I, "there is justice still to be had !
Thanks, I'll send for the dress." Bachmann had given
herself some trouble in helping me to change my
dress on the different occasions, and had shown
herself so obliging that I made her some little return.
The picture was to remain in the studio till the birthday.

A slight degree of stage-fever seized me, however,
when the day came upon which Carl was to be surprised. On the previous afternoon Professor Paulsen
came himself, when the picture was to be hung up in
our best sitting-room ; he wished to see it placed in a
proper light, so that even in this respect nothing was
omitted. Afterwards I locked the door and took away
the key. Betti was all expectation, and kept singing
to herself, a thing I had not heard her do for long.

In the morning we had our coffee with a cake, as upon
any other birthday, and we gave Carl several useful
things, which pleased him very much. Then I went
and unlocked the room and called through the door,
"Carl, there's someone in the best room wanting to see
you."—He seemed a little vexed at being disturbed,
but hurried out and we followed him on tiptoe
quietly. There he stood as if lost in contemplation
of the picture, but Betti's shoes creaked and he turned
round and saw us. "Wilhelmine," he said, with emotion, "my good wife, you could not have given me a
greater pleasure than this." He drew me to him and
kissed me on the forehead and mouth. Betti clapped

her hands in delight. "Was I not right, mamma? If only parents would always follow their children's advice!"—Carl turned to her and smiled, and then put his other arm round her. This was a birthday such as we had never had, we were so utterly, so heartily happy and content.

"Do you like the portrait, Carl?" said I, for of course one likes to have an opinion. "Do you think the likeness good?"—"It is you to a nicety," was his answer, "and yet there is something more in it than that; it seems to me as if I had you there again as you were when my bride, as you looked in the days of our first love, do you remember?"—"You mean I look too youthful there, Carl?" — "No, not at all, but it awakens my old recollection, and now when I look at you yourself, I see exactly the same expression still in your features. The artist has succeeded in bringing it out more distinctly than we are accustomed to see it."—"So now you are no longer vexed about my having been late for dinner that day? I had just returned from my first sitting——" He laid his hand gently on my mouth. "The storm passed by very quickly, and it has never really come down upon us, although, at times, there has seemed a good deal of thunder in the air."—"Carl, remember I have often had the big washing in my head, and——" —"Wilhelmine, is the picture to have its laugh at you? Look how kindly and pleasantly the painted Frau Buchholz can look down at me."—I laughed and said: "Well, I have hung up a nice warning to myself."—The door-bell then rang. "Children," I exclaimed, "there are visitors coming—probably Emmi and Dr. Wrenzchen!"

And so it was. My son-in-law wanted to offer his good wishes before going off on his rounds, and left

Emmi with us for the whole day. The portrait pleased them immensely. Dr. Wrenzchen asked me in private what it cost; I pacified him by saying that it might one day be his. In the evening we had a pretty large gathering of friends, and Carl—that best of men!—had actually arranged for us to have "Johannisgarten;" this came as a surprise for me, and so the merriment lasted far into the night.

Before getting into bed I went to take a last look at my portrait, and said: "I will do my utmost—this I vow; but to be superhuman is a thing that can't be expected of me, not by any portrait in the world." Carl, who came to see what was keeping me, said: "Why, Wilhelmine, this is ghostly in the extreme; you look as if you were playing the part of the White Lady, in the picture gallery among the portraits of her ancestors!" However, I could not reveal my deeper feelings to him at the moment—he was in too jocose a mood.

NEW CONNECTIONS.

They are going to live in the Privy Councillor's part of the town, with a flower garden in front, and a green-house, stables and coach-house at the back, and the gardener is to wait at table, and to have six pairs of white cotton gloves in addition to his wages. He is, however, to pay for the washing of them himself, as he is not likely to be so extravagant with them. The furniture they have purchased belonged to some baron who disappeared; it is meanwhile all in the loft. The marriage is to take place as soon as the workmen are out of the house, and when the young couple return from their wedding trip—they are either going to Paris or to Vienna—they are to take up their abode in their grand residence. All their china is of the onion pattern, and the kitchen sink in white marble with gilt. No prince could wish for anything finer.

All this was told me by Augusta Weigelt, who came to call; I had not seen her for some time. But, of course, she cannot well leave home now that she has another little baby. The boy is getting a splendid little fellow; and the second child, a girl, is such a nice-looking little thing! It has got well over its vaccination troubles, though I should never have advised its being vaccinated at so young an age. Augusta, however, thought that what had to be done was best done soon, so that she might have the necessary certificates.

"You are, no doubt, already thinking about your daughter's future marriage," said I jocosely.—"Not exactly that," she replied, "but when the little thing is lying in her cradle dreaming, and I am sitting by her with my sewing, I do sometimes begin to speculate. Time passes quicker than one fancies, and I mean her to have the best education possible. One can never know in what sphere she may eventually come to live. My brother's marriage will change a good many things in our family."

"His bride must be enormously rich," said I, "if, as you say, they are to have a whole house to themselves in the Thiergarten quarter, and to keep a carriage; this represents a lot of money. Your brother Emil may well talk of good luck."—"Undoubtedly! and is sure to be very happy; he will, so to say, find himself in a nest of gold. When one considers that he has absolutely nothing but himself, and that she, with her countless wealth, is marrying him out of pure affection . . . ."—"Where was it that they became acquainted?" I asked, interposing.—"First of all at a lawyer's ball which Emil was invited to by a friend of his, with sisters, for he is an excellent dancer. And she has rather a liking for the legal set. Emil, she says, must take his doctor's degree, and, if it does not cost too much, must eventually become a professor or something tip-top. She is quite bent upon this, Emil says."—"But he is no scholar!" I exclaimed, "she has made a mistake there."—"Well, at all events, Emil is a most good-looking fellow, you must admit that."—"Remarkably good-looking, no doubt," I replied; "but as far as I know, good looks are rather at a low demand with professors: it's more the brain that tells with them, as is proved with scientific accuracy after their death. However, I shall be well enough pleased if she succeeds in being one day able to style herself Frau Professorin, and can only hope that Emil is not marrying a mere money-bag, and is more on the look-out for a good heart, and a soul without wrinkles. Are you sure he is quite happy— I mean content and happy at heart?"

"I do think he is," replied Augusta, "and why should he not be? He is getting everything he can possibly wish, and he will be able to assist his parents and the rest of us also. He knows well how difficult it is for us to make both ends meet."—"Now that I like in him," said I, "and if he manages to get the purse strings into his own hands, he will, no doubt, do what he can for you all."—"Of course he will!" exclaimed Augusta cheerfully; "mother thinks so too! And father will then no longer need to slave away at all sorts of extra work, and our troubles will come to an end."—"That is not bad at seventy," I added, "if things were but all finally settled."

"It won't be very long now before they are," replied Augusta, "and I myself wish that the wedding-day were over . . . it comes rather hard upon us."—"In spite of all the brilliant prospects?"—"It's just the brilliancy of it that causes the trouble," replied Augusta, "for, of course, we cannot appear as dowdies beside all the grand folk that will be invited to the wedding—that would never do. My husband cannot go in his old dress-coat, and my best dress is completely out of fashion. Moreover, if we give them a present, it must be either a pair of sugar-tongs, or salt-cellars, or something of silver from a goldsmith. Mother did suggest a dinner service, it is true, which would make a goodly show; but we cannot manage that, it comes too expensive."—"Do not take it ill, Augusta," said I, "but that mother of yours is the very essence of senselessness. Where can she expect you to get the money from?"

These words of mine, which were nothing but the positive truth, put Augusta out rather, and she said, stuttering: "We have calculated the matter out most carefully, and only considered what will be absolutely necessary. A hundred thalers would cover all the expenses."—"I call that quite unjustifiable in your position," said I; "think of the future, Augusta." —"We have done so," she added gaily; "if we do not attend the wedding, this would at once put an end to any intercourse between us and our grand connections. And then where else—except among such people—are we likely to get to know persons who may one day be of use to our boy, when he will require good introductions to help him on in life? Is it a wise thing to appear indifferent to connections in a high position, who, as Emil says, could invite princes and other celebrities to their *soirées?*"

6

"Augusta," said I seriously, "do you think you have the proper polish for such feudal entertainments? Do you not yourselves belong to the Lansberger Strasse? But this much I see . . . a Bergfeldt will remain a Bergfeldt all its born days."

"I know that you have a pique against my mother, but you have never yet shown me any of the ill-feeling you have towards her——."—"The ill-feeling is all on her side," said I, interrupting her, "for whenever there was a quarrel it was she who began it. But do not let us rake up that subject, do not let us upset ourselves with things of the past ; let *us*, at least, keep calm and composed. . . . . So you really think you cannot manage to get out of the wedding ? "

"We must positively be there. What excuse could we give to our acquaintances were they to ask why we had not attended the wedding? Dear, good Frau Buchholz, we cannot possibly do otherwise ; and now I am going to ask a very great favour of you—but you must not misunderstand me—and you will not be angry, will you ?—could you lend us the hundred thalers? "

If any one had told me that she wanted me to fetch her down the clock from the Town Hall, I could not have felt more dumfounded than at this attack of hers. "Augusta," I replied after a somewhat longish pause for reflection, "it is certainly true that a drowning man will clutch at the first straw within reach, but why need I be that very straw? If you were really in distress, you or your husband, you might assuredly count upon me, but I have no sympathy with your high-flown notions. In any case, I should have to talk the matter over with my husband. But consider, a hundred thalers are just three hundred marks—and that is no small item in these bad times. One hears on all hands of troubles in business life, and of the social abyss that has slowly been opening for years." —"It is only a loan I'm asking for," said Augusta in a low tone of voice. "We'll manage to get the money elsewhere, and Emil will give us back all we have to lay out ; this we hope for certain."—"Augusta," said I in a warning tone, "hope is of no value whatever at the Imperial Bank. I think that you should have a fashionable back put on to the skirt of your black silk dress ; two widths of material would be sufficient with enough over to alter the sleeves. Your husband could get the loan of an elegant dress-coat from his tailor for a couple of shillings, and instead of thinking of silver plate, choose a pretty flower-pot, and present it to them in a somewhat dignified way. That would do quite as well."

Augusta shook her head. "His bride doesn't care about flowers," she said, "and greatly prefers what is valuable and expensive ; and it is of no use your trying to persuade me that my dress could look anything but as ancient as the one my grandmother wore when she was confirmed."—"Do not talk so irreverently, Augusta," said I ; "I remember your grandmother quite well—she was one of the Neumanns in the Linien Strasse, and I do not think it well-mannered of you to use the good old lady as your last trump card, in order to have your own way. I can tell you this : money is easily spent, but not so easily made."

"I am sorry if I have applied to you at an inconvenient moment," said Augusta a little huffishly, and, rising from her chair, she added : "it's high time I were at home again to see the children." Whereupon, I said, "Sleep well over it again is my advice to you ; I'm sure you could manage more economically."— "No," she replied, "I'm sure we couldn't, for I did

not even include twelve-buttoned gloves in my calcu-
lation.   If I did as you want, I suppose I might
present myself in cotton gloves.   In grand houses,
however, it's only the servants that do that!" I did
not repeat her own words about considerate conduct,
although I confess I felt myself boiling up. I merely said: "I mean it all more for your own good
than you seem to imagine; you can sew three buttons to the end of every finger of your gloves, for all
I care; that, at all events, would create sensation
enough!"

She replied that I was perfectly at liberty to act thus,
if ever I got into the dilemma of being drawn up into
tip-top society.   " Gusta," I called out after her, "you
don't mean to say you are crying about a couple of
plums.   Don't make yourself ridiculous!" But she
had already gone, and did not hear me.

How right Carl is, after all!—for he has often said :
"Money matters put an end to all sentimentality."
As a rule, when Augusta came to see me, we were as
one heart and one soul, for I have a very good opinion
of her.   Darwin has proved wrong in her case, for her
part of the Bergfeldt characteristics seems to have
been transmitted to a lateral branch.   But now that
rank and giddying wealth is to be married into the
family by Emil, she too is beginning to become de-
luded, and the mother's nature seems to be coming
out in her, like wisdom teeth that appear late in life.
Any lasting kindliness of feeling towards Frau Bergfeldt is one of the seven impossibilities in this world,
as any one may know who has discovered her narrow-
ness of mind, after having been long acquainted with
her.   When one sees a woman like her trying to rise
out of her station, and yet so wanting in culture that
she is perpetually giving glaring proofs of her igno-

rance, it is exactly as if a hen were trying to imitate a
skylark.   It can't be done, in fact !

I told Carl of the business that had induced Augusta
to apply to me for assistance, and did not omit a single
syllable that had passed between us, as I wished him
to support me in my resolve to refuse them the money.
For as I said, have we got the money to throw away ?
Who knows but what coffee and petroleum may be
hurled up to an unattainable height, by the new tax
upon corn ?   Each one is bound carefully to look after
what he has, unless he means to end his days in a
workhouse.

"Wilhelmine," said Carl thoughtfully, after he had
let me have my say, and a word or two more ; "have
you felt these bad times so very heavily that you bring
them forward in justification of your action ?"—
"What do you mean by justification and action ?   If
you can't express yourself a little more clearly, I
sha'n't be able to understand you."   He took my hand,
as if by accident, stroked it affectionately, and said :
"Now tell me, would it not have been better to have
offered Augusta the money ?   Aren't you a little sorry
already to have said her nay ?"—"Carl, do you mean
to say you want the Bergfeldts to make a show by our
emptying our pockets ?   Twelve-buttoned gloves, indeed !   She'll either have that or none.   It was just as
if her old mother had been talking out of her, *per*
telephone !   No ; I say that if any one is to have
twelve-buttoned gloves it's me or Betti !   But we are
not ambitious of any such piece of extravagance !"

"Now, do not excite yourself, Wilhelmine.   What
does it matter about the gloves ?   A more important
matter is at stake—the Weigelts' whole happiness."—
"Are you in earnest ?" said I uneasily, for my husband
at that moment did not look at all disposed to jest.—

" Perfectly in earnest," he replied. " When women set their minds upon having a thing, they will have their way, even though mischief should come of it."— " Carl, what do you know about women ?" I asked severely.—" We were talking of the Bergfeldts, weren't we ?" he replied.—" I could have wished that subject left untouched."—" What I wish to say is that Augusta will get that money, whatever happens."—" Well, then she'll get what she wants."—" Not altogether, I am afraid."—" Carl, do me the favour, and don't talk in riddles ; tell me briefly and clearly what it is you fear."—" What I fear is that the Weigelts will fall into the hands of money-lenders and be completely ruined. Let us lend them the money, Wilhelmine. If Emil has promised to assist them later, he'll do it. At all events they would be out of their difficulty for a time, and be prevented from taking some foolish step. What do you say, Wilhelmine ? "

I considered for a moment, and then said : " Carl, do you think Augusta imagined I refused her request from unkindness, or because I grudged her the pleasure ?"—" The childlike trust she has always felt towards you, will have vanished now, I think."—" The Weigelts are so wanting in independence ; if one did not watch them, they would be sure to commit more stupidities than might even be God's will. So, after all, we had better spare them the few hundred marks, especially as your business is in woollen wares. I'll go to Augusta to-morrow—it is too late to-day."—" If you mean to offer help, do not wait," said Carl, by way of warning, as I left the room.

I felt much comforted in mind after my talk with Carl, and went to see about supper ; it seemed as if a weight that had oppressed me ever since Augusta's visit, had suddenly been taken off me. I sent the

servant-girl out for a red herring, and prepared it for
Carl with my own hands, using a whipped egg and a
pinch of white pepper, that being the way he likes
them best.

My husband had advised me to send Augusta a letter
by the tubular-post, to say that I would call on the
following afternoon about the money matter; however, I thought that the twenty-five pfennigs might
as well be saved, especially as I did not know whether
the Acker Strasse, where the Weigelts lived, was provided with that blessed postal arrangement. I wish
now that I had sent one of Stephen's officials with my
message, for there are some people who cannot fly
quickly enough into trouble, and the Weigelts are
among the number.

On the following afternoon, at about three o'clock,
when I had climbed to the top of their stairs, I heard
music in the house, only a couple of squeaking notes,
it is true, but still enough to astonish me, for they had
never yet discovered anything in themselves or the
children that indicated the existence of an undeveloped
Beethoven. I rang the door-bell, which Augusta
opened, and at once gave her the good news, by saying: "Child, everything has been arranged; you can
have all you require most willingly."

Curiously enough, it did not have the effect I anticipated. Augusta merely replied: "Come in, and
take off your things, Frau Buchholz."—"Have you
changed your mind about the money, Augusta?" said
I, upon going in.—"Oh, no!" was her answer,
"we've already got what we required; fortunately the
world is not made up of stinginess." I took a seat.
"What musical box is that your boy has got there?"
I asked, pointing to the child, who had the box on a
chair and was grinding away at it in delight. Augusta

looked embarrassed, and carried the boy and the
musical instrument into the next room. When she
returned she said in a matter-of-fact kind of way:
"The little organ was part of the bargain, of course."
—"How so? From whom?"—"From the money-
lender."—"Well, I must say it's very kind of him;
he's no doubt fond of children, and, the box being a
useless thing to himself, he gave it to the boy, I suppose?"—"I did not say that," interposed Augusta;
"I mean he did not charge much for it. Don't you
think it is quite worth fifty marks? Well, he let us
have it for thirty, and it plays five tunes."—"Thirty
marks for that squeaking thing!" I exclaimed; "how
could you let yourselves be taken in like that?"—
"We couldn't well help it."—"Gusta," said I, "sit
down and give me a proper account of what you've
been doing; there's something wrong, that's clear."

She sat down beside me and told her story. After
having applied to me in vain, there seemed nothing
left for them but to go to a money-lender, who advances sums of money to men of small means in return for some voucher with a signature. - "Is the
man a usurer?" I asked.—"No," she answered, "usury
is too strictly prohibited."—"Thank God," said I,
breathing freely again. "But, Frau Buchholz, in the
case of persons with small incomes like ourselves, of
course there is not much security, so one is obliged to
take half of the money in goods, so that the man may
have some compensation for the money he advances."
—"Barrel-organs and such useless rubbish!" I said
sharply. "There are some useful and very valuable
articles among them," she replied, pointing to a number of packages in the corner. "There's a damask
table-cloth large enough for a table to seat twenty-
four persons—a wonderfully cheap thing; some excel-

lent rep for furniture covers; three dozen pocket-handkerchiefs; four blue silk umbrellas, six aprons and several smaller articles."—"Will you let me look at the table-cloth?" I asked. Augusta fetched one of the packages and opened it. I examined the table napkins and the table-cloth. I looked at them again and again before I could make up my mind to tell her the inevitable truth in an inoffensive way. At last I said: "Augusta, the cloth is splendid and will last for ever if you never take it into use; but this I can tell you, that if ever a drop of wet falls upon it, the pattern will vanish. It is nothing but a common printed article—a genuine piece of swindle—not worth a penny."

Augusta looked at me in amazement. "That's impossible," she exclaimed; "it's valuable damask."—"It has not even lain among linen, I should say," was my reply. "I must tell you," said Augusta, "that in order to obtain the 300 marks we had to purchase to the amount of 400 marks."—"And all upon credit?"—"All at eight per cent. interest, which we shall have to pay every month."—"And where are the 700 marks to come from?"—"It will have to be paid off gradually as my husband's salary becomes due."—"Augusta," I remarked, "could you not have waited a little? I see now, unfortunately, that I have come too late. How, in all the world, do you mean to get rid of all these debts?"—"We trust to Emil helping us."—"But supposing he dare not touch the money, remember it's hers."—"Well, but my husband's income goes on increasing year by year."—"You will need all he makes yourselves; as the children get bigger, you will find your expenses increasing at the same time. Moreover, a rise in his office isn't like climbing a ladder, it's more like a slow drive through sand."—

"All that's going to be changed. My husband says
that unless he gets an increase soon, he means to
go over to the Left, and the Government will then
come to see that it is standing in its own light. He goes
regularly to his political club; liberty, he says, must
come off victorious in the end."—"Augusta," said I,
"do not talk of things you understand as little as
damask table linen. Take all this rubbish back to the
man, and let him quit you of the 400 marks, or, better
still, back out of the whole agreement, and trust to
us."—"That's impossible now."—"If I offer you the
money, you surely have only to say Yes!"—"I
daren't."—"Now, then! just tell me who dare say you
daren't?"—"My husband."—"What can he mean?"—
"He says that circumstances will be very different when
the Opposition have the helm in hand; taxes are to
cease, salaries to increase, and living to be made cheap;
that we shall then not need to go a begging, and to
expose ourselves to getting a refusal. First, it was
you that wouldn't listen to us, now we won't listen to
you. If only the Opposition could have its turn now!"
—"Augusta," said I, "this is all stuff and nonsense.
Have I not always proved myself a motherly friend to
you? When I hesitated about giving you the money,
I was merely considering what was best for yourselves. Now, do follow my advice."

She cast down her eyes, and said in a low voice:
"It can't be done now. I have already bought material for my dress, and sent it to the dressmaker.
The money has already been partly spent, so matters
must remain as they are. And who knows but what
we may yet win in the lottery, for which the man
made us take tickets? He told us that very often
those who were deep in misfortune were the luckiest
in such things."

If only I had not said them nay; or if only I had sent them a message last night; if only I had . . . . yes, if only I had ! There was little use in blaming myself now; and yet I felt as if I had been as much to blame as Augusta herself. " We must wait and hope for the best," I said, rising to go. But before leaving the house, while standing in the dimly-lighted passage, I threw my arms round Augusta, and neither of us could restrain our tears. What we really were crying about, cannot exactly be said ; probably, however, it was the thought that the happiness and contentment which had hitherto dwelt with them up on their fourth storey, was being driven away by their new and grand connections. I could not recover my cheerfulness, much as I tried to ; my mind's eye seemed perpetually dwelling upon that would-be damask cloth, and for long I couldn't get the sound of the barrel-organ out of my head, for which a debt of thirty marks had been inflicted upon them.

THE CHRISTMAS FAIR.

ONE of the prime mysteries in nature—as one may read any day in the newspapers when Michaelmas comes round—are the birds of passage; long before the invention of the compass they have regularly flown straight away to foreign countries, and, in the case of the swallows, these journeys are made even on the very same day and hour of the year. Inexplicable it does indeed seem to me that the birds should all go off together, but as to the reason of their leaving, that cannot be so very incomprehensible to any one with an imaginative turn of mind—they go for their own pleasure's sake; we know that mankind does the same.

In the spring, as soon as the first warm Sunday tempts
him, he wanders about his own neighbourhood; on
Good Friday he must be off to the Spandau Restaurant; at Whitsuntide he wanders out to the Grunewald, on other occasions to Stralau or Treptow; and
as soon as the frost has made the ice firm enough, the
Rosseau Island in the Thiergarten is the object he has
in view. His locomotive organs seem affected in this
way from childhood upwards. Then, when Christmas
comes round, off he must go to the Christmas Fair,
whither some inexplicable power seems to draw him—
four horses couldn't hold him back. It would seem to
be precisely the same as with the birds of passage,
except that the Christmas Fair cannot be said to offer
unalloyed pleasure, especially when a thaw puts in an
appearance, and one comes home with a border to
one's garments as if some higher power had dragged
one through the slush.

We had arranged this Christmas to go with the
Wrenzchens, Uncle Fritz, and the Krauses, although
the Wrenzchens are rather uncertain people, owing
to his being a medical man. The arrangement had
been made more especially on account of the Krauses,
who much needed some diversion, for that boy Eduard
of theirs has again been causing them a good deal of
vexation. Can there be anything harder for a father,
who is himself a school-master, than to have to send
his own son to another school to do his work there?
It never entered Eduard's head to do anything at
home. Not he! in place of learning his Latin he
would run off and play at Robbers and Soldiers in
the Friedrichshain with other boys, or would dawdle
about the streets, and, when locked up by way of
punishment, would play tricks with the lamp, which
might have caused a fire. Then, too, when he was

thought to be really at work, because he was quiet
and seemingly out of mischief, it would be found that
he had a secret Robinson Crusoe or some such story
book by him, and his exercises would be a mass of
mistakes and ink-blots. It was inconceivable to me
that in spite of all this, his mother was for ever trying
to shield him. Did she wilfully blind herself to the
fact that his first baby-shoes had long since been worn
out, and that he no longer wore a little velvet tunic
and little white drawers? She would say: "It is not
right to torment the child with such hard work," and
would say this even in the boy's presence. Eduard
only needed to pretend that the Latin gave him headache, for his mother to say pettingly—" Papa will give
you a note of excuse, my darling, and will say that
you were not well ;" whereupon Eddy would creep
away to the rocking-chair and give himself a swing
just to while away the time. Herr Krause, of course,
did not dare to make any objection, else she would
immediately bring up the subject of over-working
young children, and he would have as little to say for
himself as an untidy recruit. What a miserable speci-
men of a man he is !

Things would have remained in this state, goodness
knows how long, had it not been that the young scamp
created a pretty disturbance one day. It happened
thus. Close to the Landsberger Strasse is the St.
George's Churchyard, which has been turned into a
garden, and benches are placed there, where old people and sick folk can have a rest, for into their little
rooms the sun shines perhaps but for one short hour
a day, and maybe not even as long. Of little folks,
there is, of course, no dearth, and no prettier scene
can be imagined, than when a grand wedding takes
place, and the young couple—in their deep emotion—

come out of the church forming one group with the nursery maids, and nurses with little infants in their arms—a group which is, indeed, but a passing one, and yet promising much for the future.

At such moments the bigger children are, of course, left without supervision, and Eduard Krause made use of a moment of this kind for his disgraceful piece of mischief. On a heap of sand, where most of the little children were grubbing about, he placed a small can of lamp-black, and it is still a mystery where he got hold of the stuff. Now, as we all know, children, unfortunately, look upon everything they find as playthings, whether it contains lamp-black or any dangerous material, and thus, scarcely had ten minutes elapsed, when the sweet little creatures had completely covered themselves with the black stuff, and looked like a pack of little negroes : hands, faces, clothes were all full of it, and the original white of pinafores and stockings had vanished, probably never to be seen again ; certainly not, at their first washing, in any case.

But the Nemesis had not been asleep. An old man sitting on one of the benches, sunning himself a little, had noticed that Eduard had placed something on the heap of sand, and then hurried off ; however, as the bride's carriage drove up at the moment, he did not pay any further heed till the mischief was done, and the only thing was to get the little dirty pigs home, which was not accomplished without scoldings and pushings, and a great amount of crying. The old man then related what he had seen, and as young Krause's ways were well known, it was at once suspected that he was the culprit.

Several excited mothers and some loud-voiced fathers afterwards went to Herr Krause's abode, and offered to sell him the children's besmudged clothing, and he did, in some cases, agree to repay them for the damage done, although not very willingly. Eduard's misdeed was the talk of half the Landsberger Strasse for some time afterwards, and the Police-lieutenant's wife told me her husband had said that if the police had been appealed to, the case might have been made a criminal misdemeanour, and that the father had acted wisely in taking the matter in hand and settling it quietly. Herr Krause has, since that day, tightened the reins a little, it must be confessed ; but nothing much will be gained by it. His reins are mere threads of cotton.

Hence it was more than right that the Krauses should have some diversion and amusement, and the proposal of a walk to the Christmas Fair seemed very welcome to them. We expected them to call for us about six o'clock, as had been arranged, but it was half-past before they came. Frau Krause excused herself by saying that at the last moment she had missed her Japanese tray, and that she had been looking for it, but could not find it. I said that such things were apt to get lost, or to slip behind some piece of furniture, and that she would probably find it in the morning, or, at any rate, before long. It did turn up again, but in a very different way from what we had anticipated, and, I may say, it was in a most calamitous way. However, of this all in good time.

We did not wait long after we had all assembled, and we walked away in the direction of the Schloss Platz, for that was, of course, the principal part of the market. We were somewhat slow in getting there, partly because of the crowds, partly on account of the shops which had to be looked at. First one of us and then another kept calling the other's attention to what pleased us best. "No, but do look at this!"--"Oh, I should like to have that!" —"Just look, how lovely!" And so it went on turn about. Many of the shops really surpassed themselves. In one confectioner's there was even an artistic castle made of nothing but gingerbread, and some equally artistic-looking men made of plums to represent knights.

Then, too, the drapers' establishments and the china shops, and those with bronzes, and the silk mercers; every one of them were exhibiting their choicest wares and displaying them to the best advantage. At Christmas time everything looks brilliant, and the ap- pearance of the shop windows would almost make one fancy there was some special illumination, every jet of gas and every lamp that will burn is lighted, and the brightest and most glittering things are placed in the windows: there's no getting by at all. One hears so constantly of the treasures of the East, and of the splendid bazaars there. There's little rhyme or reason in that. Before Christmas, isn't all Berlin, with its immensely long and brilliantly lighted streets, one monstrous bazaar?

In the midst of all this modern splendour, lies the Christmas Fair like a bit out of the good old times. It was the same in the old days when my parents took me there for the first time, and it is precisely the same at the present day. There are the same long narrow rows of booths, the same toys are exhibited; the peo- ple selling their goods have noses as red with cold as in the olden days; and wear the same sort of warm caps; and the younger folks selling their three- farthing lambkins, sawing-jacks, monkeys, and jointed wooden-dolls, and whatsoever else there may be, have exactly the same kind of thin voices as in the old

days. And how deliciously balmy is the smell of the
dark fir-trees, whole forests of which are standing
about, and the light green pyramids decorated with
bright tinsel, and covered with lights. And how comforting is the smell of the fresh pancakes and the
pastry ! And what numbers of people, big and little,
are enjoying themselves as if they had never before
seen such a glorious sight, gazing again and again in
admiration, at what, after all, cannot be anything altogether new to them. Jumping-jacks are still to be
had at the same corner as of old ; they are painted
red, yellow, and green, with a feather in their hats,
and their legs and arms clatter at the pull of a string,
just as in years gone by. The hawker's cry, too, is
still : "Front-ways he'll nod to you, backwards he'll
jerk to you, and all for a penny, the splendid Jack.
Buy him, my lady, he's the last I've got !" It all
sounds so friendly-like, as from the far-off days of
childhood ! Oh, the dear, good old Christmas time !

What has always made upon me an indescribable
impression, is the solemn, silent Royal Palace standing there like a giant, towering above the market
stalls that look dwarfed beside it. Round the Palace
is a confused hum of human voices, and a red glim-
mer of a thousand little lights, as if the shuffling,
scuffling Present could not find a better shelter than
by the side of the unalterable Past. "And, in fact,
this is the case," said Herr Krause to me ; "for upon
the self-same places where the people in former times
flocked together for their sacrificial feasts, the strong-
holds of Rulers, or Christian churches were eventually
built. Hence, even at the present day the annual fairs
are held almost exactly on the very same places, and
the same days upon which the idolatrous worship of
the heathen once took place. Who knows but what,

7

exactly where we are now standing, human beings
were once sacrificed at the time of the winter solstice,
while those who watched the tilting matches and
shouted to their gods, probably stood somewhere
about the part which now goes by the name of the
noisy corner of the market?"—"Herr Krause," said I,
after he had talked himself out, "I think you can't be
feeling quite yourself! Do you fancy a King of
Prussia would have tolerated such heathen worship,
and human sacrifices, and turmoil, in front of his windows? What would have been the use of the
Royal Guards?"—"I must beg you to remember
that all this occurred in prehistoric times, when iron
was still unknown, and people used stone knives."—
"Here, in Berlin?"—"Assuredly, here as well as elsewhere."—"Who do you think will believe such
things?"—"You may see the stone implements any
day in the Museum; they are obvious proofs of what
I have told you."—"Well, granting that people may
at one time have eaten with stone knives in Berlin,
surely it can only have been from pure stupidity."—
"Prehistoric investigations corroborate what I say."
—"Herr Krause, you are a teacher, and know all this
better than most people, no doubt; but I can only
hope you do not impart this kind of universal history
to your pupils."—"Certainly I do, young people must
be made acquainted with the first beginnings of a
nation's life to understand themselves and their
position in the body politic."—"To my mind universal
history begins with our great Elector, while the times
of Frederick the Great are far from being the end of
it," said I, "and if you want any pupil of yours to
understand what he is as a body politic, he need only
know that he is a German, and that his duty is to love
his fatherland and his Emperor with his whole heart.
That's about enough."

What is it that makes men's minds confused? It's a superabundance of cleverness, and Herr Krause seems to be suffering from that.

We had not, however, gone to the Christmas Fair to quarrel, but to buy useful things. Tradespeople want to dispose of their goods, and hence come from far and near, and offer a great selection of useful, domestic utensils at a cheap price. Herr Krause, for all I care, may use stone knives, if he likes. We separated, therefore, and turned our attention to business.

Emmi and I set about purchasing a sieve which she was much in need of, as, of course, it greatly facilitates the making of pease-pudding which the Doctor is fond of having on a Thursday with pigs' feet. Uncle Fritz meanwhile was at another booth buying honey cakes with inscriptions in sugar, to please us; he'd better have done no such thing. On my cake was written: "Old lady, don't grumble!" on Emmi's: "For ever will I stick to thee, hurrah." The one Dr. Wrenzchen got he quickly put in his coat pocket, not, however, before I had noticed that he had coloured up. "Fritz," said I, with a touch of annoyance, "I must say that this sugared poetry is not at all to my liking."—"Then scrape it off," he replied, "and get Leuenfels to write something else. The cake will be none the worst for it." Fritz, in fact, is incorrigible.

We wanted also to see the Breite Strasse, to have a look at Rudolph Hertzog's establishment; in the first place, because the most brilliant display imaginable is always to be seen there; and, in the second place, because my Carl provides that enormous establishment with various kinds of fancy articles which are woven expressly for the firm. But happy as was the thought, the getting there had its difficulties, for no greater crushing and pushing can be met with anywhere, than at the corner where the Schloss-Platz and the Breite Strasse meet. Nevertheless, we did succeed at last in getting through; for it is the custom in Berlin, when there are great crowds upon holidays, always to keep to the right in the streets, hence it is only strangers that are to be seen fighting against the stream, till some one calls out, "You, there, keep to your right, else those huge beetle-crushers of yours will be trodden to bits." That quickly has effect.

When we could breathe freely again, and had got safely out of the crush in rather a tumbled condition, we passed a long line of persons selling a variety of small wares. "I'm going to make some purchases here," said Uncle Fritz, "I find I want all sorts of things, and I dare say all of you must have come across people with a host of children, but little else in the world, what do you say?" And strangely enough each one of us could remember some such case! How flourishing their business became, when we all drew out our purses, it was delightful truly. Uncle Fritz bought up everything that was left, and one of the lads cried out—"Hurrah! I've sold everything; what'll mother say to that!" And off he scampered. What joy, about a few pence!

Another youngster scampered off too, leaving Frau Krause with a Japanese tray in her hands, speechless and horrified, like a petrified pillar of salt. Herr Krause flew off after the runaway. "My dear Frau Krause," exclaimed I, "what's the matter with you? Whatever's happened?"—"It's our tray," she moaned. "Oh, Eduard!" She staggered. Uncle Fritz hurried to support her, gave her his arm, and said: "Try to recover yourself, and look at the matter from the brighter side." This, however, she did not do, but pulled out her handkerchief, and we had a nice hysterical scene.

Meanwhile, Herr Krause returned. "He's escaped me," he called out angrily. "Who has?" I asked. "Eduard," he burst out. "What a boy he is! He has helped himself to my cigars, and been selling them here at the Christmas Fair. The tray also he took . . . . bored holes into it . . . . ran a cord through it . . . . and hung it round his neck. And there he stood among those poor children! When I caught sight of him, and thought I had got hold of him . . . . out he slips his head from between the cords, and off he flies! The police shall be sent after him!"— "How can you be so inhuman?" Frau Krause began. "Come, let us go home, Eduard's sure to be in a terrible state of fright."—"No," said Herr Krause, "I shall remain where I am; were I to settle matters with him at this moment, I might, perhaps, be too severe with him. To-morrow morning he shall have his reward."—"You don't mean to beat him, surely?" whined Frau Krause. In a gentler tone Herr Krause then said: "I shall set him a task for each day, and" —he added in a more sorrowful tone—"he shall have nothing for Christmas."—"Surely you'll let him have a tree," the mother cried out. "No tree at all," sighed the father.

"If those words were a bridge, I, for one, wouldn't venture upon it," my Carl whispered to me. "In three days it will all have been forgotten," I replied, "yet, in my opinion, Krause ought to give the young scamp such a thrashing that nothing would be left of his jacket beyond the button-ho'es, otherwise nothing reasonable will ever be made of the boy."—I am on principle averse to every kind of flogging as a means

of punishm nt, because it is an unenlightened proceeding and inhuman ; but thrashings there must be.

After this occurrence we had no proper interest in
looking at any more of the brilliant Christmas displays
exhibited in the shop windows, and so we followed
Uncle Fritz, who—by way of making us a little return
—had invited us all. to Dressell's restaurant, as he
cannot well show us any hospitality at his own rooms.

We might have been a very merry party had not
the Krauses been in such utter distress : he with the
furrows of anger on his brow, she with her tearful
looks and spoiled Japanese tray. Uncle Fritz had
ordered Dressell to provide a sumptuous supper, with
all kinds of delicacies that, as a rule, do not find their
way in among the homely fare of ordinary folks. He
can, of course, indulge in such things, as his business
is more flourishing than it ever was, and he is inclined
to be lavish with his money.

But although everything was excellent, we were a
pretty silent party at table out of consideration for
the Krauses. At last Uncle Fritz could not resist exclaiming : "Good Gracious ! are we then to be so
merry, who have little need to be so ! "—"That you
may well say," replied Herr Krause, " but if your own
flesh and blood played such tricks with lamp-black,
and then . . . ."—" He didn't mean any great harm by
it," broke in Frau Krause.—" Really ! " exclaimed
Herr Krause, as sharp as vinegar. Whereupon Frau
Krause retorted excitedly : " You know yourself that
Eduard takes unusual interest in foreign nations. I
can honestly say that no boy of his age is his equal in
that ! and how well he remembers every detail about
Columbus and Robinson Crusoe . . . ."—" Now,
Adelheid, what has all that got to do with the lamp-
black, and his destroying the children's clothes, which

I had to pay for pretty heavily," exclaimed Herr Krause.—"Well," she answered snappishly, "he told me, for he confides in me, because I'm not so violent and unfeeling as you . . . . that he wanted to see those children represent a scene in Ara Pequenna, where the negroes live. . . . ."

Herr Krause looked at his wife as if he meant to ask her whom she thought of bamboozling with such stories. This silenced her, and she even looked a little embarrassed. Uncle Fritz, on the other hand, maintained that it was undoubtedly a very amusing game, and added that it promised great things for Eduard's future, when matters might be arranged with a little less black, and ended by saying he thought Eduard had an uncommon degree of inventive genius. Frau Krause, however, took offence at this, and asked whether any one of us doubted the truth of what she had said; that, at all events, she did not mean to be insulted in that manner, and up she got in a huff and insisted upon going. Neither of them could be induced to remain, and so off they went, and we blessed their departure.

We others remained. Herr Dressell, elegantly attired and with a white waistcoat on, presented us ladies each with a lovely bouquet of flowers, and took the trouble to see that there was plenty of ice for us, both vanilla and strawberry, the coolness of which was irresistible ; so we soon recovered our good humour. The Doctor filled our glasses with the utmost amiability, and even peeled me an orange with his own fingers. When he chooses he certainly can be most agreeable; except about those Thursday evenings.

We ended the evening by drinking to the toast, that next year we might again have a Christmas migration, but only a family party. I could not resist adding :

"and let us follow the example of the birds of passage when the time comes ; every one must come, no matter whether it be from across the ocean or from the Landsberger Strasse, and thence on to the Schloss-Platz and to Dressell's in the Linden. A few kilometres more or less won't matter. The main thing is the proper sentiment in the human breast ! "

"Wilhelm !" exclaimed Uncle Fritz, "that was capitally said, and if you were a man I would certainly have you posted up in our electoral district ! "

Of course, healths all round were then drunk again, and our glasses made to ring.

FASHIONABLE SOCIETY.

THROUGH my son-in-law we had become so intimately acquainted with the Lehmanns that we were very soon on a pleasant footing with them without any formalities between us ; in fact our intercourse with them was quite friendly, we invited each other without any of those stylishly got-up cards with the formal " *Genöthigt wird nicht* " * which have become the fashion. For the mere sending out invitations has now come to be considered a pleasure. The Lehmanns, however, at times fall back into their old formal ways, as we experienced, much to our regret ; this they ought all the more to avoid doing, as Frau Lehmann is much too timid to manage large entertainments, and her husband seems always to act as though he were his own guest.

* Until recently it was in Germany the " good old custom " for the host and hostess to *urge* their guests to partake of what was on the table. The word used now on invitation cards, and even on small banners decorating the dishes, mean simply that at supper guests are requested to attend to themselves.

A fortnight beforehand we received a card the size of a calendar for hanging on a wall, with the words :

"Assessor Lehmann and his wife do themselves the honour of inviting Herr and Frau Buchholz and daughter to tea on the evening of Saturday, the 17th of January, at 8.30 o'clock. R. S. V. P."

"Carl," said I, "this is a case of a dress-coat and a white tie for you, and a very important matter as regards dress for Betti and me. I can manage easily, for I shall only need to have my claret-coloured silk, the one I had for the wedding, a little altered."—"An erection stuck on behind, no doubt?"—"Carl," said I, "it is very improper of you to speak of such things, and, indeed, I should much prefer your not observing ladies' external arrangements at all. As to Betti, we have found in the last number of the *Modenwelt* a gem of a dress, which will do admirably for the season."

"Season," exclaimed Carl, "what do you know about the season?"

"If the Lehmanns give a tea party, then it's the season," I replied; "Frau Lehmann herself told me that they had to do as others did, their social position demanded it."—"Isn't it more likely that she persuades herself to believe such things?"—"Carl, they have an old Excellency in the family and want to show him off; whether they give their guests any enjoyment by it, we had better not say."—Carl laughed, and replied: "Excellencies are always well worth seeing."—Whereupon my remark was: "I heartily wish them joy of their Excellency. Heaven knows what good they get of such things. Costly surroundings and a very meagre effect."

The Wrenzchens were, of course, invited too. Emmi, who did not know whether we had all been invited from the Landsberger Strasse, came round to inquire;

she wanted also to leave her little dog—she had invested in one after all—at our house while she was out, as the animal cannot bear being left with the cook. "Emmi," said I, "that innocent creature might be a warning to you from higher regions, that your cook is a bad character, and it would be wise for you to give her notice to leave. Dogs have a very fine knowledge of mankind; your cook must one day have given the creature a secret kick in its ribs, which it cannot forgive. I can sympathise with it there."

"Mamma," replied Emmi, "Maffi does not really like anybody except Franz and me, and is so fond of barking that he snarls at everyone, especially when my husband is called out of an evening to a patient. Herr Greve, who lives on the floor above, has already written to us complaining of the noise our dog makes. Otherwise, there's not a nicer little animal in the world than Maffi Pamph."—"That's a matter of taste," I remarked; "to my mind its eyes are too horribly like Lucca's."—"Maffi likes you, Mamma, because of the biscuits you bring him, and he would be quite quiet here, I'm sure."—"But it can't be, Emmi, for we're all going to the Lehmanns. Give him an extra good meal before you leave home."—"Pugs seem always to be hungry," said Emmi.—"They are greedy beasts," said I agreeing with her.

All this trouble about the pug the doctor puts up with, owing to those Thursday evenings; he even went himself with Emmi to choose the material for a new dress, and was not as stingy as usual. When I praised him for this in a jocose way by saying, "Now, now, dear son-in-law, such outlays are altogether out of keeping with your domestic arrangements," he replied: "They would be double what they are had we gone into a large house, as somebody suggested." I knew very well that that was a hit at me, but I smiled, saying: "If the house is small there are beer parties enough to make up for it!"—And thus he got what he deserved; but in spite of my momentary triumph, I felt more convinced than ever that before long there will be a clash between us, and neither the pug Maffi nor Emmi's dress will prevent it. But Emmi will then know what she owes to herself and to her family.

While we were thus busily engaged about our dresses, as well as our worries, the first frost appeared. Skating-ponds were opened in all directions; for, as soon as it begins to freeze, the gardens round the beer-houses are immediately flooded of an evening, and next morning skating can be had in the very heart of the town. When my two daughters were still attending school, I had no objection at all to their going to one or other of these places, with their girl-friends, for a penny apiece. The only misfortune that could befall them was that they might run against a tree or a lamp-post. However, as they got older I only allowed them to skate at the Rousseau Island in the Thiergarten, because it is there that the more elegant portion of Berlin society is accustomed to meet for the exhilarating enjoyment of winter.

Our old family physician used always to maintain that there was not a more healthy exercise than skating, and, in this respect, Dr. Wrenzchen may be said to belong to the same school of medicine, for he is fond of a run on the ice himself, and flies across the shining surface like a veritable humming-top, with this difference, of course, that he is wiser and is gifted with sense. And, certainly, it is a pretty sight. Round about the sheet of ice, the Thiergarten looks like a forest, and through the grey wintry branches of the trees the sky is often of a rosy red, with a touch of yellow like a melon, when the sun sinks down on the horizon behind Spandau. The trees on the banks are decorated with gay flags, every nation being represented, and the effect is all the more enlivening as most of the crowd of people are attired in dark costumes. When the military band strikes up some cheerful melody, all the skaters pass in and out among one another in time to the music, as well as they can. Some parties even arrange regular quadrilles, and intricate dances with taking hands, turning round, letting loose, making chains and again taking hands, and one feels astonished at their skilfulness.

The greatest adroitness in skating, as in other such exercises, is displayed by the military men, and the lieutenants develop this rapidity of motion equally well when skating with the wife of a superior officer, as when acting the part of an ice-cavalier to a young lady of whom it is reported that she will not have much under a million marks at her marriage. So here again we have an instance of that dutifulness which distinguishes the service, and can never be sufficiently appreciated. Fräulein Kulecke, who is pretty well up in such matters, drew my attention to this, and pointed out a line of skaters where lieutenants alternated with goodly dowries, and they all had tight hold of one another by the waist. Some people, no doubt, think it unbelievable that any girl could slip straight from the Rousseau Island into matrimony, and with a thaw these attachments are apt to melt away too, as fathers rarely show any great appreciation for the loveliest of eights cut upon the ice, for such skill, although eminently artistic, is a very unremunerative accomplishment. Sometimes, however, as Amanda Kulecke declares, it is managed, for on the way home, through the slushy Thiergarten, the cava-

lier may come out with the word, and she may not say
nay, because, in fact, the girl imagines marriage, too,
a blissful gliding through life.

But it's not always a case of gliding. Life expects
many a one to run down a steep staircase on skates.

The day of the Lehmanns' tea-party had meanwhile
arrived.

As our invitation was for half-past eight o'clock, we
went at about ten o'clock, and arrived in very good
time, for the grander an evening is to be, the more
abominably late the guests appear. We were far from
being the last to arrive, but his old Excellency was
already there, and, to a certain extent, formed the
brilliant centre of light, owing 'to his bald head and
his numerous decorations. We were presented to
him at once, and His Excellency expressed himself as
being very pleased to have the privilege of making
our acquaintance. Whereupon I replied, with the
most formal of curtseys and visible solemnity, that
the privilege was all on our side. By so doing I
wished him to see that although we belonged only to
the middle class, we were by no means overawed by
Excellencies. His Excellency then entered upon a
long talk with my Carl about business in general,
which I considered wanting in tact, as he might have
known that ladies took no great interest in such subjects. I moved aside, therefore, with a less deep but
well-measured curtsey, and amused myself by watching the other guests. The number of persons the
Lehmanns had invited was endless. To remember
them all one would need have been born with a memory the size of an omnibus.

The only persons I knew were the Hamburg doctor
and his charming young wife, who was dressed in grey
silk dotted over with rose-buds, and cut à la Marie

Antoinette, which suited her to perfection. Betti had been at once taken possession of by two lieutenants, and was engaged in conversation with them. Emmi, on the other hand, felt drawn to the wife of the Hamburg doctor, and I must confess that, although young girls may be lovely, young wives are far more bewitching. There seems so much depth of feeling about them.

After a time I found myself near the seats of honour, namely, round about the sofa where the elderly and most voluminous ladies made a solemn impression by their very dignified appearance and the brand-new ribbons of their caps. Tea was taken without so much as the sound of a word, and with it there was handed round a fruit tart and small narrow knives to eat it with.

What was there to talk about? All of us being perfect strangers to one another, no one, of course, cared to open their mouths with a remark about the weather; then one don't seem to know enough about the theatres; and household affairs are naturally too inferior a subject for the occasion. Guests were, moreover, still coming in, and the crush was so great, one might have supposed the Lehmanns had annexed the waiting-room of a railway station, and that some official would presently be ringing a bell and calling out: "Take your seats, please!"—I kept thinking to myself: "I wonder what's to happen next. If we had been in the Landsberger Strasse we should all long since have been sitting round the supper-table, and would know what we had been invited for."

The room was now crammed full, and I was secretly beginning to denounce the season and these fashionable gatherings, when some one began to play on the piano. The Lehmanns had managed to secure the

services of a youth from one of the conservatoires; he
wore huge linen cuffs, only three pairs of which could
go to the dozen. This youth then attacked Mozart
and the audience too; it was a perfect banging. This
roused the canary out of its sleep, and it forthwith
began singing at the top of its voice and utterly
drowned the music that followed. In fact the musical
entertainment could not be continued till the bird's
cage had been covered over. A young lady then rose
and filled the room with her shouting. Of melody, in
my opinion, there was nothing to be heard, but the
effect was all the more melancholy. As soon as the
applause ceased, she commenced a second perform-
ance. It was of the same doleful colour, enough to
give a drill-sergeant the blues. When the accom-
panist had wrung out a few melancholy chords by
way of conclusion, I said to the lady on my right :
"There now, the second child's dead too !"—"Whatever do you mean?" she asked.—"Oh," I replied,
"that's what we say when a mournful piece of music
comes to an end."—"It was my daughter that was
singing," she retorted in a stinging way, and turned
her back upon me.

In order to show her that her behaviour had left me
perfectly cool and indifferent, I turned to the lady on
my left and endeavoured to start a conversation with
her, and began by speaking of a flaxen-haired youth,
above life-size, who had at that moment entered the
room, and seemed a fitting subject for remark.—"What
kind of genius is that, I wonder?" said I.—"Whom
do you refer to?" replied the lady.—"That very long
young man standing there at the door," said I; "you
just wait and see if he doesn't cause mischief."—"I
am not aware that my son has given you any reason
for such a remark," she answered snappishly.—"Par-

don me that ever I was born," I replied, remembering
that what one calls out into a wood, the echo brings
one back.

I vowed to myself not to utter a single word more,
as I could not possibly know in what relation all these
people, whom the Lehmanns had collected in honour
of His Excellency, stood to one another; so I allowed
my thoughts to speculate about the ways of fashionable society. From these gloomy reflections I was
fortunately aroused by supper being announced.

In the next room, which had been kept locked all
the evening, a side table had been arranged with all
possible kinds of eatables, and presented a very inviting appearance when the doors were thrown open.
The gentlemen hurried in and gallantly attended to
the ladies. Those ladies, however, who had no special
gentleman to attend to them, and who did not choose
to push themselves forward, got nothing. I was
among the last to reach the manger, and succeeded
only in snatching hold of a small dessert plate and a
knife and fork; at the same time I saw that all such
dainties as caviare, *patés de foie gras*, and chicken, had
already vanished. Of the turkey nothing was left but
the skeleton, and of the fillet of veal only the mark on
the dish where it *had* been. There was, however, still
some Italian salad to be had, also some cold sliced meat
which, upon closer inspection, proved to be American
tinned meat and Brunswick sausage. The jellies, too,
had scarcely been touched. I took a small helping of
what was left, and while eating it in discomfort in the
midst of a standing crowd, it struck me that one
needed experience in this kind of stand-up supper, as
not a soul thinks of pressing one to take anything; in
fact the whole proceeding seemed to me a kind of
murderous attack, and so I quietly envied the sub-

lieutenants who had been in front of the battle. Betti told me afterwards that her lieutenant had brought her a delicious bit of the breast of a chicken, while he had preferred venison with a goodly supply of caviare. The younger folks had, it seemed, been making engagements with one another, as there was to be dancing later. The Lehmanns thought it better taste to let His Excellency depart first, so there was a little delay. Wine and punch were handed round, and this brought more life into the conversation; His Excellency was meanwhile standing beneath the chandelier, holding a kind of audience.

At the beginning of the evening I had stated that that unusually tall young man would be likely to create trouble, and I proved to be right. When I have a presentiment of anything, it always comes true, and moreover, so precisely like what I had imagined, that I should assuredly have been anointed a prophet had I lived in the Old Testament.

All of a sudden a fluttering, flapping noise passed through the rooms, and it very soon turned out that the canary had escaped. The young man just mentioned, having nothing better to do, no doubt meant merely to amuse himself with the little creature, but his huge awkward hands must have so bent the cage door that it would not close again.

And now the fuss that was made in trying to catch the bird. Several brooms and a pair of steps were fetched, and an endeavour was made to drive the creature into the adjoining room so as to catch it if it were to settle on the cornice. The bird, however, would neither go into the next room nor on to the cornice. The chase became more and more eager and determined, and the bird became the more bewildered. The young man who had caused the mischief took part

8

in the chase, and in this way tried to make up for his awkwardness; but just as he was about to make a very vehement thrust with a broom, as if he were playing billiards in the air, he accidentally struck the glass chandelier beneath which His Excellency was standing, and fragments of glass came pouring down upon His Excellency's shining pate.

Although His Excellency was in no way injured, he at once intimated a wish to withdraw, and thus left the company which harboured so dangerous an individual. This greatly distressed the Lehmanns, who seemed quite to lose their heads. They accompanied His Excellency to the door, and the Hamburg doctor meanwhile caught the bird, and the dancing commenced. The young people enjoyed themselves immensely, as usual on such occasions, but I did not breathe freely till we were on our way home in a second class " rib-breaker," leaving the stifling heat, the badly arranged refreshments, the host of people to whom we were utterly indifferent, in one word, fashionable society, behind us.

When we reached home, my Carl said : "Wilhelmine, if you feel as I do, you'd butter us some bread and let us have a couple of bottles of wine. I'm quite hungry."—"That's just what I do feel," I answered. So there we sat down at three o'clock of a dark winter's morning, in a cold room with ice on the windows, and refreshed ourselves after all the hardships we had endured.

While we were all of the opinion that the Lehmanns could not have given themselves or any one else any pleasure with their tea-party, and were speaking of the various persons in the way they deserved, I asked Betti if Uncle Fritz had not been invited.—" Invited, he was," she replied, " but he told me he had no great liking for stand-up suppers, and that he wouldn't readily be found crawling into such traps."

Upon which I remarked : "I do not consider his words well chosen, but if he means them to refer to the fashionable entertainments of the season, I must confess I approve of what he says ; for, honestly said, I consider this evening the most profitless one I have ever spent in my life."

ON THE WAR TRAIL.

If Uncle Fritz had ever told me, when I was a girl, that at some later period in my life, when I had become a sedate woman, and married moreover, I would one day go out on the hunt after a man without Carl's knowledge, accompanied only by the Police-lieutenant's wife, and that we should do this after the manner of the Red-skins whom we read about in those old days in Lederstrumpf's stories, where it is said they crept stealthily upon their enemy on all fours, and then scalped him amid hideous war-cries . . . . I should certainly have said: "Come now, you've been wearing a new cap and got a chill in your head, no doubt."--But, although it really did come to pass that I had to go out on the war trail . . . . can it be said that I was to blame ? Certainly not ; it was simply owing to the new arrangements that have come to be a necessity in Berlin, now that it is year by year growing bigger, yet these arrangements had been made for well-intentioned persons and not meant to be abused by people without consciences. Or, can Herr Kleines be said to possess a conscience ? I, for

my part, doubt it, but if he has, it must have a loop-
hole. The Police-lieutenant's wife lays the blame on
my shoulders, and says that I should never have introduced him to them ; this, however, I denied with
all the strength in me, for it was she herself who asked
me to introduce him, the day when he came up to us
at Pichelswerder, and her curiosity would not rest till
she knew who the young man was who was talking to
me, dressed in the very height of the fashion. Then
only did I venture to introduce him. If she maintains
anything else, she will at some future day have to
answer for it, when our hearts come to be laid open ;
for the result will not be altogether in her favour.
Still I do not wish to say a word against a lady in her
position, for I value her friendship. And, after all, we
are none of us without our failings, although no one
can say that I have ever made any one responsible for
what other people had done, or exposed them to the
dangers and changes of the weather, merely because,
from a feeling of respect, they made no reply, and
preferred to suffer and endure, rather than over-step
the bounds of social propriety. If Frau Bergfeldt
had met me in that way I should not have forgotten
my superior culture, no, not by any means, but should
have thanked my stars that I was not in her shoes.

The matter in question was as simple as possible.
The Police-lieutenant's wife had noticed that her
daughter Mila had latterly been writing an unusual
number of letters to her girl friends without the postman bringing any answers. This made the mother
suspicious, especially as Mila has really very beautiful
light brown plaits of hair, and has become altogether
very pretty. In my opinion a little too fully formed
for her years ; still, slim enough, and particularly neat
about the feet; this she no doubt has from her father,

who is still very fond of casting a pleased look down
upon his well-fitting boots, although he has long since
passed that period of life when tight shoe-leather is
considered one of the pleasures of existence. Mila
certainly has not inherited her nimbleness of walking
from her mother, any more than she has those neatly
tripping feet of hers; for I'm convinced that since
her mother has been tramping about the world, the
price of leather must have risen. But no one need
take offence at this, for, of course, natural gifts are
natural gifts, and I, for one, consider it condescending
in a lady of her position to promote any special branch
of industry.

When her suspicions were once aroused, and she
felt sure that all was not as it should be, the Police-
lieutenant's wife became watchful; yet, although she
looked all through Mila's possessions, she could not
find a trace of anything. However, on the day of the
big cleaning, when all the furniture is turned upside
down, it came to light—for there among the mattress
springs of an old couch which Mila had in her room
as a sofa, stuck a packet of letters tied together with
a light blue ribbon. All of them were addressed *poste
restante*, and the make-believe friend to whom Mila
had been writing was no other than—Herr Kleines.

When she had recovered from her horror, the Police-
lieutenant's wife locked herself into her room, and
read all the documents through, so she told me afterwards: "exactly like what one reads of in novels,"
she said, "and there was poetry too; Spielhagen
couldn't have done it more effectively himself, I think."

What was to be done? Should she tell her husband,
place the letters all in a row on the table, get him to
sit on the sofa behind, call Mila in, and hold a regular
inquisition that would end in angry words and scold-

ings? Or should she go more cautiously to work ; leave Mila in optical delusion as if nothing were known, and lay hold of Herr Kleines and give him his well-merited deserts? She decided upon the latter course, and therefore rolled the blue silk ribbon round the sinful literature, and confided it again to the sofa springs. She could thus from time to time watch how matters were proceeding, and by always knowing what went on, could, as it were, be her child's own guardian angel in disguise. Of this she was con-vinced—Herr Kleines was a mere family deceiver, who took delight in making love to young ladies, and in breaking off the connection as soon as he noticed that the family were beginning to consider the matter be-yond a joke. This is one of the dark sides of life in a large town ; if anything of the sort happened in a small town, such a man would at once be excommu-nicated by every respectable family, till he made up his mind to marry the girl, or if that couldn't be man-aged, he would be dismissed from his post, and some younger and more honourable man would obtain his place, with a prospect of an increase in salary, so that there might be no excuse for his hesitating to accept the offer.

Herr Kleines' character was sufficiently well known to the Police-lieutenant's wife, for the day after he had taken Mila out in a boat on the Havel in the dark, the Police-lieutenant paid a visit to Herr Kleines' lodgings, and as Herr Kleines happened to be out, the Police-lieutenant had a long chat with his landlady. This landlady became as talkative as he could have wished, for it was clearly a relief to her, once in a way, to be able to blurt out everything uninterruptedly. " He didn't owe her anything, that she must admit ; but as to order—there was nothing whatever of that in him ; if she didn't tidy up everything herself, his room would look as if it had been tumbled up by an earthquake. And then his dreadful and endless smoking ! It was a wonder the house hadn't long since been burnt down ; her new table-cover was full of holes in no time, and a bed-quilt he had also set fire to. When she had complained of this, his reply was 'that she could insure the things against fire if she chose ; he wasn't responsible for such damage.' Was that a proper way to speak ?"—"About what time did he usually come in of an evening ?" the Police-lieutenant had then asked.—"He goes his own way in that more than in anything else," the landlady had answered ; "no Christian way of reckoning time could keep any account of his way of treating day and night. Yet she herself was of a respectable family. Her parents, however, had left her nothing but the house to live upon, and she had been advised to let out the apartments ; it was a hard way of earning a living ; a bitter, miserable kind of life. She never dared be ill, and had to put up with a great deal ; for those young men who were modest and easily pleased were apt to get behindhand in paying what they owed : and those gentlemen who were punctual in paying were full of pretensions, and impudent. Otherwise she would never tolerate the coffee parties they gave, that was certain, for her father had held a good position."

"What were these coffee parties ?" the Police-lieutenant had then asked.—"They call the ladies their cousins," the landlady had replied, "but she knew them to be shop-girls whom they had met at public dancing-rooms."—"Who do you mean by 'they' ?"— "Well, Herr Kleines and Herr Pfeiffer, who has rooms here too. I have to make the coffee and to provide the cakes, and they are all as hungry as young wolves ;

at times I have had to supply them with as much as two marks' worth of cakes. What will be the end of it all? Yet if I drop a word about extravagance, there is at once an uproar, with abusive language. When one has to live upon furnished gentlemen, one gets to know what goes on in the world."

I felt my coiffure standing on end when the Police-lieutenant's wife told me of these goings on, and afterwards, when I had an opportunity, I asked Uncle Fritz if he had ever heard of such things, and whether young men were all as bad as that.—" There's some of one sort and some of t'other," was his reply; and then he added : " but the fault's not theirs alone. If families were to welcome young fellows to their houses, without regarding them merely as matrimonial speculations, many a one would, maybe, be more steady. But as things are, if a young fellow behaves at all in a friendly way towards any of the daughters in a household, the aunts immediately set about making up a match, which makes the man fight shy, and off he goes howling. It's no wonder that he goes and plunges into the stream of Berlin life! What's the good of perpetually regarding society as a mere marriage market?"—What Uncle Fritz got from me in reply to his last remark was not milk-sop, that's certain.

The main point was, however, that we now knew enough about Herr Kleines; and when the plans of the Police-lieutenant's wife were matured, she paid me a visit and said: " Things have come to a point now." —" What?" said I.—" Well, he has invited her to meet him at the confectioner Müller's, to have chocolate there."—" The place opposite the Central Hotel," I asked, " and celebrated for its cakes?"—" That'll be it, for they are to meet at the Friedrich Strasse Station." —" It's shameful," I exclaimed, " to disgrace so welcome an arrangement as a city railway station by such wicked doings ! "—"Yet it was you that introduced him to us."—"It was not," said I.—"It was."—"It was not."—"It was so."—"Well, I never!" I replied, with as much nonchalance as possible, in order not to cause any provocation.—"Frau Buchholz," she resumed with all her innate refinement, "you are, at all events, in some degree responsible, and must, therefore, help me catch Herr Kleines at the station. I have taken our tickets already ; now do be good enough to put on your things and come with me."

I had hitherto always considered a railway journey a kind of pleasure, except, of course, when travelling in one of those crawling trains that stop at every telegraph post ; but I see now that all depends upon the why and the wherefore, and whither one happens to be going, and that speed is, after all, only a secondary consideration.

I should not have been sorry if our engine had had a fit of explosion, or if our train had come to a standstill ; but, as always happens where I am concerned, there was not any such good luck in store. How often I have wished, as a child, when our last holiday had come, and some unfinished work had got to be done, that the school would fall in, or be burnt down, or that the teacher would break his leg—but no such joyful wish of mine was ever fulfilled ; on the contrary, it was sure to happen that the girl next me in class would be asked to repeat the very lines I knew best, and that I had to stutter through the verse which I had felt positive we should never come to at all that day. So, of course, on the present occasion, likewise, not a mortal thing came to my rescue, not a vestige of anything like slipping off the rails, nor the faintest bit of a collision, and before I had sighed myself out, we had reached the Friedrich Strasse Station.

' We shall have to cross over to the other side quickly," said the Police-lieutenant's wife, "for he sent her a ticket to Potsdam, of course, for fear of any one noticing anything, in which case we should have waited in vain at the station on the city line. However, I had read his letter and have seen the ticket he sent her. " Horrible," I exclaimed.—" And, of course, it is doubtful whether the confectioner Müller may not, after all, be a blind, and that he may have the intention to carry the girl out into the wide world."—"Let us hurry, dear friend," said I, "there is some crime in view here that must be prevented. He shall come to know what Frau Buchholz can be !"—" And," added the Police-lieutenant's wife, "he'll think of me too, when the crash unexpectedly comes down upon his head."—"Yes, undoubtedly, we are the thunder-clouds," I said, continuing her train of thought.—" I was not aware that there was anything thunder-cloudy about me," she replied curtly, " and if my new mantle is too good for such an expedition, I need not make myself any reproaches. It was you who introduced him to us."—"No, it was not."—"It was so."—There was no help for it, she persisted in her wilful opinion.

Away we went down the stairs, winding our way through the various passages, past the wigwams with the ticket-collectors inside, first round a pillar here, and a corner there, exactly like Indians on the war trail, till we had found the right entrance, and reached the main-line platform, out of breath.

Meanwhile, daylight had all but come to an end, and the electric lights were lit. The effect was as if moonlight were shining into the huge vaulted building that runs along in a curve, somewhat in the form of an architectural sausage, open at both ends for the trains to fly in and out. The wind, too, comes driving through the gigantic funnel, and persons who have a liking for shattered healths need only run themselves hot, and then sit in one of those stations. In three minutes the first symptoms of a cold in the head will put in an appearance, or the chill will be felt in one's back. In my mind's eye I could already see myself being rubbed with opodeldoc, and taking hot lime-blossom tea ; yet surely the human organism has some other destination in life than merely to catch cold from a feeling of respectful affection. And one's temper, too, does not get any the better from the waiting and standing about ; there are constant tinkling and rattling sounds, and a continual moving to and fro at every turn and corner, just as if the place were regularly haunted, for no human eye can see the electrical wires that regulate all the communication.

The darker the evening got outside, the more eerie things appeared in the station. On looking out from the moonshiny light in the station into the darkness which seemed scarcely larger than a hole in an oven, suddenly something in the distance with a couple of fiery eyes that got larger and larger and rounder and more brilliant every moment—would at last come rushing in, panting like some huge monster, and then as suddenly stand still. As soon as it comes to a stop, of course it is at once seen that the apparition is nothing but a railway train ; but when it first came rushing from the darkness into the light, hissing and spitting, I could have fancied it some supernatural creature about to crush to atoms everything that came in its way.

Then, on every side there is a pushing and driving, to the right and to the left, in front and behind, as if the devil had let loose all his attendant spirits to frighten one ; we meanwhile sat there in a cutting draught, on the watch for our enemy, our plans of action ready for the coming attack. Escape he could not, for as soon as he set foot on the platform the Police-lieutenant's wife intended to encircle him, while I was to stand at the top of the stairs with my arms stretched out sideways, to cut off his retreat. He was as good as caught already—of this there seemed no doubt whatever.

Just as I was beginning to feel the campaign intolerable, something at last did happen, and although it was not Herr Kleines that appeared, it was his boon companion, Herr Pfeiffer. " There is one of the two," I whispered, " let us to the attack." And before Herr Pfeiffer knew why or wherefore, the Police-lieutenant's wife had met him face to face, and when he was about to make off by turning back, there he had me with outstretched arms before him, as had previously been arranged. Our victory was a splendid one ; he collapsed like a jelly taken out of its mould too soon. But he was hypocrite enough to pretend that he was pleased to meet us. We, too, said that we were very glad to meet so very steady a young man, and thus we bandied about a lot of polite speeches that were positive untruths, the one party endeavouring to conceal his fright, the other their wrath.

He tried in various ways to beat a retreat, but found it impossible ; he said that he must positively go and speak to one of the porters for a minute. But we stuck by him ; thus any communication by which he might wish to warn Herr Kleines was nipped in the bud. At last he made a final effort to frighten us by speaking the truth: " Excuse me, ladies, I must be off to meet a friend, otherwise there will be a calamity." —" May I ask you who your friend is ?" inquired the

Police-lieutenant's wife. — "It is my friend Herr Kleines," replied Herr Pfeiffer in his deepest and most assuring tone of voice.—"Wear him in your cap, for all we care," said I. And scarcely had I flung that piece of ridicule at him, when Herr Kleines himself came bouncing up the stairs two steps at a time; a piece of glass, of course, stuck in his left eye, and the outer man was clothed in an overcoat the colour of wash-leather, like a scavenger's, with reddish-brown checks all over it, which made him look more odd than captivating.

We had thought that, by means of the manœuvres we had practised upon Herr Pfeiffer, we should be able to catch Herr Kleines with the utmost ease, but when he saw us he made off by the way he had come, and scampered backwards to the point where the station ends and the danger of being run over commences. Can he be going to throw himself on to the rails, to be dashed to pieces by the first chance demon of an engine? thought I in horror. But this was not likely, for whilst he fled, he kept turning his face, with the eye-glass, towards us, and hopped from one leg on to the other in a most inelegant fashion, at the same time making most inhuman and contorted grimaces. The Police-lieutenant's wife maintained afterwards, for certain, that he had even stuck out his tongue, and said she supposed it was at me, which favour, however, I modestly thrust back upon her. The whole affair had, moreover, passed so quickly that she may have been deceived, especially owing to the moonshiny light and the presence of the many people about, who, of course, could not imagine what had happened, and gazed in amazement at Herr Kleines' war-dance.

Surely we shall have him yet, thought I, for he

couldn't go much further unless he preferred death to
our society. We had even raised our hands towards
him, when he seemed to touch an iron handle, whereupon immediately and before our very eyes, Herr
Kleines disappeared into the depths, taking off his
hat, and smiling in a bland way as he vanished. The
fact was he had got down the luggage-lift; fancy our
having to witness that !

" Thank God he is safe," exclaimed Herr Pfeiffer, as
the boards closed over Herr Kleines' head, and he had
vanished as if by magic. "You are glad of this?"
said I ; "really I could pity you, Herr Pfeiffer."

If the train from Alexander Platz had not come
up at that moment, with Mila in it, I think the Police-
lieutenant's wife would be standing there still in a
dazed kind of way (as if she had dropped a tray with
dishes), and trying to understand how Herr Kleines
had managed to escape. She did not, of course, know
that his business took him continually to the railway
stations, and that he was intimately acquainted with
all the arrangements there. Otherwise how could he
have made such unconscionable use of the luggage-
lift, which was meant for the convenience of passengers, and had not been put up by the State for the
escape of miscreants. Language has no words for
him ; there is no designation contemptible enough for
such conduct as his.

Mila must have nearly dislocated her neck in trying
to catch sight of the checked ulster with which Herr
Kleines meant to fascinate her ; when, however, in
place of seeing it, she perceived her mother and me,
her head disappeared from the carriage window as
suddenly as if it had snapped back on an india-rubber
string. That was of no use, however, for what has
once been discovered remains discovered, and out she

had to come of the carriage, out of her romantic
dreams of secret meetings with chocolate and the best
of cakes at Müller's, out into real life with electric
lights, out on to the platform for local and main-line
trains.

"You're a nice daughter," exclaimed the Police-
lieutenant's wife in the purest of Landsberger Strasse
dialects ; "come here with you at once," and took hold
of Mila firmly by the elbow. Mila looked as miserable
as if she had been one of Castan's blear-eyed wax dolls
walking in its sleep. I wanted to have a word with
her, but her mother said : "Leave her to me, Frau
Buchholz ; I shall address my daughter as becomes a
mother. The best thing we can do is to pack her off
to a boarding school in Switzerland, and that as soon
as possible. From all I hear they are strict there, and
such places as city railway stations are unknown."—
"That is a great advantage," said I.—"One word
more, Frau Buchholz, you will be discreet, won't you ?
Not a syllable to any one about all this ? Thank you
very much, good-bye ! "

When the mother and daughter had disappeared
down the stairs, I meant to have addressed myself
again to Herr Pfeiffer, partly to give him a final word
of warning, partly also to bind him over to silence.
But he was off "on four dimensions," as Uncle Fritz
has lately taken to saying when anything has vanished.
Probably in his fright he jumped into the train, and
not having a ticket, I can only hope his railway mis-
deeds will not altogether escape punishment. Maybach attends to the comfort of travellers in every
possible way, but any offence committed against the
mighty railway corporation itself, he punishes mercilessly. Let Herr Pfeiffer and Herr Kleines remember
that ! It is quite possible that, in some such case and

in the interest of families, Maybach might order the luggage-lift to be nailed down, and any such result of our war trail would be welcome news to aggrieved mothers. To attain such results, the German people have been given the right to raise complaints, and who can prevent them? But these complaints generally lead to one's being told that all such things are better managed abroad than in our country. Woman, too, has her political rights, and does not need to allow herself to be imposed upon.

The Police-lieutenant's wife told me two days afterwards that Mila is soon to be sent away to Switzerland, where she is to receive instruction in languages and comportment. The mother said she had torn Herr Kleines out of the girl's heart by the root—indeed the girl confessed to have found him more comic and amusing than anything else, and seems not to have taken the matter very seriously. So this love affair of a summer's day may be considered at an end. Nevertheless, I approve of the precaution taken in sending Mila away from the neighbourhood where her admirer resides, and we are, therefore, not likely again to be called upon to go out on the war trail. Mila, too, will make progress with her studies, which is very necessary, for, although we do not make any pretension to occupying as high a social position as the Police-lieutenants, I can truthfully say that in literature, history, and such knowledge, our Betti is a good bit in advance of Mila, in fact as far as the Belle Alliance Platz is from the Wedding.

FORTUNATELY the season was now behind us again, and we were living a harmless kind of life. My Carl had to devote more time to his books than he had ever done before, and seemed to entertain the wish of extending his business and to depend more upon his own manufactures, if only he could have obtained the right sort of help. As, however, he seemed unable to find a suitable partner, the business had to remain as it was, and he had to manage alone. Betti and I, of course, did our best to make his life as pleasant as possible in various ways, for it was, in reality, only for us that Carl kept busy at his books far into the night. He, on the other hand, seemed specially concerned about Betti's welfare, and would say he wanted to see things comfortably settled regarding her future. When I reproached him by saying that he was overworking himself, he would reply: "Do not worry, child! Before the day comes for me to close my eyes, I want to be sure that neither of you will want."—"Carl," said I, "do not talk in that way, it pains me. Whatever should I want with Mammon without you? Do take care of yourself. Keep warm, and do not have such melancholy thoughts; you'll become hypochondriacal, and lose your appetite."—"Well, well, Wilhelmine, as you like, but there's no use trying to conceal the fact that we are neither of us young people any longer."

Of such conversations Betti, of course, was told nothing. She, quite contrary to her former ways, was now taking an active interest in the household arrangements, and no grass was allowed to grow under her feet. And I had the satisfaction of seeing that, of

9

an afternoon, she occupied herself with literature. Her attempts at verse-making were still not very successful, although Herr Leuenfels came from time to time to instruct her in the fundamental principles of poetry. In these lessons I silently took part, sitting at my work table, for one can never know in what way poetry may prove useful some day.

Poetical instruction of this kind is by no means an easy matter. At first Betti was made to select a number of convenient words, such as : wall, warm, pearl, and flower, and had to think of as many rhymes to these as she could find, and then make verses of the collected words. The verses did not become beautiful, some hadn't even a vestige of sense, but even Herr Leuenfels declared these exercises to be utterly indispensable, inasmuch as persons not quick at rhymes would never produce anything great in poetry. He said that even the so-called classic writers (and Leuenfels somehow had a mighty pique against them) were bunglers at rhyming, and had, moreover, perpetually borrowed from the ancient Greeks, and other such careless poets.

"You must be mistaken there, or be thinking of some one else," said I, disputing his remark. "Do you mean to say that Schiller—that noble soul—decked himself with the feathers of others? 'No,' say I, his earthly sojourn was too honest for that."

"Pshaw! He honest, indeed!" exclaimed Leuenfels disparagingly; "why, he had his cellars full of the best of wines."—"And he deserved to," I replied.—"For those commonplace rhymes of his?"—"It's not every one can make as good ones," said I, getting personal ; "and as to his having copied others, I don't believe it." In place of answering me, Leuenfels took a volume of Shakespeare and one of Schiller out of the book-case, and turned up certain passages where he said Schiller's dishonesty was most distinctly evident. "In 'Hamlet,'" he said, "we find the words 'Fare well,' and in Schiller's *Cabale und Liebe* 'Fare well.' In the same way in 'Hamlet' we find, 'there comes the King,' and in Schiller's *Jungfrau von Orleans* precisely the very same words. And his Louise Millerin says 'Oh,' and 'Ophelia' says 'Oh,' and there are numberless instances of the kind."

"Now you see, Mamma," said Betti, who had been helping Herr Leuenfels compare the passages, "if Schiller had done this at an examination, he would never have been allowed to pass."

"And to think that for all this length of time his works have nevertheless been described as classic!" I exclaimed in dismay; "whom can one trust nowadays? Everything is false."

"We can tell to a nicety, in the case of all of them, where they have been light-fingered," said Leuenfels; "but we younger poets do not let anything escape us with regard to their so-called heroic minds; we are pitilessly searching in our work."

I felt as if struck dumb at this discovery, for, honestly said, I loved my Schiller; he was more to me than any other poet. "Did he steal his 'Song of the Bell' too?" I asked.—"Of this we have as yet not obtained any reliable information," replied Leuenfels. —"That is, at all events, some comfort, for I know it almost all by heart, and it would be very disagreeable to think one were carrying stolen goods about in one's memory."

"It is time that this excessive praise came to an end," added Leuenfels. "Why is it that the public extol the ancient writers and neglect the younger school of poets in such an unwarrantable manner? The works of ancient writers are purchased, while we are left to grow mouldy in editors' desks. The feeling for genuine poetry has died out among the people.'—"Do not be too hard upon the people," said I, by way of consoling him; "depend upon it, you will be admired when you are dead." He threw himself into an arm-chair, pushed all his ten fingers through his fair hair, and said, moaning: "I feel it; I was born into this ungrateful world a century before my time!" Thereupon, with a scoffing laugh, he exclaimed, "Why did I not think of starting a beerhouse!"—"You can do so still," said I, "if the people absolutely refuse to have their tastes purified. Moreover, I do believe they understand beer better than poetry. Test them by putting a book of poetry by the side of a beautiful cool pint of beer; you will see which they will grasp at first."—"They are not worthy of our writing poetry for them. And for all I care, let them sink into the slough of their own vulgarity. I will shatter my harp, and leave the people to perish."—"What cruelty!" I exclaimed; "do try once or twice again in kindliness of spirit, as Abraham did with the people of Sodom and Gomorrah, before God cast His dynamite upon them."

"How can I do so, when no one will listen to me?" he began again. "Into the paper-basket they have cast my songs, and—oh, woe is me!—among the 'Editor's Gossip' have I been scoffed at!" The poor creature—I really began to pity him. "Need everything be written in rhyme?" said I, meaning to speak compassionately and cheerfully at the same time; "there are people who cannot stand the smell of onions, and others who, before midsummer day, like eating the green herbs above the earth, and after midsummer the roots from below the ground. It may be the same with poetry; it may be one person's favourite dish, while another mightn't care to touch it even with his fingers. To speak honestly, I myself prefer what is not written in rhyme, for it's only very rarely that people speak in verse, and then they do so only when their imaginations are too active, and leeches have to be applied, and ice put on their heads. I would advise you to try and write plain intelligible German prose, instead of rhymed verses; I'm sure it would be more welcome "—" Prose !" he cried out in a voice of despair—"wretched prose !"—" My daughter, too, has more talent for what is simple, I think; don't you think you have, Betti ?"—"Poetry has certainly not come within my grasp yet," Betti replied. " Let Herr Leuenfels hear the little story you have been writing." —"It's too trivial; I should feel ashamed of it."— " Please, let me hear it, Fräulein Buchholz," said Leuenfels; " I did not say that I considered prose to be absolutely superfluous." He will give in by and by, thought I.

Betti went to fetch her story; it was one she had presented to her father at Christmas, and it had pleased us immensely, for she had done it all out of her own head without any help. The tree that she wrote about she had seen in a shop—that was all. The mother, the father, and the children were all un- known to her; she had invented them all herself. I was therefore very anxious to hear what Feodor Wichmann-Leuenfels would say to it; but Betti was a little bashful, for she stuttered rather at the begin- ning in reading out the title, " The Patent Fir-Tree." " That is pure nonsense !" exclaimed Leuenfels, inter- rupting her.—" It is not," I replied; " the thing ex- isted, and what has existed is not nonsense. But you are not to interrupt her again, else I shall be annoyed." Betti continued :

"It had come from America carefully packed in a box. The several parts were numbered, so that they could be put together in the manner intended, and when all the different parts had been fitted into one another, there stood the patent fir-tree trim and ready. The trunk looked almost exactly like a real trunk, only it was a little more glossy than the reality, for it had a coat of sp'endid patent varnish : the branches too were very much more regularly placed than is generally seen in a poor forest tree, they were all curved so evenly and regularly one would have supposed they had all enjoyed the same lessons in deportment. And how beautifully green the branches were ! In place of needles they were covered with fine soft chenille, which the dyer had coloured with his brightest of greens. There was not a tree in the wide world as green. Every one of the wire branches had a candle-holder, and there were small hooks for fastening on the sweetmeats, silver apples, and golden nuts. The nuts and apples too were made of metal by some patented process. They could not, of course, be eaten, but on the other hand, could be used over and over again as Christmas came round. Then, too, the stand upon which the tree was fixed was of cast-iron, nickel-plated, and had an inscription which informed every one who could read, that the tree was a patent one. The stand moreover had a spring, the secret about which was not to be revealed till Christmas Eve came ; for even this secret was a patent.

"In fact, there never was a more patented fir-tree than this American piece of mechanism.

"Christmas Eve arrived ; and while the children were anxiously awaiting the moment for the doors of the room containing the tree and the presents to be opened, the parents were in the room arranging the tables. Affection had assisted in the selection of the various gifts, and again it was affection that lent a hand in placing the gifts in as pleasing a manner as possible, in order that the eyes of those who were to receive them should at once catch sight of what they had most wished to possess. Again, several of the gifts were carefully hidden, so as to be discovered, and by this means a new surprise was created after the first delight had subsided a little. In the midst of all these gifts stood the patent fir-tree.

"The parents, in quiet and expectant joy, gave a last look round at the pleasant scene which they knew would make the children's hearts beat with greater glee than upon any other sight during the year.

"'I do not see anything wanting,' said the mother, 'yet it strikes me that I miss something, but cannot make out what it is.'

"'It is the brightness of Christmas, I think,' replied the father ; 'let us light the candles, their brightness will give the finishing touch.'

"When the lights on the patent tree were lit, the doors were thrown open and the children stood on the threshold dazzled by the brilliant scene. When, however, they were led up to their several little heaps of presents, each one to a separate place, they burst out in joyous exclamations ; again had come that moment of blissful giving and joyous acceptance.

"'Have you examined the fir-tree carefully?' said the father after a time.

"'Is it a real fir-tree?' asked one of the boys.

"'No, but much more beautiful. Now watch how wonderful it is.'

"With these words the father pressed a little button attached to the nickel-plated stand, and the tree slowly commenced to turn round ; a musical box too began to play a lively dance. This was the secret of the patent fir-tree.

"A Christmas tree that could turn and play tunes by itself was a thing the children had never seen. 'How do you like it?' asked the father, and again wound up the clock-work.

"The children did not answer at first, then one of the boys asked : 'Did this tree ever stand in a forest among other trees, and ever listen to the stories the fairies tell, like those in my story book?'—The father smiled, and said : 'No, this is not a fairy-tree, but was made by a clever man in America.'

"'It doesn't smell like Christmas,' said his sister. 'Now I know what it was I missed,' whispered the mother to the father, 'the tree does not give out the aroma that the firs of our forests do. It wants the fragrance.' Whether it was that the patent tree noticed that it was being spoken of disparagingly, it is difficult to say, but just at that moment something cracked in the clock-work, and while a new and merrier tune commenced, the tree, too, began turning round quicker than before. One might have fancied that the tree wanted to show off all it could do. But this only seemed so, for, in fact, the new tune and the quicker movement were patents also.

"The mother had meanwhile gone out, and when she returned after a short time, she was carrying a small real fir-tree, the very last one to be had of a man in the street who had been offering it to passers-by, but had been unable to sell it, owing to its looking too miserable and poor. The mother took the sweetmeats from the patent tree and decorated the little tree she had purchased ; paper nets and gold paper chains were also hung upon it, and candles were fastened on to the branches. A little table covered with a white cloth was brought in for it to stand upon, and soon its candles were lighted and the children gathered round it. ' This is a real Christmas, now ! ' they exclaimed. And when one of the candles in toppling over a little, set fire to the needles of a neighbouring branch, making a fizzing noise, the fire had to be blown out. A light streak of smoke rose from the tree. ' Now it is Christmas more than ever ! ' the children again cried out.

"The patent fir-tree had meanwhile been standing still again, as no one had wound it up, but the little forest tree with its fresh aromatic smell sent a perfume over the whole room. The candle that had leant over a little had helped in this as far as it was able.

"When visitors came during the holiday week, the patent tree was exhibited and had to perform its feats. Every one thought it very wonderful ; but as Christmas Eve was past no one seemed to notice that it lacked what was, after all, the best part about the real tree—the power to awaken memories, the memory of former Christmas Eves, and of the green forest that was slumbering beneath a white covering of snow, awaiting the resurrection of spring.

"Some days afterwards the patent fir-tree was taken to bits, packed in its box, and placed in the loft, every numbered piece of the trunk, every numbered branch being carefully rolled up in tissue paper. I doubt, however, whether it will be fetched down this Christmas and put up again, for I have heard that a beautiful large fir-tree has been ordered, so tall that it will almost touch the ceiling, nuts also, with real kernels, and apples that can be eaten, are to be gilded over and silvered of an evening after the children are asleep.

"These are bad prospects for the patent fir-tree."—

Betti ceased and cast down her eyes as if she had been thieving or had committed some silliness that she was ashamed of ; but I enjoyed hearing the little story again, although I knew every syllable and comma in it. However, I did not say a word, and waited anxiously for Leuenfels to express an opinion ; but he said nothing. " Now then ! " I said at last and a little impatiently.

Leuenfels shrugged his shoulders and said, with a critical air : " Is that all ? How can any one think of writing about such commonplace things ? "—" But she's managed it very nicely," I ventured to remark ; " or are there faults in it ? "—" There is absolutely nothing whatever in it," he exclaimed, " no proposition, no periphery, no proper rounding off, and above all not a vestige of poetry. Where is the Christmas angel, with its poetic, white gleaming wings ; where are the church bells, with their harmonious music ; where is there anything about faith, hope, and charity ? And what I consider most unpardonable is her imitation of Andersen and those other scribblers of fairy tales. My advice to you, Fräulein Buchholz, is to give up any further attempts at writing ; you have talent, certainly, but of genius not a spark ! "

During this downpour of abuse I felt as if dust were being flung at me all round, especially in my face. Betti sat there looking utterly petrified, and did not venture to stir, she felt so ashamed and disgraced, for Leuenfels was right ; her story did not contain any one of the things he had specified. I, myself, could now scarcely imagine how it was that we had all enjoyed the story so much, and that Carl had maintained that Betti might be uncommunicative, but that she had depth of feeling ; how utterly mistaken, too, I had been in supposing that Betti might yet find happiness, and a kind of profession, in literary work, since it had become evident that she had no inclination for becoming a governess, or for studying music or painting. An owl—as I may say—had clearly been sitting in our midst.

Betti did not venture to make a remark; she is not apt to give in readily, so I had to risk a speech. "Herr Leuenfels," I began, "as her story does not appear good enough for you, I should like you to tell me what you consider true poetic style; it is well that one should know the difference."—"Nothing is easier than that," he replied. "There are two poems of mine published in the 'Eolian Harp,' the editor of which—Hunold Müller von der Havel—himself requested me to become a member of the National German Rhyming Society. And I have become a member. My last poem carried off the prize. Do I need to say more?" —"Oh no, certainly not."—"I composed it in the Winter Garden at the time of the Press Festival. True genius is not bound by time or place. Let me recite it to you."

With this he leant against the stove, pulled out his cuffs, pushed back his hair, put on a look like apple jelly, and then commenced:

A SORROWFUL SEPARATION.

(Prize poem by Feodor Wichmann-Leuenfels.)

"A palm-tree in the far-off north,
   In a lone green-house is standing.
How very much hath changed its worth!
   Its leaves are now all vanishing.

"It dreams long dreams of a pine-tree,
   On the distant Congo-strand;
Yet long has that tree ceased to be
   On the desert's fiery brand."

"Now just listen to that," I exclaimed, when he had ended in a doleful tone; "grand the poem cannot be called, and neither can I call it new."—"Not new! An improvisation of mine on that evening, not new!"—"No, new it is not," said I. "Betti, you surely remember Heine's poem about a dreaming pine-tree. Isn't it almost exactly like this one of Herr Leuenfels'?"—"There's not the smallest resemblance!" he exclaimed in an offended tone. "In the wretched production you refer to, the pine-tree stands in the north, in my poem it is the palm-tree, and you call that the same? Ridiculous! Those who do not possess sufficient knowledge ought not to presume to pass judgment."

This made my blood boil up. "You say that my Betti has borrowed from others, while you yourself crib things in such a way that one might fancy the police must be at the door. And yet you talk about genius and pathology, and goodness knows all what other ologies! That's more than I'll put up with in my house! So do me the favour to see if your greatcoat is in the hall; if it is, take it out for an airing, that the moths don't get into it. I should think you'd drop writing poetry now, once and for ever!"—"If my poetry is to be thus scorned, I shall let people know what I can do. If they will not honour me as a poet, they shall learn to fear me as a critic. Now I recognise my destination in life, and it is to you, Frau Buchholz, that I owe this discovery." With this he made a formal bow, and walked out haughtily.

How right Uncle Fritz was after all; if the words "patent humbug" had not been invented already, they would have had to be specially invented for that idiot. And to think that it was Dr. Stinde who packed him on to my shoulders. Just you wait, my boy, I'll pick a crow with you yet!

The result of all this was that Betti no longer found any pleasure in writing, and that the world was one critic the richer ; I do not exactly wish Leuenfels to run his head against a wall, but God grant he may! Had it not been for his insolence, Betti might have innocently continued her literary pursuits, and her work would have kept off wearisome thoughts about her lost happiness ! She would have found distraction without seeking it far from home, at the theatre or at concerts. We very rarely go there, for it is a most expensive kind of pleasure when other folks have to show one how to be pleased, and we do not care to throw away our money in that fashion. If once in a way we go to the opera-house to hear " Lohengrin," or to the theatre, those are eventful evenings, long to be remembered. At times, too, we go to the Wallner theatre when something really funny is being acted ; but, as a rule, those operettas are too shocking.

Things therefore went on much in the old way, and as Mila, too, was away, there were hours during the day that seemed as heavy as lead. However, when there's nothing to alter, there's nothing to will, and we both of us had to bear the same burden, Betti on her young shoulders, and I on my old ones, and neither of us cared to admit which found it hardest to bear.

My thoughts were occupied also with the mysterious remarks Herr Max had made to us on the day of the regatta, and I do not know what I would not have given to have got to the bottom of that subject. However, I asked myself by way of consolation, Does human life always flow on in a stream as clear as crystal ? No, indeed, it is more generally as muddy as ditch-water.

The day of revelation came at last, however, in the form of a letter from Herr Max, who asked me to grant him an interview. I appointed the following Friday, as Betti was to be at the Kuleckes, and I received him punctually at six o'clock in the best sitting-room. "Now, pray do not make a long preface," said I, after having placed some port wine before him, by way of rousing his spirits, for he made upon me the impression of being somewhat nervous. "You can speak out plainly without beating about the bush, I am prepared for the worst."—"I have come with good news, I hope," he replied. "Then let us have it without more ado."—"As I have come as spokesman for my friend Felix, I must enter a little more into detail than you may perhaps like."—"Do as you wish then, but take a little wine first."—He took a sip and then continued : "You got to know him—"—"And to be deceived in him ! Never shall I forget seeing him in the fresh courage of youth and with quick determination risk his own life to save that boy's. I admired him then, and his modest and yet manly character upon closer acquaintance won my whole heart, and not mine alone, and that's what was wrong in him. He knew what he had done, you knew it too, and after rejoicing in having deceived an innocent girl's heart, he vanished, never to appear again. That's what's false in him, and that's my opinion of him now."

Herr Max replied with animation : "I can justify his behaviour."—"I cannot believe that."—"I think you will believe what I, his friend, have to say for him."—"Tell me with whom thou goest, and I will tell thee who thou art," I observed distrustfully. Herr Max clenched his teeth firmly, and looked at me almost angrily. "You wrong him !" he burst out ; "I have known him from my early school-days. He was strong and powerful, and protected me, the weak boy, from persecution ; he looked after me when I lost my parents; I owe everything to him. There is not a truer nature than his, and that is why everything that affects him affects me. How my heart rejoiced when he told me he had found the joy of his life! And he himself cannot have suffered more than I did, when he told me that it had all to come to an end."

"Had to?" I asked in astonishment.

Max was silent for a time, and then added in a low voice: "We had both of us only been in Berlin a year or two; our week-days were devoted to work, and on Sundays the large city with its environs offered recreation in abundance. Can you find fault with young men, who are full of life and good spirits, for taking part in the amusements that are offered?"— "I see no reason whatever why they should not enjoy themselves; but would, nevertheless, not have them follow the crooked paths that Herr Kleines does."— "I do not understand!"—"Who gives parties for lady-cousins that are no cousins at all." Herr Max cast down his eyes, and remained silent. "Well, are you not going to speak?" I asked in dismay.—"He met her first out at Treptow and danced with her . . . "—"What 'her'?"—"His ruin."—"Now I know enough," I replied bitterly; "you need say no more." —"I must," he exclaimed: "you must hear all I have to say. The day we returned from Tegel, where we met you and your daughter, Felix said to me: 'Max, from this day henceforth I break with the past' . . . " —"That he may have said, but he didn't do it."—"He did his best to break off the connection, but she would not let him. She threatened, if ever he became engaged to any girl, to come forward and make some claim against him."—"Had she any right to do so?" —"No, and Felix laughed at her threats, but she vowed she'd create the greatest disturbance possible, on his wedding-day, even though it should be inside the church. She declared she would swear that he had promised to marry her, and added, that no one would be able to prove the contrary. He asked her whether she meant to ruin his whole life; whereupon she replied that she belonged to a respectable family, and did not mean to be pushed aside by any one, and that in her hatred she was capable of anything, he had better remember that. This was why he avoided any further meetings with Fräulein Buchholz, whom he loved with his whole soul; he was afraid that words he dared not utter might escape his lips, words that might draw her to him and expose her to annoyance. The only thing he could do was to leave Berlin."—"But first get as much amusement out of it as he could! Do you mean me to believe that the Bock music-hall is a place for persons with broken hearts?" He looked at me in amazement, while I continued: "Well, you may think what you like, but I saw him there myself, and moreover in very strange company, I had time enough to notice that!"—"He had reason for acting as he did. His object was to get that young woman off the right scent; after that evening she ceased following him about any longer."—"Berlin, Berlin!" I exclaimed, "is this what you make of mankind! And Herr Max, is this what you call good news? Truly, I am much obliged to you!"—

"I have good news, certainly," he replied calmly; "the troubles that have kept Felix away are now all at an end; yesterday that acquaintance of his married an artizan in a good position, and Felix commissioned me to tell you all that had happened, so that you might not misunderstand him."

I said nothing. Could I declare him free from blame? No. And yet I felt he had not acted dishonourably towards us. He did not press himself upon us; it was I that encouraged him; he had never spoken to Betti of love, had never promised her anything, or asked any promise from her. Of that I was convinced. And yet in both their hearts there had quietly and secretly bloomed hopes that had as secretly and quietly withered—destroyed by the levity of Sunday amusements.

"Has Felix acted so very badly, that you have no word of pardon for him?" asked Herr Max.—"Of what good would my pardon be to him?" I replied.—"It would be everything to him, it would enable him to hope that he might again present himself at your house."—"It is too late now, Betti has resigned herself to her fate, and lost love is not apt to return."

Herr Max rose hurriedly: "I cannot and will not tell him that," he said excitedly; "he hopes for a kind message. He must have it."—Herr Max spoke so warmly and feelingly for his friend that I could not but be affected myself, and therefore said: "I cannot decide this matter alone, others have a word to say as well," and with this I rang the bell, and sent Doris down to Carl, who was in the office, to ask him to come up to me. He came at once, and when he saw Herr Max, greeted him in a very friendly manner, and said: "Well, and how do matters stand now, my young friend?"—"The marriage took place the day before yesterday," was his answer.—"Now, Carl, how's this?" I exclaimed astonished; "how is it that you know about all this?"—"Herr Felix Schmidt was honest enough to tell me the circumstances that compelled him to leave Berlin; and I could only approve of his actions."—"And me—you have kept all this from me? Carl, I do think . . . . "—"Now, Wilhelmine, do me the favour and look up at your portrait for a minute!

10

Why should you have been worried about the matter
unnecessarily? I myself had begun to doubt whether
things could ever come right, and therefore considered
it better not to recall the past. The question now is
whether Betti has forgotten him or not?"—"She
doesn't seem to think of him at all!"—"Yet it may
only seem so," interposed Herr Max. "Well, I will
try and find out; still, I do not think there will be
much use now; as soon as she hears all the particulars,
she will draw back. She has her pride." Whereupon
my Carl replied: "When the time comes, he will tell
her all himself. We have no right to abuse the confidence he has placed in us. He has repented and
atoned for his folly, by having had to conceal his love
for her. Can you ask more? He who is without sin
let him cast the first stone!"—"Carl, I hope you'll be
able to cast the stone yourself." He laughed, and
said: "My wife has already given in, I see; come and
fetch your answer to-morrow, Herr Max."—"Do not
come yourself, that might strike Betti as peculiar,"
I urged; "if things look promising, I will put this red
hyacinth on the ledge between the windows."—
"Thank you," replied Herr Max; "I will pass your
house the first thing in the morning, and will look up."
Thereupon he took leave of us and went away. I could
not help thinking that any one who had so devoted a
friend could not possibly be a bad man. If only youth
were not so overflowing with spirit and thoughtless-
ness! Yet, perhaps, were it not so, that little boy
would be lying dead in his grave.

I could not help letting Carl know a little what
I thought of his egoistical silence, but my words
seemed as good as thrown away upon him, the future
seemed all so rosy-coloured to him now. He wanted
to have Felix Schmidt as a partner, and would not

think of anything else. "I should have such a support in him, Minchen, for he understands the manufactures. Away in Saxony, where he now is, they
want him to become a partner."—"How do you know
that?"—"The firm applied to me about him, as he
had referred them to me."—"And what did you say?"
—"First and foremost, that he was an upright man,
and that I should place full confidence in him myself."

After supper, Carl went out a little for a glass of
beer, and I waited for Betti, who came in at the usual
hour. She was in very good spirits, for she had read
her little story to the Kuleckes—as had been arranged
—and they had all spoken favourably of it, especially
Amanda, and so Betti meant again to try her hand at
writing, in spite of Leuenfels. Amanda had, it is true,
said to her: "Betti, a story must have something
about love in it, no matter whether it ends happily
or unhappily, but of love there must be something."
—"Well, Betti, won't you try?" said I, by way of re-
connoitring, and I felt my heart beginning to beat
faster.—"Am I to write about happiness and love
with tears in my own eyes, Mamma," she replied sorrowfully.—"You might," I added, continuing my own
train of thought, while my heart beat faster and faster;
"you might describe two young people loving one
another without acknowledging it; make the lover
go far away to earn a livelihood, or something of the
sort, meaning to return when he had made enough,
but finds then that the girl has meanwhile forgotten
him."

"Forgotten him!" exclaimed Betti, looking at me
in astonishment; "then she could never have really
loved him."

"Then do you love him still? And do you know
why he went away?" I blurted out thoughtlessly. At

that moment a stroke of apoplexy would have done me good, for I felt sure that Betti would be upset. However, she remained quite composed, and said, in a scarcely audible voice :

"Perhaps he thought me unworthy of further notice."

My hands were clutching tightly hold of the sofa, for, indeed, I needed support; gradually I loosened my hold, and drew a breath : "Betti," I said, "be good enough to put that red hyacinth in between the windows, its scent is too strong for me."

Betti did as I asked her; and now I knew that she would forget and forgive, whatever she might hear, and I also saw how right Carl had been in keeping the matter quiet, for how easily one finds oneself off at a gallop.

"Have you had visitors, Mamma, that you are sitting here in the best room ?" asked Betti.

"A business friend of papa's has been here," said I, with as much indifference as possible.

And then we talked of all sorts of things that weren't specially interesting to either of us ; Betti avoided talking about her literary work, and I took care not to let anything further escape me. At last sleep sprinkled its dream-dust in our eyes, and we went to bed. The red hyacinth, of course, was in its proper place.

THE FIRST OF APRIL.

I WAS not aware that I had in any way offended Augusta Weigelt, and could not understand, therefore, why she avoided our house as if we had had scarlet fever. It vexed me ; so, a short time ago, when I met her accidentally, I put the question as to why she never came to see us now, upon which she made a number of excuses, as if she had been practising the art of lying. "If you don't care to come, I can't force you," was my reply; "and if you have ceased to care about us, why, we had better begin to address each other more formally. So 'Good-bye' to you, Frau Weigelt."

How matters really stood with the Weigelts I could not make out ; nor whether they had received the expected shovelful of sovereigns from their wealthy sister-in-law, or whether a debtor's hawk had taken up its abode on their roof, as Uncle Fritz says when there are bills that have to be paid for dear life's sake, and there is nothing but wishes to pay them with.

To my subsequent joy, however, I found that I had been wrong about Augusta. She herself was not to blame for the coolness that had sprung up between us, it was altogether the fault of her husband, who did not deserve to have so good a wife. Who would have thought that that simpleton of a student, as he used to be—and who ought to be thankful that he obtained an appointment in a Government office— could have become so uppish. The reason is simply his dunderheadedness, although it nevertheless seems inexplicable.

It had seemed very strange that he should have forbidden Augusta to accept money from us, but I ascribed this behaviour of his to my having at first refused to give them what they wanted, when she applied to me ; some people cannot stand being denied anything. However, Uncle Fritz discovered what was the true state of matters.

Young Weigelt had, in fact, got among a set of fellows who fumed away to him about the evils of the

present state of society; and they succeeded in rousing him to such an extent that he believed anything,
so long as it wasn't to be found in the Bible. He
owed debts that he would gladly have been quit of,
and simply because things had gone badly with him,
owing to his own stupidity, he now fancied the whole
world must be in a bad way too. The State, he said,
was of no earthly use, and Government made mistake
upon mistake; goodness knows with what else besides
they may have talked their beer sour.

The consequence of all this was that young Weigelt
became careless in his work, and disliked by his su-
periors, and thus spoke of starting business on his
own account, meaning, as he said, to upturn the State
altogether; yet a Prussian Government office cannot
be said to be the most appropriate place for such en-
deavours. Did he really imagine that he had got his
appointment because of his beautiful eyes? Young
men like him could be had in plenty—fifteen to the
bushel. He might be glad he was not turned out of
the office; in fact, that his wife and child had been
taken into consideration, when he was on the point
of getting his *congé*. And yet he set himself on the high
horse, when others were given posts ahead of him,
and he had to wait for another chance.

Every one may be said to be the maker of his own
good fortune; but any one who has not learned his
business properly, can accomplish nothing but mere
bungling, and this was the case with young Weigelt.

"If our State isn't to his liking," said Uncle Fritz,
"he's at liberty to go and find one that is. But it
seems to me he knows that he's not likely to find meat
anywhere without bones, and that oxen don't run
about in America as ready-made sausages; and that
if we have to work here, they have to shift for them-

selves over yonder. Let him emigrate with his little
bit of learning, and his legible handwriting. He'll
be able to suck his thumbs! It might be the best
thing for him to go abroad, to learn what bosh has
been talked into him by those soft-brained idiots who
call themselves his political friends. To think of that
nincompoop—who can't manage his own affairs, who
has to put himself into the hands of money-lenders,
and has to take useless goods from a swindler—to
think of him presuming to talk politics! He wants
to govern, does he? He teach the State wisdom—a
blockhead like him!"

"Why do you vex yourself so about him?" said I to
Uncle Fritz; "he's too insignificant a creature to
make one angry."

"I've just been to ask him to join in the torchlight
procession, and to come and spend the evening with
me and my friends afterwards. His reply was that
such proceedings were against his principles."—"Is it
possible?" I exclaimed.—"Yes, indeed," said Uncle
Fritz, "but truly the freaks of nature are marvellous
sometimes."

This happened a few days before the last of March,
when the torchlight procession was being arranged in
honour of Prince Bismarck, which was to take place on
the evening before his 70th birthday. We heard a
great deal about the preparations long beforehand,
and were looking forward to the evening with the
greatest delight, especially as Uncle Fritz was so enthusiastic about it. But then, to be sure, Fritz had
served during the campaign in France, and knew
what it meant to risk life and limb for one's country.
"Wilhelm," he said to me one day, "not a drop of
blood has been shed in vain, every drop has brought
honour and power to our country. None can equal

us now ! Germany is greater than she has ever been before, and this we owe to our Emperor and to his Chancellor."

On the evening of the torchlight procession we went to the Linden in good time. Carl, Betti and I, and half Berlin seemed to have assembled on that broad, open space. Head upon head might be seen at every window and on the balconies, and numberless people had taken their stand on the road, the riding-path, and on the pavements. Every one of these persons needs a means of existence, and can obtain it only in times of peace, and this is what Bismarck has managed to obtain for us, and will see that we have it in days to come as well.

" Let us try and get to our old place again, close to the Friedrich Strasse," said Carl. When we had got there, he said to me : " Wilhelmine, do you remember our standing here to see the King when he came from Ems ? The Queen, who was at his side, could scarcely restrain her tears."—" I remember it well, Carl ; what terrible days those were. Uncle Fritz had to be off with the rest. The French were considered the first and foremost among nations, and they vowed and vaunted they would raze Berlin to the ground. Who could say how things would go ?"—" The King, and Bismarck, and Moltke knew though. And do you remember that we stood here again when our King entered the city with his victorious army as an Emperor?"—" How can I ever forget that ? What a day of rejoicing it was. And what a sight Uncle Fritz was to look at, covered with dust and bedecked with wreaths !"—" Well, to-day's procession is a solemn offering of thanks to the mighty Chancellor for his fidelity to his Emperor and to Germany. But look over there towards the Palace ; the procession has started."

And so it had. A cloud of smoke could be seen at the lower end of the Linden, a red light was glowing in its midst like a fire, and this became larger and larger, till it got to look like a huge fiery serpent creeping nearer and nearer, and at last reached the point where we were standing. Bands of musicians dressed in historical costumes, on foot and on horseback, alternated with groups of men carrying torches, and the representatives of the various corps of students, all in full toggery, occupied endless carriages, and were followed by the bulk of the students on foot, all of them young men, the Chancellor's hope for the future and the inheritors of his legacy. In front of the students walked a grey-headed man carrying a bright torch ; he was wearing a student's cap in black, red and gold, the colours of the olden days. His heart must have preserved the freshness of youth, and been full of enthusiasm to-day.

Endless masses of persons carrying flaming brands, illuminated inscriptions, banners, flags, and badges, kept passing by. Then came the artist's chariot, in the form of a gigantic ship, bearing Germania wielding her uplifted and protecting sword, while on the deck of the ship stood representatives of every district and province of the Empire, who greeted her with shouts of rejoicing. Then came the ambassadors from Cameroon, with camels carrying gifts such as Africa has to offer ; and they again were followed by endless lines of persons on foot with flaming torches in their upraised hands.

An hour had passed, but still there was no sign of the procession coming to an end. Thousands of spectators stood there, deeply affected, and overpowered by the marvellous scene. The procession ended by all the men from Schering's manufactory coming up with their hundreds of magnesium lights, which made the streets look brighter even than by daylight ; and scarcely any one at that moment but had his eyes moistened with tears. It was with deep emotion that the people paid this homage to their mighty states-man, their Bismarck.

Carl did not feel at all disposed to have supper at any public place after this sight. "Let us celebrate the evening by ourselves," he said ; "I shall like talk-ing over all the glorious past among ourselves."

So we made ourselves comfortable at home, and when I appeared with a bottle of good "Johannis-garten," Carl declared it to be a very happy thought of mine. He went out, but came back soon with a little book called "Prince Bismarck," by Ernest Scher-enberg, which he afterwards read aloud to us.

It seemed to me and Betti inconceivable that Ger-many could ever have been so shamefully treated in former days. It had silently to endure seeing its rights and its honour violated, merely because, in its dilapidation, it did not know its own strength. But now, thank God, we're all in one box.

Then came the day in Versailles when the Chancel-lor read out the Emperor's proclamation, which con-cluded with the words : "We and our successors to the Imperial Crown do pray that God may enable us to be the promoters of the German empire—not by warlike conquests, but by the rewards and gifts of peace, in connection with the nation's welfare, free-dom, and culture."

" Those were the Emperor's words," said Carl, "and Bismarck will see that they are fulfilled. For fifteen years now we have enjoyed peace and all its blessings, and this we owe to German trustworthiness."

At these words we all three rose from our seats and

emptied our glasses. Whose health we drank need hardly be said.

"Now, do you see," said Carl, returning to the subject again with animation—"France, with her Republic, is again offering up her children to its old idol *Gloire ;* England, with her Parliament, is shedding inglorious blood to its egoism ; they both of them now appeal to us, and ask Bismarck to decide matters —Bismarck, who in Versailles swore with his Emperor, and before all the world, that there should be *Peace !* The days in which we are living are so great, that we can scarcely comprehend their importance ! The young people of our day are growing up in a very different Germany from what I knew in my young days. It is no longer the poor Fatherland whose sons grieved over it the more deeply the more they loved it."—"What a pity we have none," I exclaimed thoughtlessly.

"We shall have to be satisfied with sons-in-law," replied Carl jocosely.

In order to remove the impression which these remarks of ours might have upon Betti, I endeavoured to change the subject, by saying :

"Daughters would, after all, have acted much in the same way."

HOW IT ALL CAME TO BE SO DIFFERENT.

I HAD not exactly forbidden Carl to associate with old Herr Bergfeldt, for it would have been impossible for me to have seen that my prohibition was attended to, there being so many places in Berlin where they might have met in spite of everything ; an excuse to go out on business about dinner-time can, of course, easily be manufactured, and restaurants for a morning glass of beer are to be found at every third house ; one need only drop against the door to find oneself inside. Then, too, old Herr Bergfeldt was far less to blame for all the disputes than was that wife of his, with whom nobody can get on for any length of time, for if she hasn't any one else to quarrel with, she'd take to quarrelling with herself.

Why is it that I can live in harmony with other people, and she cannot? Because any one wanting to stigmatise me as stupid would have to get up two days before me, if not sooner. And then the way she tries to look down upon us simply because the husband of the one has an official appointment, whereas the other is only a merchant ; she wants also to make show with a scanty income, and has to be as sparing as possible with her coffee, in order to have one or two pence for a few pleasures.

Has she not always, when invited anywhere, made great pretensions, and acted as if she had been the chief person present? And when she didn't manage to get what she expected, off she would go into the dumps, and all pleasantness would come to an end. Then, too, she would act as if she knew what culture was, and would dispute points that had long since been settled, as she once did with me on the subject as to whether petroleum was masculine, feminine, or neuter. I remember when we were discussing this and other words, that my fingers regularly itched to be at her, and I felt pretty much as if I had been sitting upon red-hot needles ; but properly cultured folk keep quiet even under such provocation. To forget such things, however, is quite another matter.

In spite of this, Carl ventured one day—in the happiness of his own heart, and as if there had never been

a dispute between us—to give me the latest piece of
news, in the shape that Frau Bergfeldt was really a very
stately-looking woman, and had a very good figure
He afterwards said that he meant nothing special by
this remark ; but I did not let him off with that. He
said he thought that we ladies had got to like each
other, and to feel as kindly disposed towards each
other as they, the husbands, did, for they had stuck to
each other from their boyhood. "Well," said I, "your
dear friend Bergfeldt would need to have married a
totally opposite kind of woman. For all I care, she
might have been crooked and deformed, but to suit
my taste she must have been a woman of culture and
feeling. Had she been that, I should have felt a sisterly affection for her." The upshot of all this was a
long period of irritation against the Bergfeldts, which
lasted till we next met. Thereupon, however, she
played me that trick behind my back about Betti's
engagement ; and when her son Emil found an opportunity of marrying an heiress, her true character came
out, for my Betti's happiness was of no more value to
her than a bad four-penny piece, and—pardon my
saying so—she coolly thrust us Buchholzes into the
dust-bin. Hence I can never in my life again become
reconciled to her, although at one time we were on
very friendly terms ; now, however, she has offended
me too mortally.

For old Bergfeldt, on the other hand, I really feel
sorry when we meet by chance. How prematurely
grey he has become ; how he totters in his walk, as if
some unseen burden were weighing upon his shoulders. My Carl does, it is true, get a grey hair now and
then ; but trust me for pulling it out ; and as for the
way he holds himself, he might any day be taken for a
drum-major in civilian's dress.

Yet what can old Bergfeldt have to worry about? Are they not all going to be as rich as Crœsuses? Instead of going to his office, he'll be able to sit and spit at the swans ; and as to her, she needn't leave her bed till eleven in the morning, and can take him pancakes in a silver-gilt pan. With anything less than that she'll never be content.

But it all ended differently—oh, how differently !

When I think of it, I could almost fancy that what I lived to see cannot be true, cannot have happened, any more than the sun could go out suddenly, or a grand-looking, beautiful tree topple over without any warning. And yet a human being is more to one than the sun, more than a tree whose flourishing branches promise glorious fruits. It is difficult to believe that he is gone, and where he had no right to have gone.

My Carl had often hinted that he was afraid trouble would come of Emil's having engaged himself to that heiress, and also thought that the Bergfeldts were deceiving themselves as to the consequences ; Herr Bergfeldt certainly less so than his wife. I cannot say that this astonished me, knowing as I did that the woman had been born totally devoid of sense and had never learnt anything since. At first when Emil had become engaged to the only daughter of the immensely rich widow, and the girl was perfectly crazy about the good-looking young fellow, the Bergfeldts were in a supreme state of joy. Emil had managed to win Fortune's favour, and had come in for the prize. Frau Bergfeldt, of course, at once flung herself at the future mother-in-law, and the two became one heart and soul. The old lady, as well as her daughter, had no intimate friends of their own, notwithstanding their wealth, so they were glad to make use of the Bergfeldts ; and, at first, there was no lack of present-giving. Emil's betrothed gave him a large gold watch with a chain, and he obtained credit at his tailor's ; for the daughter liked to see Emil dressed in the latest fashion. Frau Bergfeldt had, with the utmost friend-liness, been presented with several dress-lengths of silk, but it had cost her a pretty penny to get them made up. The Weigelts and old Herr Bergfeldt, on the other hand, got nothing, as of course there was no need for their making any show. The women-folk did not perceive that there was no genuineness in that kind of affection, and allowed themselves to be enticed on to the swampy declivity, by the show of wealth ; old Bergfeldt, however, seemed half con-scious that things were not as they ought to be. Emil probably felt this even more clearly, for it was he who had finally to settle the matter.

It cannot exactly be said that Emil had acted frivol-ously; he was really a good-hearted fellow who never had any ill-feeling towards anybody, except those who had invented head-work. Study was a trouble to him. Old Bergfeldt had, indeed, managed to scrape money enough together for him to attend the high-school, but much had still to be done ; the real difficulties began with his university career, with his first year's military service, with the delay in getting him an appointment, for nowadays there seem to be more lawyers than law-suits. It was then that the heiress appeared on the scenes, a very God-send. Emil would no longer need to bother about his examination, and hoped, at all events, to be able to repay his father abundantly for what had been spent upon his education. This he had intended to do; he had promised his father, his mother, and his sister to do so. But he had made a wrong cal-culation.

I never knew his wife; I had only seen her at a distance when they were engaged; but from what I managed to get out of Augusta, I know what to think of her. Where other people have a heart, she must have had a money-bag, which she opened only when it suited her own purpose. Even before their wedding she had begun to consider Emil's relatives beneath her notice; and the grand people at the wedding, Augusta said, had turned up their noses at them so, that she felt miserably unhappy among them, and her husband had, in fact, never ventured to move from the wall, when once he had taken up his position there. Augusta also told us that Emil had confided a good many things to her, that he would never have mentioned to any one else, when he came to see her occasionally. He had told her how hateful it was to him to have perpetually to stay at home with the two women, and to be obliged to put up with their whims; that not a day passed without their dishing up his poverty to him, and that they were for ever harping upon the subject.

During the very first days of their honeymoon, she had begged him to try and make a name for himself, to work and study so as to win some title by which she might be addressed. For affection's sake he might perhaps have made an effort, but there was no affection on either side. And when, one day, he had asked her for a larger sum of money than usual (not for himself, as Augusta told me sorrowfully afterwards), she sneered at him, called him a nonentity, and asked him what he wanted money for.

He had sold himself, and she now refused to honour the bill of exchange. This was the beginning of the end.

It must have been an awful life that those two led, a very hell upon earth ! Did any one, I wonder, in passing the villa in the Thiergarten, with the rare flowers in the front garden, the tubs with laurels and orange trees—suspect that no happiness had ever taken up its abode behind those plate-glass windows? Did any one know that for weeks past, another and hideous inmate had been creeping in and out among the corners of those show-apartments, an inmate whose step no one could hear but Emil, the supposed master of the house? .

He certainly had discovered a means by which he could close his ears, a means that he had found in the wine-cellar, and which he made use of even when out on supposed pleasure trips, and he—for respectability's sake—had been allowed to carry the purse. Yet there were hours when he was sober, and when he felt his misery doubly; it was then that the watchful inmate in his home would creep up to him, and begin to whisper words to him—words that were gradually uttered louder and louder, and with increasing persuasiveness: "You will have to do it! You cannot help yourself!"

And so the awful thing happened, and it then became clear who the unbidden guest had been—Death!

To me it seems but yesterday. Evening twilight had set in, and the bustling noise of the daytime had begun to cease, when Carl came in more abruptly than usual. I noticed, at once, that something must have happened, and asked (before he had time to utter a word), "Carl, what is it? What misfortune has happened?"—"My poor, poor old friend Bergfeldt!" he said sorrowfully.—"Has he lost his place?"—"He has had a greater loss than that—his son Emil."—"Lost! do you say?"—"Emil is dead."—"Impossible!" I exclaimed aghast.—"It's only too true, he has shot himself. I have just come from Bergfeldt. He is utterly broken down, Augusta is with him "—"And

11

where is she—the mother?"—"Where else could she be, but with her dead son?"—"Alone?"—"The two ladies have meanwhile gone to an hotel; they left the house, abusing the poor, dead man for having brought this disgrace upon them."—"Left alone!" I exclaimed. "Carl, I must go to her. Such great sorrow she cannot bear alone. If I cannot give her back her son, still I can mourn with her."—Carl embraced me, and had to support me, this news seemed to have robbed me of all my strength. We had been fond of Emil; he had at one time stood closer to us than many thousands in this world.—"Go to her," said Carl softly, "I have told my old friend that I will attend to all the melancholy business that will have to be done. When it is dark I will come with the men."

Sooner than I thought, my cab had driven up to the gate. I got out, lifted the latch, opened the gate and closed it again quietly behind me. In front of the house a man-servant was waiting, and let me in in silence. I took off my things in the hall, where two large Moorish figures were holding lamps in their hands, and had a grin on their faces; this alone made me feel uncomfortable. To have to put up with such artificial company every day, must verily have been a penance. The man-servant opened a door for me, and I walked in hesitatingly.

Only one gas flame, and that half turned down, was burning in the chandelier, probably in order that the room might be kept cool; nevertheless, the gilt frames of the mirrors and pictures glistened in the semi-darkness, as did also the bright majolica vases and porcelain figures, of which there was an over-abundance on the cabinets. All this I noticed, but could not see Frau Bergfeldt. I was about to move into the adjoining room, which was separated from the one I was in

by a heavy plush curtain, when I became aware that
something was moving in one of the darkest corners of
the room. I stood still. It was she. Miserable and
utterly broken down, there she sat in an arm-chair embroidered in gold, and her eyes, which had a dull and
vacant look, were turned towards me. "Is it you?"
she said in a scarcely audible voice, "I knew you would
come!" I sat down beside her. I took her hands in
mine, I smoothed her hair and stroked her cheeks, but
she took no notice, and seemed to fancy herself still
alone. I tried to speak, but couldn't.

After a little while, she rose and said in a hoarse
voice: "Would you like to see him?" I merely nod-
ded. She took me by the hand and drew me into the
next room. There upon a little table burned a spirally-
twisted red candle, such as have become the fashion;
it was standing in a silver candle-stick, and threw a
flickering light over a couch, across which an Eastern
shawl had been placed. She moved back the shawl
and gazed motionlessly upon the pale face of her son.
He lay there as if asleep, except that in his left temple
was a small dark wound where the ball had entered
his head. I struggled in vain with my tears, they
burst forth unrestrainedly. "He will never wake
again," she began, "the doctors have been here; they
said his aim must have been steady. Why did not his
hand tremble? He might be alive now. Why did his
hand not tremble?"

How could I answer her? He, no doubt, wished to
free himself from a hateful life; that is why his aim
was so certain. "Hadn't we better go back now?"
she asked. "I have been sitting beside him, but a
scraping noise over there by the stove frightened me.
It may have been mice."

One look more, one last look. Then I drew the

shawl over the corpse, and led the mother back to her
old seat. From time to time a carriage might be
heard driving past, otherwise the house seemed as silent as midnight.

"Frau Buchholz," she said at last, breaking the
silence, "I am so terribly thirsty; I have been all the
time. I didn't like to tell the servant, he looks so
grand. I should so like some white beer, only a
mouthful. You are so fearless—Emil always said so
—would you mind asking him?"

I went out and ordered the man to get what she
wanted. He was about to raise objections, by saying
that he couldn't leave the house, but an abrupt *Allez*
from me made him take to his heels.

When he came back I took the glass of beer myself
and gave it to her. With a look full of thanks, she
took a long, long draught. How thirsty she must
have been! How she must have suffered, poor woman! She drew a deep breath, and her whole body
trembled. "My son, my son!" she cried aloud, and
her voice then became choked with sobs.

Oh, Emil! if you had thought of your mother's despair, your hand would have trembled, you would
have hurled the weapon from you. Unhappy child!
you did not strike yourself only, you struck the hearts
of your parents as well. Was there no other path by
which you could have escaped from your misery?
God in heaven forgive you—your great sin! It was
only by degrees that I succeeded in pacifying her a
little. By the time Carl came she had become composed, and was willing to come away. Once more she
went into the room where Emil lay; she knelt beside
the dead youth and kissed his pale lips for the last
time. Then she let us put on her cloak and bonnet as
though she had been a child. A cab was waiting at

the door. Carl and I took her between us, so that she did not see the men who were standing in the garden, in the dark, with the bier. Carl returned to the house and we drove off townwards. I held her in my arms till we reached their house, where Augusta came to meet us. "Oh, Frau Buchholz," she sobbed, "dear Frau Buchholz, how differently it has all ended—how differently!"

THE EVENTFUL THURSDAY.

Nature has certainly acted wisely in having made the earth round, and in setting it revolving, for in this way old times come to be turned down and new times come to be uppermost. One drawback, however, is, that everything gets crushed in the process, sorrow as well as joy, and that nothing lasts for ever. Yet, where do we find anything perfect throughout?

By degrees the Bergfeldts became resigned to the trouble that had fallen upon them; Betti went frequently to see them, and chatted away to the old father of an evening. This was not an easy task to her, especially at first, but when she came to see how it comforted the father to talk about Emil's childhood —telling her first one thing and then another, with many a repetition and digression—she was only too glad to be a patient listener. The old man, she said, never spoke of the last occurrence, and seemed as if he had scarcely realised what had actually happened. Betti sacrificed herself, but she did it willingly; her painting, writing, work for bazaars, and the many other things with which young ladies occupy themselves, had all to be set aside, for all her spare time

was devoted to the sorrowing parents. Even the Police-lieutenant's wife hinted to me that Betti was neglecting her.

But why need we always be ready to do what she
wishes? Why need we feel flattered at her sending
round for us and entertaining us with talk about her
connections and their family-tree?

That might have been the case in former days, but
no longer now since we have learned that the Buchholzes are one of the oldest families in Berlin. This
was discovered by Herr Hermann Vogt, among the
city archives, while he was making his researches
about the history of Berlin, and it was he who told us.
The first known Buchholz, called Claus, was a town
councillor in Berlin from 1449 to 1451, and lived in
the Stralauer Strasse. Another, George Buchholz, a
dean, rendered great services to Berlin in connection
with the introduction of the Reformation, and even in
those days couldn't swallow the idea of going to Ca-
nossa. These services of his were rewarded, for, on
the 15th of August, 1540, he received a considerable
increase of salary. Further, one Kersten Buchholz, in
the year 1452, was head of the Guild of St. Mary,
which erected and maintained at its own expense an
altar in St. Nicholas's Church, to the honour and glory
of God. All this is stated in the ancient records, where
there is also a coloured illustration of the Buchholzes'
coat of arms; in the upper field, silver, half of an iron
knight holding a beech-tree in his right hand, in the
lower field, silver, two red planks with a beech-tree between them. The self-same knight forms the crest of
the helmet.

Thus we are certainly not mere people of yesterday.
What I mean to do is to set Betti to work at em-
broidering our coat of arms on silk, and she shall take

this work to the Police-lieutenant's house, when next we are invited there. If the Police-lieutenant's wife should ask what the work is, I shall simply say : It is only our coat of arms—that will stagger her, I should think. On our visiting cards and note paper the crest will look both charming and aristocratic. But people need possess the faculty of appreciating such things ; unfortunately Dr. Wrenzchen and Uncle Fritz are altogether wanting in that respect.

In fact, as regards Uncle Fritz, the world might as well be standing still without a vestige of revolving about it. For a few years ago when, by way of advice, I said to him : "Fritz, you ought to be getting married," he replied, "Wilhelm, that would be too much for me ; I'd rather buy myself a musical box." —Yet, although, I know that he has had enough of a bachelor's life, he takes absolutely no measures for altering his ways. So I made up my mind last Thursday to give him a regular talking to. We always have some friends in on Thursday evenings, in order that Doctor Wrenzchen may come to see that by persistently remaining away he will at last draw the displeasure of the whole family upon him.

As good luck would have it, Uncle Fritz came in somewhat earlier than the others, so that I could not have wished for a better opportunity for giving him a bit of my mind. After he had answered my inquiry, as to how he had been keeping, in his usual way by saying, "So-so-ish," he sat down and began playing with my work-basket, till he had made himself one big toy out of all the reels and needles, as was always his way.

"Fritz," I began, "are you for ever going to remain a child ? Surely some day you're going to show you have got some sense !" Instead of giving me an answer he set his toy a-spinning, and seemed to be greatly amused with it.

"What can people think of you?" I continued. "Is your present mode of life so very much to your liking that you can't give it up? Are you still perfectly content with having to dine at a restaurant every day?" —"You know I never liked that," he replied; "five changes of plates and never a thing upon them! That's not an arrangement to please any one of Germany's sons, who, as a rule, are accustomed to simple but substantial eating at home."—"Well, then," said I, "why don't you start a dinner-table of your own?" He was silent, and merely kept spinning his toy. "How far have you brought matters with the old grandmother in Lingen?" I said, at last, aiming straight at the point. "Well," said he, "I suppose I may say we're half way; I've done my half of the road."—"Fritz, I do beg of you to be serious. If you have firmly resolved to marry Erica, let this dilly-dallying come to an end, otherwise look about for some one else."—"I'll not dream of any such thing." —"What's the reason then that matters are at such a standstill?"—"It's the old grandmother—that's the long and the short of it. She's taken it into her head that Berlin is a nest of wickedness, and that I am the blackest gaol-bird in it; that her grand-daughter's soul would be ruined for ever if the girl were withdrawn from her care."—"But what does Erica's father say?"—"Nothing. He has to do what the old woman wills. Her money is in the business, and so she has the whole tribe under her thumb."—"Then he's a mere night-cap?"—"With tassels!"—"And I think it presumption in her to want to have the reins in her own hands still. Old people may have their own opinions, but so have young people, and they ought

to be allowed to act freely."—"How right you are,
Wilhelmine! and that's exactly what Dr. Wrenzchen
says himself."—"I didn't mean in everything," I added
hurriedly; "a certain amount of guidance is indispensable. That's evident enough from your own case,
Fritz. Now, I think you ought in some way to make
up for the bad impression you made upon the grandmother, and thus win her respect."—"I can't possibly
go to Lingen merely to show her how well I can stand
being thirsty."—"Tell me one thing, Fritz—is Erica
really fond of you, and likely to stand by you?"—
"She? why, she wouldn't give me up, not if she were
to get grey-headed before matters were settled! And
I—I don't mean to give her up—that's as sure as a
gun."—"Well, then, you both mean to go to your
wedding on crutches, I suppose?"—"If only Erica
were not so submissive. In her pious simplicity she
imagines that to leave her home without her grandmother's blessing, would bring disgrace upon her own
people; otherwise the way she is tyrannised over at
home would long since have come to an end. I have
tried everything that can be done, but the conclusion
of all her warm-hearted letters is always: 'hope and
trust; our love will yet overcome all difficulties.'"

"That's very touching, certainly," I remarked; "but
what's to be the end of all this tomfoolery? Are you
sure, Fritz, that it's not more obstinacy than affection
on your part that makes you so set upon that one
girl?"—"Wilhelmine, you know I took a liking to Erica the very first moment I saw her. I felt myself
drawn to her at every turn and corner."—"You were
for ever at the Krauses while she was there, certainly,
I know."—"She was so simple, so childlike, and kind-
hearted. I soon discovered that her life at home
hadn't much pleasantness for her; the very country it

self is not much better than a morass, a road lined with trees, and a heap of earth which they call a hill."—"Probably as high as our Kreuzberg."—"Half a meter lower, at least."—"What about the town itself?"—"Clean and pleasant-looking, but not quite as big as Berlin."—"That I could have imagined, without your ingenious observation. Yet the life there may be pleasant enough for all that."—"If the family circumstances permitted, no doubt it might. But Erica's existence must be a wretched one. That she has to work from morning till night is the least part of it; but she never gets a kind word for what she does, and is told a hundred times a day that every one has his or her duties in life; and a fearful hullabaloo is made about the slightest piece of forgetfulness, as if it were a veritable crime. That's what makes her life unbearable. Avarice and malice seem to rule the household; everything that costs money they call sinful, and what they can stint their bodies of, is considered piety."—"So she is not as happy as might be?"—"I mean to get her out from among that set. Everything she has had to put up with, hitherto, shall be made good to her. Life is new to her still; by my side she shall learn to know what it really is. I will show her how beautiful it is; in her eyes I will read how happy she has become; she shall be mine yet, that gentle dove. You see, Wilhelmine, that I've made up my mind; it's the grandmother that won't."—"Fritz, does she know anything about cooking?"—"Who?"—"Why, Erica, of course."—"I never asked her."—"Well, I could teach her; I know your favourite dishes."—"We've not got as far as that yet, however."—"If it can't be managed otherwise, I'll go to Lingen myself, and let them hear what I've got to say. Let me but meet that grandmother face to face—— !"—"You'd take her by the heels, I dare say."—"Fritz, is that an expression fit for the delicate proceeding in question, and one that can be managed only by a woman, because it demands tact and feeling? But mark me—either this affair is put into proper order, or that old woman will get to know who I am."

The Krauses came in just as I had finished speaking, so there was an end to our conversation. Herr Krause was dressed in so-called Jäger's clothing; it is said to be good for the health, and allows worry and vexation to ventilate out of the body better than ordinary clothing. This is very necessary in Herr Krause's case, for Eduard's mischievous doings have lately again been carried so far, that he was one day dismissed from school. Of course he was not removed; but had it not been that Herr Krause is himself a teacher, and that the boy promised before the assembled conference to alter his ways, he would have been ignominiously expelled. So Herr Krause is now obliged to go about in wool, owing to that good-for-nothing boy of his. Uncle Fritz says that Krause looks, of all things in the world, like a worn-out old acrobat in search of an engagement. Frau Krause, on the other hand, likes the garments, because she thinks they make her husband look spruce, and, moreover, are economical as regards washing, for linen is ruined in no time by the quantity of borax and other stuffs the laundresses worry into the things. In this respect of course I could not but admit that she was right; for what is called a new method of doing up things is, in reality, nothing but a method of making things old—it so rots the clothes. Stiff the things may be, as stiff as boards, and as glossy as a tile-covered stove, but they're as brittle as glass. Hence I have never sent our fine things out to be washed, and yet my Carl is always as trim as can be.

The gentlemen sat down to whist with a dummy. Uncle Fritz, who, as a rule, always wins, played badly that evening. This put Herr Krause, who was his partner, somewhat out of temper, which it oughtn't to have done, sitting as he was in wool, as I remarked to Frau Krause. She rattled away, trying to make all sorts of excuses, and said, among other things, that perhaps the wool he was wearing came from an angry lot of sheep; however, the truth was that Eduard was really the cause of her husband's great irritability.

A little before supper-time Emmi came in, and I at once noticed that something was wrong. Here we have it, at last, thought I. I took her into the adjoining room, where supper was laid, and said : "Well, have you come to blows, already ?"—"I was weary at home," she replied, "and if Franz chooses to go out to play *skat*, surely I may go out too if I please."—"Haven't I always told you that ? You ought long since to have shown more spirit. Is he coming to fetch you later ?" She shook her head negatively. "Have you really had a quarrel, Emmi ?"—"No, not exactly; but is he always to be in the right ?"—"Why, I should think not !"—"You know, Mamma, that I conscientiously keep an exact account of every small purchase I make, even the milk for Maffi."—"By the way, did you bring the creature with you ?"—"No, he was sleeping when I came away, and I did not care to spend money for a cab on his account. But I want to tell you that Franz maintains it's not the writing down all the items that makes a good housewife, he says it's in keeping down the accounts."—"Was it about that you got angry ?"—"I merely said he could go and look in the store-room, and he would know where the money had all gone to. I had got in two hams, the string of sausages, butter, and a lot of other things

besides."—" But, Emmi, what makes you buy so much
at a time, when you can have things in fresh when you
need them ? If you have too much in the house, the
things will only spoil."—" Our cook thought we hadn't
enough provisions in the house, and Franz doesn't understand these things. It was she, too, who advised
me to go out this evening, for she said it would be the
best way of putting an end to such disputes."—
" Emmi, I cannot honestly say that your husband is
wrong in the present case," said I, for I had no wish to
take the cook's part. " One thing, however, I do approve of is, that you have made a beginning in showing
him that you can take refuge in your parent's house.
You just wait and see if we shall not all of us remember this Thursday."

And verily we did remember it. The day is one
that will dwell in the memories of us all, however old
we may live to be. How I do repent ever having advised Emmi to give tit for tat, in order to get her
husband under her thumb. How terribly I had to
atone for it all afterwards. And yet I had no presentiment whatever that the tragedy would begin that
very evening; otherwise I should assuredly have said :
" Emmi, you had better go home, things are looking
rather askew."

Emmi herself did not seem to be feeling altogether
comfortable. She had no appetite, and the later it got
the more restless she became. It was somewhat the
same with me also. I kept thinking, "What if Dr.
Wrenzchen should get wild with rage ? They had
hitherto lived in the utmost harmony—that is to say,
all excepting his Thursday evenings out. Yet, had he
not stipulated for them at the outset ? " A chilly feeling would creep up my spine when I thought that if
anything happened I should be blamed for it all, and

should never again venture to look my Carl in the face. I was on the point of saying to Emmi, " Don't you think you had better be going; Uncle Fritz will see you home," when we heard a violent ring at the front door. Emmi stared at me, and I at her. It was only misfortune that could have rung the bell in that way

My Carl, who saw that neither of us were capable of moving, and had long since noticed that things were not all square, went out to see who was there. He was a horribly long time in coming back, so it seemed to me; and when he did return, he called me out of the room. I had made up my mind, of course, that I should probably have to face Dr. Wrenzchen in some degree of wrath. In place of this I found a policeman standing in our entrance; he, in a very formal way, gave us to understand that Dr. Wrenzchen's house had been broken into, and added that he had been requested to see that the Doctor's wife was informed of the fact in as gentle a way as possible. The Doctor had also commissioned him to say that if the lady were at all afraid, she was to remain overnight at the Landsberger Strasse.

Emmi, who had hurried out of the room after us, heard all the policeman had said, but nothing would induce her to remain with us. So a cab was quickly procured, and without even bidding the Krauses goodnight, we drove off to Dr. Wrenzchen's house.

We found a pretty state of things there. Dr. Wrenzchen was trying to discover what had been stolen; one policeman helped him in this, another kept watch at the door, and a third was examining the rooms, and entering notes in a pocket-book. Emmi flew to Franz, who greeted her at once with the words: "Things are not so very bad after all. They've not carried off much money; luckily I went to the bank this morning, and the other things can be replaced in time." She was about to beg forgiveness for having left the house, but he called it a lucky accident that she happened to be out, as otherwise she might have fared as badly as the servant-girl, whom the robbers had gagged with a towel to prevent her calling out, and had also locked her up in a room, bound hand and foot; he had found her half unconscious, in this state, when he came in.

Their rooms did, indeed, present a most murderous appearance. In place of newly-married neatness and order, that affects the very bones in the larder, everything was in a state of confusion, as if an auction were being held. The robbers had pushed away the escritoire from the wall, and had damaged the writing-table. The doors of a wardrobe were standing open, and clothes were lying about on chairs and on the floor. The Doctor's best dress-suit had been taken, and an older suit left for him to wear. All the silver was gone, except the candelabra presented to the Doctor at his wedding. Uncle Fritz noticed this, and called out triumphantly, "Now you see they are only plated!" The store-room had been ransacked: the hams and sausages were gone. The thieves had not shown a spark of reverence for anything.

In consequence of the men's muddy boots, moreover, the house looked as if a caravan had marched through it.. Perfectly dreadful! And then the unpleasant consciousness that the robbers, with their thieving hands, had been rummaging about in boxes and drawers, doing so probably amid rude jokes, and ridiculing things that were of no value to them, but precious to the young people for recollection's sake. On all sides there were traces of the thieves, and the place even smelt of them. The poet, it is true, says :

"Sacred unto all time are the abodes of good men ;"
but I would say, any abode that has been touched by
bad men one will not readily like again in one's life.
The Doctor will have to move ; no long day of cleaning and scrubbing would ever destroy the picture of
horror and desolation those rooms presented.   And
the burglars—where were they?   They had vanished
like any lovely dream.

The police forthwith took a statement of what had
occurred.   The servant-girl was called, and came in
with a pocket-handkerchief at her eyes.   The people
on the floor above, too, a Herr Greve and his wife and
daughter, we asked to come down and state what they
knew of the matter.

The result of all the questionings and answers was
—that as soon as Frau Wrenzchen had left the house,
a man came to fetch the Doctor to see some sick person.   The servant-girl had told him where the Doctor
was to be found, whereupon the man had replied that
perhaps it would be time enough if the Doctor came
early in the morning, and asked to be allowed to write
down the address.   The girl said that she let the man
in, but that, at the same moment, a second man had
forced his way in, and clapped his hand tightly over
her mouth to prevent her screaming ; she said she became unconscious then from fright, and when she
recovered found that she could neither scream nor
move, as she was gagged and bound hand and foot.
The Doctor had found her in this state when he came
in.   Dr. Wrenzchen corroborated the girl's statement,
but expressed his astonishment at having, when he
came in, found all the doors unlocked, though closed.
When he saw what had occurred, he at once called a
watchman, and then hurried to summon the police ;
they immediately declared that the gagging and fet-

tering of the girl, as well as the robbery, must have been committed by several persons; that this was proved simply by the heavy escritoire having been moved from the wall. Herr Greve and his wife maintained that they had not heard any noise in the slightest degree suspicious.

"What had the rascals looked like?" the girl was then asked. She said she couldn't exactly say, but remembered that both of them had full black beards. "How could you be so careless to let in suspicious-looking men, with black beards, like swindlers?" said I to her. The impertinent creature answered that she couldn't tell what people were by looking at their noses. "Why did you not call for help?" She replied, that as I wasn't a police-inspector, she didn't need to answer me. "If you'd a clear conscience you wouldn't be so insolent," I replied. What did I mean by that? I might have my own ideas; perhaps the provisions were bought expressly for the thieves? I should have to give an account of such speeches. "With pleasure," said I; "I know you well, and think you capable of anything." The Doctor was about to interfere, but I exclaimed: "Depend upon it, she's had her hand in this business; nobody will make me believe otherwise." The girl then flew into a passion, and I can't say what my answers to her were, for she was so utterly wanting in respect. She called the police and Herr and Frau Greve to be witnesses that I had insulted her, and attacked her honour as a respectable servant. The police replied that all this would be enquired into when the case came to be investigated.

The police then withdrew, leaving us in the utmost state of excitement. The girl was despatched to make coffee, and we tidied up the rooms, in order that they

might recover some sort of physiognomy. The thieves
did not seem to have entered the bedroom; but when
we came to look and see whether one or other might
not have crept under the bedsteads, we found Maffi
Pamph lying there dead, with a cord round its neck.
They had murdered it, no doubt, amid cold smiles.
Herr Greve now remembered to have heard the dog
barking, but had not thought anything further about
the matter.

While we were drinking our Mocha, which the girl
brought in, casting a wrathful look at me, Uncle Fritz
said : "You'll see, Wilhelmine, that that girl will
bring an action against you."—" She would never presume to," said I, laughing at the idea. "You were
more excited than you had any right to be," said Carl
reproachfully. "Carl," said I, "if she had met you as
she did me about those crawfish, you'd never have
·kept quiet so long. She had to catch it from me, and
that pretty smartly."

Dr. Wrenzchen was most affectionate and gentle towards Emmi, and declared it to be a merciful dispensation that his wife should have taken it into her head
to pay us a visit on that very evening, and that a great
catastrophe had perhaps been thus warded off.

"Just so," said I, and smiled at Emmi in a knowing
way. We two, of course, knew all the ins and outs
about that "dispensation," and how it had been set to
work. It had been set agoing by Frau Buchholz, who
at that moment was dipping a bit of cake into her
coffee.

I HAVE seen Frau Krause in various forms of impulsive excitement, but never in such a state as she was the other day when she came to us. "Is Eduard here?" she exclaimed, "has he been here?"—"No," I replied; "has he run away?"—"He's been away since yesterday," she whimpered. "The teacher with whom he has been living thought that we had kept him at home overnight, and, knowing the boy to be delicate, thought that he might have been feeling unwell, as he did not appear at school-time."—"I never knew him to be delicate!"—"You are so unsympathetic," she exclaimed; "but where can he be?—where can he be?" —"He'll turn up all right," said I, by way of consoling her. "Have you set the police to work to find him?" —"My husband is having a search made; placards are being posted on the advertisement-pillars, and notices put in the papers, whatever it may cost. If only some misfortune has not befallen him!"—"Let us hope not," said I; "but now, Frau Krause, do let me offer you some refreshment."—"No, no, thank you; I cannot rest; I must go and try elsewhere." And off she went, looking as troubled as when she first came in.

What could Eduard have been about? I felt convinced he must have invented some special piece of mischief, for he was ever doing what he ought not to do. Yet it would really be a terrible thing if, after all, some misfortune had run up against him, for the Krauses have but the one child. However, I could not think this likely; such weeds are not apt to disappear. Yet, where could he be?

Yes, where was he? This question was not merely asked by the sorrowing parents, by the yellow placards on the advertisement-pillars, and by the paragraph among the local occurrences in the newspapers. A number of other people, too, would have liked to know, either from curiosity or by way of receiving the reward offered for information on the subject. All enquiries, however, proved in vain, for Eduard was not to be found in Berlin. He had clearly made off somewhere.

If there was anything Eduard disliked in the world it was Latin and Greek. He could not see what use there was in scribbling hieroglyphics on paper, and placing accents on the top of syllables, when he was himself perfectly indifferent as to whether they were long or short. There seemed no sense in it to him. As little did he care into how many provinces Gaul was divided by Cæsar. When his history lesson was beginning to get interesting, when the Romans were bravely fighting their enemies, the teacher would torment the class by enquiring into the relations of this or that vowel; and thus in place of hearing which army won the pending victory, in the hand to hand fight, the boys had to set about declining and conjugating words, and then some in the class would suffer more disgraceful defeats than any mentioned in the Gallic wars. Eduard has specially good reasons for not considering Julius Cæsar his friend.

There were other books, however, that the boy liked immensely, much better than the remarkable doings of the ancients, and these he read with enthusiastic delight. They told him of distant countries, of forests of palm and fruit trees, where were to be found quantities of parrots and glow-worms as large as one's hand. Adventures might be had there with wild men and animals, that always ended in favour of the white man; and deeds so daring were told that he could

scarcely read quick enough to learn how it all ended.
Greatly would he have liked to have a trained ostrich
to ride upon, such as was described in one of his
books. How his boy friends would stare in amazement! Not one of them would be able to overtake
him, for an ostrich is such a fearfully swift creature.
He could have guided it with reins between its beak.
A tame jaguar, too, he would have liked to have, to
run about after him like a dog. If any one then had
dared to interfere with them, the jaguar would have
stood by him; they might all come after him, the jaguar wouldn't have allowed any one to touch him. A
bow and arrows, also, he would have carried by him;
with these he could have shot right into the top school-
room window. Then, if the janitor had appeared, he
would have jumped on to his ostrich, his jaguar following, and away he would have been across the hills
before any one had caught sight of him.

He had often liked thinking about such things, when
kept in after school hours. And these thoughts did not
remain a mere wish. The longing to experience for himself what he read about, became a burning desire; he felt,
in fact, that he must be off out into the wide world. Here,
in Berlin, everything seemed against him. The teachers
were unjust, and showed a preference for other boys;
and he wouldn't condescend to sneak into their favour
by becoming a milksop, like those in the front rows.
He wasn't going to fawn and flatter. Off, therefore,
he'd better go.

Across the plains of Northern Germany sped the
night train that leaves Berlin at 11 o'clock, arriving in
Hamburg towards 6 in the morning. It rushed past
quiet places, it whizzed across the moorland, over
which the moonlight was spinning a haze that seemed
to become mingled with the distance. From time to

time bright lights became visible, these were the lanterns on solitary stations which the steam-horse greeted with a shrill whistle, although it could not make a halt. At some places, on the other hand, the iron creature got a drink, an immense quantity of boiling water, and whilst its thirst was being quenched, men with iron hammers came and knocked at every axle and wheel in the train, to hear by the sound whether any part had been injured, or a breakage was to be feared. Some of the passengers would wake and grumble at the noise which robbed them of the sleep they struggled so hard to get; others were not disturbed by it, but slept on in the most uncomfortable of upright positions—either because they had good consciences or good nerves.

In the corner of one of the third class carriages was seated a boy, his head resting against the hard wooden partition; he was enveloped in the sound, refreshing sleep of childhood. A smile was flitting round his mouth, so that any one not knowing who he was, might have fancied that kindly angels on purple-edged clouds were playing with the sleeper, and that the reflection of their brightness might be seen in the boy's face. Any one with such thoughts would have been greatly astonished had it been possible for him to take part in the boy's dream; for, in place of being in the company of lovely, angelic beings, he would have found himself transported into the midst of the excitement of a tiger-hunt. As young Krause's thoughts had latterly been more occupied with tigers and jaguars than with celestial creatures, it was natural enough that in his sleep he should have dreamt of the things that filled his thoughts when awake. The crack of the hammers on the axles of the wheels, probably aroused in the mind of the deeply slumbering boy the idea of gunshots, while the tiger would be speedily added by the quick fancy of the dreamer.

Eduard was, in fact, carrying out his long-cherished plan. He had kept his pocket-money—both that given him formally by his father, as well as the very secret and much more abundant supply from his mother—all the more carefully, as he had learned from experience that commercial pursuits are useless without success, and his first attempt to acquire capital at the Christmas fair had proved an utter failure. Perhaps he did not possess one of those lucky pennies with which so many have come to Berlin in rags and wretchedness, to become millionaires in a few years, finding life then, however, tolerable only upon india-rubber tires—or, perhaps, he did not possess the requisite talent. His business speculation in cigars (in which he had made his father unwittingly take part) was not a success, whereas his savings bank was flourishing. When threatening clouds overcast his school-heaven, his savings were almost enough to purchase a railway ticket to Hamburg, as he discovered in the Berlin A B C guide for travellers. Then, too, his watch was worth a few half-crown pieces. So he broke down the bridges in his rear by selling his watch as well as the detested Latin and Greek books of torment, together with the respective lexicons; this piece of business was transacted with a dealer in second-hand articles, who, to their mutual sorrow, could offer but a very low price for them, as he had already too much of the same sort of things to dispose of. The boy, however, took what was offered with a light heart, thinking: I shall not require much money; when I get to Hamburg I shall at once go to sea as a cabin boy. What fun it will be sitting high up on the mast and crying out, Land! land ahead! when the coast comes in sight, where the na-

tives are all black. Hurrah! What fun! The boy
meant to write home on board ship—more seemed to
him superfluous.

When morning began to dawn, sleep and dreams
departed. The boy saw the sun rise on the golden
edge of the horizon—coming up in brilliant splendour.
This was a new sight to him. His fellow passengers
woke also. They asked him where he was going to.
To Hamburg. Had he relatives there? Yes, he said
untruthfully. Whereabouts did they live? Close to the
ships. Did he mean the harbour? Yes; what was the
best way of getting there? On leaving the station, if
he kept straight on by Hofer's Hotel, and then turned
to the left, he could not fail to find it. Any one would
be glad to tell him the way if he asked; he must not
hesitate, but ask boldly. That was splendid advice.
Be sure not to hesitate! Always boldly forward!

The flat moorland came to an end, wooded hills appeared to the right and left of the railway, and the
light of the morning sun played amid the young green
leaves of the beeches. Thereupon the woods receded
to make room for a river which cut its course through
the rich meadows in graceful windings. "Is that the
Elbe?" asked Eduard.—"No," answered one of his
fellow travellers, smiling, "that's the Bille. We're
just coming to Friedrichsruh, look!" Eduard saw
this castle of Prince Bismarck's; the train passed
quite close to it. Then a short halt was made at
Bergedorf. Women in curious attire came up to the
carriages offering flowers and fruits. The boy was
told that these were Vierländer women. "What a
strange world it is," thought Eduard; "what wonderful things I shall see when I get to distant lands!"

At last the train stopped beneath a huge vaulted
roof; it was the Hamburg station.

Every one hurried towards the way out, and the stream of human beings carried Eduard out too. On getting outside, the boy stood for a moment in doubt as to which way he should go, but soon discovered the words Hofer's Hotel written in large letters on a fine-looking building. Now he knew what to do, and walked bravely onwards. He did as he had been told to do, and turned off to the left ; after a short walk he reached a market place where Vierländer men and women, in their peculiar dress, were selling vegetables. He had never seen such people in Berlin.

He asked his way to the harbour and got an answer ; but although he listened attentively the answer was utterly unintelligible to him. Latin he had learnt, but did not know anything about Low German. Was his journey round the world going to present unexpected difficulties after all ? No, no. Only boldly forward. And, trusting to luck, on he went.

He crossed bridges that led across narrow canals where men were pushing heavily laden barges slowly forwards. On both sides of the canal gabled houses rose straight out of the water. He asked if this was the harbour. "No, thur be the Fleeth," was the answer, and Eduard was as wise as before.

At last, however, he gained his object ; he came in sight of the tops of masts, the lower parts of the ships were hidden from view by a long low building. The gateway was open, and as no one interfered he walked in. There lay numbers of ships of all sizes, such as he had never seen before. And huge steam cranes stretched out their iron arms ; boxes, bales, and sacks were fastened to the chains, and the cranes raised their burdens, turned, and again slowly laid their prey down, just like rational creatures. As far as his eyes could see, these strange machines were at work unloading the ships; sturdy-looking men stood ready to receive the bales, and piled them up into endless heaps. He asked one of them whether this was the harbour. This is the quay, was the reply, the harbour is further on. Keep to the right and across the bridge yonder, and you will see it right in front of you.

There was the harbour. His heart beat fast at the unexpected sight. Numberless masts rose out of the water like a very forest. The vessels lay close alongside of one another; and upon the narrow channels of water not occupied by ships, quick little boats and swift little steam-tugs kept plying to and fro. Slowly he went on his way, his eyes steadfastly fixed upon the floating city. How vast it was! How immense.

Gradually, however, hunger began to make itself felt. The boy walked into a sailor's tavern and asked for breakfast. What he got was good : a large cup of coffee, black bread, and fresh butter. All this was much better than in Berlin. At a side table were sitting some sailors, one of whom was addressed as "captain." The boy thought to himself : "I wonder whether he could make use of me as a cabin boy? I will ask him. Boldly out with it !"

The sailor, at first, did not seem to understand what the boy wanted. When he did make out what the boy's wish was, he said : "So you want to go to sea ? Have you got your father's consent?" Eduard was silent. "Or your guardian's ?" continued the man.— "No," muttered the boy.—"Then go home again, my boy, that's the best thing you can do."

Greatly disappointed, Eduard left the tavern. "Home !" He couldn't possibly go home now. His watch and the books he had sold alone made that impossible. He would probably find some other captain more kindly disposed towards him. There were so many ships !

Not quite so hopeful as before, Eduard sauntered away along by the harbour. Where could he find the right sort of captain ? He had fancied that all he would need to do was to go on board some ship, state his wish, in order at once joyfully to obtain the work he wanted. But there lay the ships out on the water, and he was on land ! After a while he resolved to speak to a sailor. Accident led him to address an Englishman, who did not even condescend to look at him, and the boy's endeavour to obtain advice failed utterly. This discouraged him very much.

The harbour now offered him but little pleasure, so he turned aside into a road that led up hill. On reaching the top he found people sitting on benches under the shade of trees, and he determined to rest here himself.

From this hill he had a view down upon the proud river Elbe, away into the blue distance beyond the opposite bank, and down upon the busy life of the town immediately below him. One large steamer seemed just to be starting, majestically it ploughed its way through the water, away towards the great ocean. Smaller steamers, sailing ships, and boats of all kinds were coming in and going out ; how was it he could not obtain a place in any one of them ? His longing to be off somewhere became greater than ever, and he could scarcely endure to look at the view before him. A feeling of restlessness drove him onwards.

Without knowing where the road led to, he walked on, and soon it seemed to him that the way was well chosen, for he came to a very pleasant looking place, with a number of booths of every description and sights worth seeing. He was asked to go and look at a menagerie. That he could not resist. A merry-go-round, too, was a thing not to be despised. What could there be better for him to do than to have a ride on a lion? Hamburg was assuredly a magnificent town! After he had more rides on the merry-go-round than ever before in his life, he turned into a refreshment room to have something to eat. His savings were, it is true, rapidly dwindling away, but a cocoanut he must have, and a few shells. They were being sold in the streets, arranged in tempting rows on trundles.

Later in the afternoon the place became more lively still, a puppet show was given, a bear was made to perform its antics; the theatre in the square was opened; on all sides wonderful things were to be seen, and great numbers of people flocked together. Eduard no longer thought about captains.

Then, however, night set in. The crowds dispersed. Every one went off home. Where was he to go to? His purse was empty; his day's enjoyment had run away with every farthing he possessed.

Perhaps he might yet find the man he wanted at the harbour. He set off down the avenue by which he fancied he had come in the morning. Straight ahead, he could not fail to come to the Elbe.

Had he missed his way? There seemed no end to the avenue. On and on he went, then stood still: "I never was here before! Where can I have got to? Never mind! Boldly forward!"

Was not that the river gleaming over there? It must be the harbour! A few paces more, and again he stood still. In front of him glistened a large expanse of water; the moon and stars were reflected in it, and the gas lamps along the shores glimmered in the water in long streaks of light. Beyond, the houses rose like a dark wall, and towers rose up higher still into the dark sky.

"I will stay here," he whispered to himself; "over yonder, among the shrubs, I can find shelter."

He soon found what he wanted. A bench offered him a resting place.

He sat down, and gazed out over a second and larger sheet of water that lay there as if asleep. The boy, however, could not sleep; he felt so alone in that strange place, so forsaken.

He was very cold too, for the night was chilly, and he was hungry as well. The hours seemed endlessly long. When the clocks in the towers struck the hours, and the sounds reverberated through the night, he would count them, and heard how the one clock began first and the others followed. From time to time long-drawn weird sounds reached him, like fearful moans of anguish. These were the eerie sounds of the fog-signals from the steamers leaving the harbour; they seemed like the wailings of some terrible sorrow, as of farewell tears and the loud moanings of homesickness, and as they came across the waste through the silent night, they found an echo in the boy's desolate heart.

How gladly he would now have been back in Berlin.

He wondered whether he could get back on foot? He fancied that he could find his way. But the reception that awaited him at home, and the jeers of his school-fellows! He clenched his hands: "I will not go back."

Finally he was overcome by weariness, but after a short sleep the sky began to brighten, and he was awakened by the chilly breath of early morning. Eduard was shivering, and the feeling of hunger became more and more unbearable. He searched his pockets, but could not find any stray coin. There was the cocoa-nut, however—he had forgotten it ! How was he to get at the tasty kernel, and the milk which the savages lived upon? Fortunately, on the previous afternoon he had bought a knife, and this would prove useful now. Eagerly he set about peeling off the fibres. What a difficult piece of work ! He managed it at last, however, but his forehead was wet with perspiration before he had removed all the tough mass. The next thing to be done was to open the hard shell; but his knife made no impression upon it, and always slipped off, however much he tried to prevent it. Then he tried to break it on a stone, but found he hadn't sufficient strength, the nut remained persistently whole. A cunning thought struck him : " I'll sell the nut and buy bread with what I get for it." He could quench his thirst with water from the Alster, and the largest of the foreign shells would make a capital scoop. Savages, no doubt, did this too; but where were the savages? And where was he? He threw his shell away in the river when he had finished with it. His adventurous spirit seemed to be vanishing.

Meanwhile the town had become full of life; swift steamboats kept passing under the broad arches of the bridges, near which Eduard had spent the night; railway trains were running over them, tramcars, too, and other vehicles. Foot-passengers were taking healthy exercise in the prettily laid out boulevards, and business men were hurrying citywards. Eduard, too, determined to seek his fortune in this famous mercantile city.

He offered his cocoa-nut to the passers-by, but they had clearly no great desire to buy it ; most of them, too, seemed to have no time to stop even. To the boy it seemed as if all the Hamburg people were in a furious hurry. A little way off, however, stood a man who did not appear to be taking part in the universal race; perhaps he might be persuaded to buy the nut. He would go and tell the man how hungry he was.

The gentleman did not refuse to listen to the boy; on the contrary, he enquired sympathetically as to where he had come from, and where he was going, and in a few minutes had succeeded in winning Eduard's confidence. In fact, Eduard even summoned up courage to ask him whether he knew any captain who needed a cabin boy. The gentleman answered that this might perhaps be managed. "Give me your hand, my boy, I will take you to one." Who could be happier than Eduard at that moment!

The gentleman was inquisitive, that could not be denied. He wanted to know where Eduard had spent the night. "In the open air," answered the boy, with hesitation.—"Have you got no more money?"—"I've nothing but this nut."—"And you are hungry?"—"Very."—"You'll get something to eat very soon. Have a little patience."

This comforting prospect absorbed Eduard's whole attention, but still he did notice that some of the people hurrying stopped for a moment and looked at him in a curious way, some smiled in a sneering kind of manner, others seemed to pity him. And the gentleman was meanwhile holding his hand so peculiarly tight. "Where are we going?" Eduard asked doubtfully.—"Here we are already," replied his companion. They had halted in front of a large, plain-looking building of a somewhat unpleasant appearance. The gentleman pulled a bell-handle, and the heavy door opened and closed behind them at once. In the same manner they passed a second iron gateway.

"Here, I bring you a runaway," said the friendly-

looking gentleman, and leading Eduard into a room
where he had to answer a number of questions. He
confessed everything—everything. "If you have spoken
the truth you will be kept here but a short time; we
shall write to your father."—"Oh, don't, don't!" en-
treated poor Eduard.—"There's no other way, my boy;
and now come, we have comfortable quarters for you
here. Sleeping in the open air is not good for any
one." The inspector gave him a sign, and without any
resistance, Eduard followed him into a large airy passage, with yellow-coloured walls, and thence up a broad
staircase. Here the official opened a barred doorway
that led into a corridor, on the one side of which was
the room which Eduard was told he was to occupy. It
was lofty and clean, but the iron bars in front of the
window gave the room a desperately unhomelike appearance. "Over there on the wall are the rules which
you will have to observe. When any one of the officials
come in, you are to stand up and to remain respectful-
ly standing while he is in the room. The orders for
the day must be punctually attended to, and any in-
jury done to the room will be punished. You can
write to your relatives, and I would advise you to do
so. First of all you shall have some breakfast, after
that you will have some work given you."

The door closed, and was then locked and barred.

Eduard was left alone. Utterly crushed, he threw
himself upon the bed. His wilfulness was broken,
and repentance came over him. Bitter repentance.

An official brought him a basin of steaming soup,
with a slice of bread ; never had anything tasted better to him, not even at home when on festive occasions
some extra good dish was generally prepared. A
basket, too, was brought to him containing pieces of
tarred rope, which he was told to fray out till it

became oakum. He was expressly warned to be diligent.

So Eduard had set to work picking oakum. While his hands were busy his thoughts flew hither and thither. They took him to Berlin, where he had never been required to work all day long. How free he had been there, comparatively! Why had he left home? How well off he had been there! When school was over he had been allowed to go out for a country walk. His parents had taken him wherever they went. With his father he had gone out butterfly-hunting, even on that day—he suddenly stopped in his work, and stared blankly in front of him. He fancied he saw a boy standing by him on a pier, and then suddenly disappear. Eduard gave a low cry, and covered his face with his hands. He was horrified at himself.

But from the basket arose a peculiar smell of tar, which again brought up before his mind the Hamburg harbour, and this renewed in him the desire to sail out into the wide world with a fresh breeze. The sight of the water and ships had bewitched him, and he felt he should never again be content away from them.

Two days afterwards his father came to fetch him. Eduard listened submissively to all his father's reproaches. One request only did he make: not to be sent back to the High School.

"What is to become of you, if you will not study?" said the father.

"I want to be a sailor."

13

If ever a preacher in the wilderness prophesied rightly, it was Schiller, when he made his classic quotation : "Yet with the powers of fate, no eternal bond can e'er be made." These words were to come true in my own case, although, certainly, I do not know how, or where, I ever made a compact with the eternal powers. I have always striven to do my duty, and to be just and orderly, but this is no longer possible in life, the wickedness of mankind is too great.

The investigations concerning the robbery at Dr. Wrenzchen's house had been concluded, and had led to no further result than that a safety chain and a new lock were put on his front door. The Police-lieutenant's wife told me that the robbery had been done according to the usual method of house-breakers, and Dr. Wrenzchen had no choice but to submit to the loss of his silver. I advised him to ask a somewhat higher fee from his patients, so as gradually to recover his loss, but this he refused to do ; so now they take their meals with plated goods, which is in keeping with their candlesticks.

The cook gave notice that she wished to leave, and to my great relief, they did not persuade her to remain, especially as the girl gave as her reason for wishing to leave, that she did not mean on every occasion to be pulled up by the mother-in-law, and that, moreover, she meant to show that lady that there was justice to be had in Berlin. Dr. Wrenzchen tried to persuade the girl to be reasonable, but her answer was that she had been called "a low cheat," and that she wasn't likely to forget that.

I myself doubted whether she could have accused

me of using such words ; yet Dr. Wrenzchen declared
he had heard her say something of the kind, amid
other invectives, and he came round to ask me to offer
the girl some compensation in money, so as to induce
her not to make any further fuss—"Do you mean to
think that I would eat humble pie for that wretched
creature ?" I answered, indignantly ; "if I were to do
that, it would seem as if I acknowledged myself in the
wrong."—"Do as you please, dear mother-in-law, but
as the girl was acquitted of the charge of conniving
. . . ."—"She's nevertheless far from being innocent
in my eyes."—"I would advise you to withdraw your
accusations."—"I shall not demean myself by any such
act of submission ; it would be an unheard-of proceeding for her to bring an action against me. It's perfectly impossible !"

It proved, however, to be perfectly possible. One
morning after Carl had gone to his business, a letter
was handed in for me, a larger one than I had ever received in my life before, and its very outward appearance, the very look of the envelope made me suspect
some terrible communication. With trembling hands
I subscribed my name to the paper the postman had
handed in for a receipt, and then I opened the letter.
Inside were the words : Concerning the case of the
private action presented by Maria Johann Band,
spinster, against Frau Wilhelmine Buchholz for abusive language. I could not read a word more. The
letters I could see, of course, but could not make the
slightest sense out of them, they so danced before my
eyes. This alone seemed clear, I was summoned to
appear in court.

There was no help for it, I had to go to Carl, and
yet when I stood before the office door with the letter
in my hand, I hadn't the courage to enter. I took

hold of the bell, and then let go again ; I again took hold of it, but felt I did not dare to ring. Carl had, as yet, no idea what a disgrace was hanging over our heads, and that a public accusation had been brought against his hitherto blameless wife. But, of course, I could not stand there for ever. I opened the door gently and tottered up to his desk. " Carl," said I, timidly, " do read this extraordinary document—it is —it has—I can't understand it." Carl read the paper, and his face assumed a stern expression. " This is vexatious," he exclaimed, " more than vexatious! There are nine charges."—" Nine ?" I cried out in amazement, interrupting him.—" Yes, nine several points ; they are mentioned singly ; there, you can read it yourself."—" Carl, the girl's impertinence surpasses belief ; I merely said that she ought to have taken more care."—" Wilhelmine, you quite forgot yourself that day in your anger."—" I said no more than I had a right to."—" That will be proved when the case is investigated ! "—" Carl, need it come to that ? "—" Well, perhaps it may be settled without your appearing at court. Before the case is investigated an attempt might be made to settle things amicably. You will have to admit having done wrong, pay the girl some small compensation, and there's an end of it. Are you prepared to do this ? "—" Yes," I sighed.—" Don't be down-hearted, Wilhelmine, and do not worry unnecessarily ; but now, old wife, you must leave me, business is very brisk, and I have a good deal to attend to."

Not to be down-hearted is easily enough prescribed but not so easily managed. After that legal document entered our house, my life was nothing but trouble and anxiety ; I felt as if a guillotine were perpetually hanging over my head, and I could hardly swallow my food. I could not get rid of the thought that Carl merely pretended to regard the matter lightly, so as to conceal the terrible truth from me. One afternoon, therefore, I went to Uncle Fritz, who is very far from being Carl's equal in kindness and consideration, and hence I hoped to learn the true state of affairs from him. When he had read the document, he said: "Wilhelmine, the case is ticklish. You swore at the girl, and she must feel pretty sure of her case, for she has as witnesses the two policemen who were present, also Herr Greve and his wife, and Dr. Wrenzchen."— "The Doctor against me?"—"It says so here. He can, of course, refuse to stand as a witness, being your son-in-law, but who can tell but that he may not choose to let slip a lovely opportunity of having his revenge, once in a way. You have had your fling upon him often enough!"—"Fritz, do you really think him capable of such malice?"—"He might possibly be mollified if you were to promise for ever to renounce your guardianship over him as a mother-in-law."—"I will promise no such thing," I answered angrily; "now what I want you to tell me is whether you think it likely I shall lose the case."—"You may depend upon it, you will; for remember the policemen with their official oaths are against you." I had often heard of the danger of official oaths, and that if they were against one, one's case might be considered as good as lost. "Fritz," said I, "what am I to do? What can I do?" —"The one means of escape you had, you have unfortunately neglected."—"I will make up for it now, Fritz; only tell me what I can do. Most assuredly I will make up for it now."—"Well, you might maintain that you were not sober on the occasion, and plead extenuating circumstances."

That was too much even for my patience. "Oh—

you—you—cannibal!" I exclaimed, flaring up; "do you hold nothing in reverence, not even your own sister's tribulation?"—"Come now, Wilhelmine, don't go on like that. Probably they'll let you off on some of the smaller points, and there's little likelihood of your being sent to prison."—"Carl quite expects the matter can be settled by accommodation, what do you think?"—"If your accuser had consulted a right sort of solicitor, possibly there might have been a reconciliation; but she seems to have got hold of a left-handed sort of individual; he will probably persuade her to carry matters to extremities to suit his own purposes."—"But how will the girl be able to pay the cost of it all?"—"The party that loses has to fork out; you'll have to do that, my dear."—"Oh, how mean, how shameful! To accuse me thus at my own expense. Is that justice?"—"The law precisely."—"Then the law ought to be upset. Fritz, I shall never survive this disgrace! My days are numbered!"—"Console yourself, Wilhelmine; every second respectable person has been punished once in their lives. Cheer up!"

"Is that your advice too!" I exclaimed bitterly; "if you've nothing better to say, you may as well go and get yourself embalmed! I spurn such advice as your 'cheer up'!" Winged with wrath, I left Uncle Fritz, and blamed myself for having exposed myself to being the wretched target of his taunts. Yet, when people lose their heads, they are apt to act senselessly.

Uncle Fritz proved right about the girl's having engaged a pettifogging lawyer: he was a regular cut-throatish, left-handed kind of individual, so that the attempt at accommodation ended in smoke.

A few days afterwards came another legal document, demanding my personal attendance at the Royal

Magisterial Bench in Old Moabit, No. 11, 12, on Saturday at ten in the morning, Room 29. And even though I might have thought of running off somewhere, what would have been the use? The Court threatened, in case of an undefended non-attendance, to bring up the person by force; and rather than grant to my · mortal enemy the sight of my being dragged in before the tribunal between two policemen, I resolved to appear of my own free will, although my nervous system had completely collapsed.

The upsets to my spirit were never ending. Heaven only knows how people came to know that a public action had been brought against me; among our own acquaintances, the one subject of conversation seemed to be the approaching trial. Would it, otherwise, ever have occurred to Frau Krause to come and launch out her condolences to me!—"You know now yourself what it is to be persecuted by fate, although you never showed us much sympathy when our Eduard was the victim."—"Please, remember," said I, "that your troubles were of your own making; I do not think it right of you to make fate responsible for your boy's mischievous tricks, or to imagine that fate induced him to run off from home."—"Eduard has such a love for investigation."—"It's always in the wrong direction, however; he never thinks of investigating Latin, for instance."—"He has chosen his profession now, and won't require Latin any more, and it's but a dead language after all."—"May I ask for what profession he has shown a preference? A confectioner's, perhaps, so that he can stuff himself!" Frau Krause smiled in a sneering way, and said: "Eduard means to be a naval captain, and some day he'll have a handsome salary; and captains are always very much respected. He has bought himself a compass already,

and up in our loft he climbs about the clothes-lines in
an astonishing way. A captain's post is the very thing
for him."—" He's not one yet, nor do I believe he'll ever
be one," said I.—"That's because you always think
you know better than other people," she replied hotly;
" but your wisdom is not infallible, else you'd never
have spoken punishable words, I should think." –
" That's a subject you do not understand," I answered
excitedly. " Very possibly," she replied snappishly;
" I only repeat what people say, I would not venture to
pronounce judgment, for we've never yet had anything
to do with law courts." When she had gone, I said
to Betti : " She has shown herself in her true colours.
Never let her come in again; my unhappiness is too
great for such hyenas to come and feed upon it."

The following day I had a visit of condolence from
the Police-lieutenant's wife.—" Much depends upon
the judge," she said, " and the way you represent the
case. What are you going to wear?"—"Simple
black," I replied.—" The less showy the better, in
order that the distinction between you and the plaintiff
is not made to appear too great, and your higher
social position is not considered an aggravating cir-
cumstance. The coat of arms you were having embroidered will not be of much use to you in the dock."
—" I never thought it would. When we keep our carriage I meant to have it painted on the door."—"And
I only meant to say that ancestors and emblems will
not be of much use if you are found guilty; such disgrace sticks to one for ever."—" We've not got that
length, however," I remarked.—" But you will surely
admit that my husband knows something about such
matters, and he said that the thunder-bolt was as good
as down upon you already. Yet we are above all pre-
judice, and I may add that I do not see any reason

why we need give up our old intercourse with you."
In the eyes of the world, therefore, I was already con-
demned. I felt positive the Police-lieutenant's wife
would never again drive us out to the Grunewald.
Henceforth I should be one of the outcasts of society.

This thought robbed me of all the sustaining power
I had left. After this I could do nothing but creep
about the house if I wanted exercise. I hadn't even
the heart to sit at the window, for it seemed to me as
if the passers-by pointed at me with their fingers.
Betti tried to persuade me that this was a delusion;
but one day, with my own eyes, I saw Frau Heimreich
walking up and down the other side of the street with
her eldest girl, and casting spiteful glances up at our
windows. That was intolerable to me. I became
more and more of a sufferer, and it was, at last, so impossible for me to get any sleep that Carl had to have
a bed made up in another room as his snoring disturbed me so.

Frau Bergfeldt, too, paid me a visit; however, I cannot say that she cheered me up, rather the contrary.—
" Good gracious, Frau Buchholz, to think of your
having got into the frying-pan ! But why need you
have struck about you so with the poker ? "—" What
sort of speech is that to me ? " said I indignantly.—
" Well, it's said you belaboured the girl so, that a
bloody head was the end of it. So you'll certainly get
six months."—" There's not a word about blows in the
matter; how can you talk such rubbish ? "—" I'm sorry
for you, Frau Buchholz, but that's what the whole
town is saying; yet wherever I go I take your part, and
say: 'It's a mercy the cook had a thick skull, else
they'd have had to drag Frau Buchholz on to the scaf-
fold.' "—" You call that defending me ? "—" Yes, I do;
weren't you always considerate to me . . . . when Emil

.... so it would really have grieved me were you to be put on the rack, or anything of that sort."—"Good God, protect and defend me! I can swear I never raised a finger against that girl."—"Frau Buchholz, don't perjure yourself. How could the report have got about, if there was no truth in it? Maybe the hand in which you held the poker slipped a bit; at all events, that's what I would say to the judge, if I had flown into the ditch as you have done."

"Frau Bergfeldt," I said in a weak voice, "I cannot bear any more of this kind of talk, I would rather be left alone."—"I'm in no hurry," she replied, and kept sitting there, and continued: "It's only at first that you'll feel it, afterwards people will forget it; one has to forget things. Yet what's in a person the rain'll never wash off."—And in this style on she rattled. It was not till I was miserable both in body and mind that she went. "Betti," I said, with a last effort, "I'm not at home to any one after this, not even though the Great Mogul himself should come running up on hands and feet."

One exception had to be made, however, for Frau Helbich, the tavern-keeper's little wife, would not take a refusal, saying she had an important communication to make. She had heard all the particulars. The *skat* players had discussed the case to and fro, so that she had become quite interested in it. "Frau Buchholz, it is to you that we owe all our good fortune, and we are deeply grieved to think of you in this dreadful trouble. It's enough to turn the heart in one's body. And I am positive that you are innocent."—"That I am, Frau Helbich; but no one will believe me."—"I believe you," she replied briskly, "and that's the reason I have come here. I want to tell you that whatever may be said, the point about the dog is suspicious."—

" It's of no use saying that; the lawyers sifted the whole matter thoroughly."—" Well, but every one knows that the first thing burglars do is to poison a watch-dog."—" That doesn't tally, for the dog in the present case was a mere lap-dog."—" That's just it; watch-dogs are outside the house, and might be got at; the dog at Dr. Wrenzchen's was a lap-dog and was inside the house. Now, who gave it the poison? That can only have been done by some one in the house."— " That doesn't tally either, Frau Helbich, for the dog wasn't poisoned, but throttled by having a string tied round its neck. You are mistaken."—" One of our regular midday customers, a student, was positive about this. He said, that if the poisoning could be proved, you would be acquitted."—" Frau Helbich, I am much obliged to you for your sympathy, but the lawyers are likely to know more than a sudent and we others who haven't experience in such things. Everything was, of course, thoroughly examined, and nothing was found."—" And I had so firmly hoped to render you some assistance, Frau Buchholz; you cannot think how grieved I am for you." With this she began to cry, and I cried too. Of all the attacks upon me this was the most affecting one; we both felt so utterly helpless. And the following day the case was to be inquired into.

I was so downcast that I went to bed before it was dark. My Carl came and sat down beside me. He spoke very kindly, and said that I oughtn't to make matters out worse than they were ; but then he hadn't had the many visits of condolence that I had had, " Try and get a good rest," he said, " and do not worry so. When the trial is over, you will quickly recover your old cheerful spirits. You look so snug and comfortable lying there, now do try and be happier."—

"Carl," said I, "you surely don't want me to purr like an old tom cat? Even though I could, I wouldn't, in my present state of misery."

Betti came in and asked me if I cared to have anything to eat. "You might bring me a little milk and biscuit later, just enough to support life, but I'm in no hurry."

I had no appetite. Terrible thoughts seemed to have driven hunger away. In a kind of doze, I dreamed of prisons and executions, and although I tried to persuade myself that this was only the result of Frau Bergfeldt's chatter, as soon as I closed my eyes, the same horrors again rose up before me.

Carl came in to wish me good-night, and Betti insisted upon my taking some food. To please her, I forced myself to take something, and found it tasted better than I had expected. The milk was freshly boiled, and the biscuits crisp. The child also brought me in a night-lamp, which she lighted, and after having kissed me, she too went away. Again I was alone.

Before me was the last night of my hitherto irreproachable life; henceforth I might never again be able to look any one straight in the face. And if I saw two persons nudging each other, and jeering, I should always suspect that it was about me. And if people should look at me rather doubtfully, might they not be quite right in doing so? Could I ever again condemn a fellow-creature without saying to myself, "You have yourself sat in the dock, and have had sentence passed upon you." Then a proverb crossed my mind, Heaven only knows where I had heard it: "Woe, woe to thee, Wilhelmine! the righteous will turn their faces from thee." Sleep was what I wanted; oh, how glad I should have been to get to sleep.

I lay first on one side, then on the other, and just as I
fancied I was about to drop off to sleep, I became con-
scious that there were crumbs of biscuit in the bed,
and my slightest movement made them irritate and
annoy me. Every moment, too, there seemed to be
more, till the torture became unbearable, and there
was nothing for it but to get out of my bed and re-
make it. This, I felt, did my spirits some good, but
of sleep there was none to be got.

I lay and tumbled about as much as before. There!
Wasn't that a crumb again? Yes, to be sure it was.
A few must have got on to the mat in front of the bed,
and stuck to my bare feet. And truly the whole lot of
them seemed to have come marching back again. I
felt desperate, and cried in my vexation and helpless-
ness. By what small means God can punish us—a
single crumb of biscuit is enough! I knew that I had
not always done what I ought to have done, but had I
really deserved such terrible chastisement? It was
long since I had folded my hands in prayer; now they
found their way to each other of their own accord, and
I humbly prayed for help. Then I crept out of bed a
second time, and remade it with the utmost care. When
I lay down again a gentle peacefulness seemed to have
come over me, and sleep came with it.

Early in the morning I was awoke by noises in the
adjoining room, which was being cleaned. I heard
Doris opening the window, moving the chairs, and
putting all into order; Betti too was up. She came to
me quietly, thinking I might still be asleep, and was
surprised to find me awake. "Child," said I, "with
trouble in one's heart, and crumbs in the bed, there's
not much sleep to be got." She helped me to dress.
Later Uncle Fritz came in, he was to be my witness;
and, slow as the clock seemed to go, at last it became

time for us to drive off. The last act of the tragedy was about to begin.

Never had I even seen the law court in the Moabit district, and now I was actually to appear as a delinquent there myself. "Over yonder is the court-yard where the executions take place," said Uncle Fritz, pointing to a wall. I shuddered. But Fritz continued : "As long as Krauts keeps on his white gloves he's not dangerous ; when, however, he begins to take them off . . . ." Carl here forbade Fritz to talk in that manner, and gave me his arm. He asked for Room 29 ; we were shown the way, and at the end of a long corridor, we reached the antechamber. Some people were sitting there on benches, others were standing about. Herr Greve and his wife were there, also some policemen and Dr. Wrenzchen. And that wretch of a girl too I caught sight of, she who was the cause of all this worry and trouble.

The door of Room 29 was then opened, and a lawyer's clerk read out from some document the words : "Ahrens *versus* Meier." Several persons who had been waiting went in, and after a short time came out again. They had come to terms at the last moment, fortunate people that they were ! "Band *versus* Buchholz" was then called out. My brain was all in a whirl. I tottered forward, my limbs feeling as heavy as though I had been walking in dough, and more like a dead toad than a human being. A small square place like a box was pointed out to me, and there I sat down upon a chair. This was the barricade to separate the accused person from the rest of the world.

At a raised table covered with green baize, sat the magistrate, his assessors, and the clerk of the law court. The latter read out the indictment. On the right sat the plaintiff, in the middle were the witnesses who had been called, and behind them sat the public, a barrier separating them from those taking part in the proceedings.

Everything that I was supposed to have said was then read out. And, oh! how offensive the words sounded in the mouth of a man who knew nothing about the matter and who hadn't even been present. And this I had to listen to! The magistrate, looking very solemn in his black gown, then said that the statements of the witnesses would have to be confirmed on oath, and after giving them an impressive exhortation, they were asked to retire. When they had left the room the magistrate addressed the plaintiff and me, and gave us to understand that it would be much the wiser plan for us to settle the matter quietly by accommodation, and asked if we would agree to this.

"Yes," I sighed.

"No," said the girl ; she had her reputation as well as grander folks, and didn't mean to be trodden upon.

No such thing had been done, replied the magistrate, and moreover, what advantage would it be to her to persist in the punishment of a lady of irreproachable character? Frau Buchholz was willing to retract her words, and to bear the costs of the trial, whereby her honour would be perfectly satisfied.

The servant-girl maintained that she would not agree to this. Frau Buchholz should be imprisoned and pay 3000 marks damages, that's what she demanded. The magistrate thereupon replied in a very severe tone of voice : "You have nothing whatever to demand."—Her solicitor had told her she had.—Then she must have employed a very strange kind of solic-

itor.—He knew as much and more than other lawyers.
—That remains to be proved.

As there was thus no likelihood of any amicable set-
tlement to the dispute, the proceedings commenced.
Dr. Wrenzchen was called in as the first witness. The
magistrate drew his attention to the fact that, as a rel-
ative of the defendant, he had a right to decline to
stand as a witness. "What will he do?" thought I.
"Will he take his revenge, and thus bring about an
eternal breach between us?"

The Doctor said he should refrain from making any
statement, but wished to express his surprise at the impudence of the plaintiff in claiming him as a witness
on her side. This remark of the Doctor's seemed to
me the greatest possible proof of nobility of soul, and
never shall I forget it.

Herr Greve was then called. He was asked his age,
his social position and his religion, and had to swear
not to conceal any fact, or to add anything to what he
knew, but to speak nothing but the truth, so help him
God. While saying these words, he had to raise his
right hand, and all those present had to take part in it
by standing up.

The magistrate then asked Herr Greve whether he
had heard the defendant call the plaintiff a low cheat
on the evening in question. Herr Greve replied that
he could not remember to have heard exactly those
words. He was further asked whether he had heard
the defendant say of the plaintiff that she was a brazen-
faced huzzy. Herr Greve replied that he did remember this, it having struck him as strange that a lady of
culture should have used such an expression, and he
attributed it to her being in a state of great excitement.

"Mr. Magistrate and gentlemen, I can furnish a true
statement of what happened, and beg you to hear what

my witness has to say. That girl always behaved in a rude and impertinent manner towards me." Uncle Fritz was then called. As he came forward the abusive creature exclaimed: "That's a witness I won't have."—"The admissibility of a witness is determined by the court," said the presiding judge.--"I don't care, I won't agree to it. He once wanted to pinch my cheek, and I gave him a crack across his fingers for his impudence; since then he has always been against me."—"I hope no one will credit me with such bad taste," was Uncle Fritz's reply. The magistrate, however, requested him to be serious, and to keep to the point in question.

Uncle Fritz then stated that the plaintiff, without any obvious reason, had invariably acted in a reprehensible way towards the defendant. This had struck him whenever they had met at Dr. Wrenzchen's house. "What reason had the defendant given you for acting thus?" asked the magistrate.—"Well, I can't bear any one coming peering into my pans when I'm cooking," was her reply.

"Of course not!" I exclaimed; "you didn't want an experienced housewife noticing how her daughter was being cheated at every turn and corner! How was it that, notwithstanding their simple life, their expenses were so enormously high, in spite of my daughter keeping an exact account of her outlays. Dr. Wrenzchen himself was becoming suspicious. Her object, Mr. Magistrate, was probably to frighten me out of the house, in order that she might prey upon an inexperienced mistress, and that, too, was probably her reason for making the fuss about the crawfish.—"That's a new insult to be added to the list," the servant-girl called out in a loud voice. Dr. Wrenzchen, however, supported my statement.

The most ticklish point in the case was, however, still to come. The magistrate observed : there seems to have been provocation for the alleged insulting speeches, but the defendant's assertion that the plaintiff made common cause with the burglars, might be likely seriously to injure the plaintiff's prospects in life.

The policemen were then examined, and stated that I had certainly declared that the provisions had been purchased specially with a view to the robbers, and also that I had undoubtedly maintained that the plaintiff had had a hand in the matter. This they affirmed on oath, as did also Herr Greve and his wife.

A buzzing sound seemed to fill my head. I felt as if the floor of the room had suddenly became aslant, and that I should not be able to prevent myself slipping down. I nervously clutched hold of the chair, as I saw the magistrate rise and say to his colleagues, "You will agree, I think, that some mild form of punishment is all that is necessary."

In the vain hope that some assistance might yet be forthcoming, my eyes wandered anxiously round the room ; and I caught sight of one face upon which all the compassion in the world seemed to be concentrated, and tearful eyes that looked at me in a dumb but beseeching way. I understood the beseeching look of plump little Frau Helbich, and, as if by some inspiration, I rose up and said aloud, "Mr. Magistrate and gentlemen, I should like to ask my accuser one more question ; let her confess why she poisoned the dog."

A pin might have been heard fall, the silence was so great. The servant-girl changed colour, and seemed to lose her self-possession. "I never could endure the animal," she burst out. "So you admit having poi-

soned the dog?" said the magistrate, giving her a penetrating look. " It was simply to provoke me that they
called the creature Maffi Pamph, because my name
was Marie Band."—"And was that sufficient reason
for your despatching the animal?"—" I couldn't stand
the name any longer."—"Mr. Magistrate," I interposed, "Maffi is merely an abbreviation of Möppel,
and Uncle Fritz added the name Pamph."—"Really,"
exclaimed the girl, casting a malicious glance at me,
" there's no one here likely to believe that!"—"But
it's true," I replied; "everything that's soft and pet-
like begins with an ' M,' surely no one would ever
think of taking a crocodile or a rattlesnake on to their
lap to stroke and fondle, and call either of them
' Mousie,' or ' minikin.' " The magistrate interrupted
me by saying, "I must ask you not to wander from
the point. I understand you had absolutely no intention of annoying the plaintiff by giving the little dog
the name of Maffi Pamph?" .

"Goodness me, of course not! We never meant
anybody by that name. That's a mere shuffling excuse of the girl's. The dog barked at every one in a
horrid way; Herr Greve can tell you that, and it was
very necessary on the evening of the robbery that it
should be quiet, else Herr Greve might have come
down, alarmed by the noise, and have surprised the
burglars. Moreover, the dog would never let her touch
it, so that she must have put the poison in its food."—
" That's a downright lie!" exclaimed the girl. " You
have, however, already half admitted having given the
animal poison," said the magistrate, turning to the
plaintiff; "it would be well for you to tell us the
whole truth. Your denying matters will not help
you; science has means of proving whether the dog
was poisoned or not."—"Well then, I did give it a
powder to be rid of it."

" And where did you get the powder?"—" From an apothecary."—" Which apothecary?"—"I don't remember now."—" Try and recollect, it would be strange if you had forgotten that."—" I didn't fetch it myself."—" Who was it did you the favour to fetch it?"—" An acquaintance."—" What was the name of this acquaintance of yours?"—"It was a man I didn't know, I asked him."—" Again one of the great unknown!" said the magistrate, and thereupon made a sign to the clerk, and whispered some words into his ear. The clerk left the room and returned with a policeman. The magistrate rose and said, " There are grave reasons for thinking that the plaintiff, Marie Band, spinster, was implicated in the robbery at the house of Dr. Wrenzchen; she must be placed under arrest, and the case enquired into again. The private charge against Frau Buchholz may be considered as withdrawn."

Marie Band had to follow the policeman and be put in prison—I was free!

We left Room 29, to make way for others. It is to be hoped that this is the first and last time I shall ever have to enter it. But should it happen that I have again to attend, I shall be able to assume a very different tone, for I have now become quite familiar with legal phraseology.

When we got outside and could breathe freely again, as if some great danger had been evaded, little Frau Helbich came waddling up to me, offering her heartfelt congratulations. "Frau Helbich," said I, " you have a very penetrating insight into things; what would have become of me had you not been in Court?" —" All happened as it was ordained," she replied; " our heavenly Father rendered you assistance, He put all things right in His own good time." I pressed her hand, and said : "And you were the seraph He sent to help me!" We understood each other.

A few days afterwards I received another legal document, announcing that the private charge against me was withdrawn.

The girl had been induced to make a full confession. Maffi Pamph was sent, like any human being, in a sealed box to a chemist, who turned him inside out, and found an inconceivable amount of poison in him, which the greedy creature must have consumed. The rope round its neck was a case of mere sham fighting, as was also the girl's being tied hand and foot and gagged. It also came out that the accomplice had, at first, addressed the girl as a lover, and that she had entrapped him partly by love and partly by stolen goods. Of course if she had not been thievishly inclined by nature, she would never have acted thus. I had always maintained that she was a good-for-nothing, and Maffi had evidently thought the same; precisely as in the case of Professor Paulsen's dog Polli, that couldn't stand the smell of the old woman who was arrested afterwards. Clever dogs sometimes have a supernatural kind of wisdom.

As the police managed to discover all this, they afterwards set a watch upon the girl's doings of an evening, and thus obtained further clues, and got on to the track of the burglars; and Dr. Wrenzchen was beginning to hope he might yet recover his silver.

All the troubles and worries of the past weeks, however, seemed to have attacked my very bones; and a tinge of grey had become visible in my Carl's hair. My dearest, best beloved Carl, had your anxiety on my account really been so great! Shall I ever be able to repay you, with all my love!

MY SON-IN-LAW.

THERE was no use fighting against it or trying to deceive myself; the experiences of the past weeks had completely damped my spirits, and however great an effort I might make to smile—like the jaws exhibited in dentists' windows—my temper became daily more and more disagreeable, and my complexion yellowish-grey in colour. After the trial I had most firmly resolved that in future I would always be most gentle and submissive towards Carl, but I found it absolutely impossible to control my irritable nature; and so I made his life as well as Betti's miserable, without really wishing to do so. A fly on the wall would annoy me, and I would scold them both for it. Frau Helbich one day brought me a small bottle of home-made Swedish essence of life, but it upset my stomach, and I took a perfect dislike to it. In fact, I was ill.

When matters had become so bad that they could scarcely have been worse, I, at last, did what Carl had wanted me to do at the outset, and agreed to consult Dr. Wrenzchen. "He was so extremely considerate towards you at the time of the trial," said Carl, " that I am sure you can place full confidence in him." But I was myself afraid that the Doctor might prescribe me some medicine to harm me. My mind had become so darkened. At last, however, he had to be called in.

The Doctor examined me very carefully, and then said that the only thing that would restore me to health was a prolonged stay at Carlsbad and use of the waters. " No, no," was my reply, " I'll not submit to be sent so far off as that What will become of things here, if I am away ? "— " You can leave us here with a perfectly easy mind, and the sooner you start, the better," replied the Doctor.—"So that I may be out of your way, I suppose!"—"In order that your complaint may not become chronic."—"But what if Emmi should require her mother?"—"If you want to get well for your own and for your children's sake, follow my orders; as your son-in-law I will consider you as far as possible; as your medical man, however, I have no consideration, and must ask you to obey me. Either you go off to Carlsbad in a few days, or I send you a notary that you may make your will."

Those words of his had effect The necessary preparations were soon made, and after a miserably sad "good-bye," Betti and I got into the train. How could I know whether I might not be hurrying straight into the jaws of death, instead of to Carlsbad?

Betti had at once determined to accompany me, and put up with my unintentional ill-humour in the most forbearing way. She had, indeed, become perfectly changed since sorrow had entered into her life. Formerly there had always been slamming of doors, and tossing of heads if anything was not to her liking; now she went about so quietly one scarcely heard her, and was all loving devotion. I had had sorrow enough myself; but in my case it had all turned to gall and bitterness. I wondered whether Carlsbad could be of any use to me! I doubted it.

And I had reason for thinking this; for during the first days of my stay, there was not a trace of any improvement. I drank the waters as prescribed, and early of a morning was one of the many hundreds who promenaded past the Marktbrunnen, having my white glass filled with the warm beverage by one of the water damsels. Afterwards a walk had to be taken, and coffee was had somewhere in the open air. Betti thought Carlsbad lovely, shut in as it is by woods and hills, and the river Tepel flowing by. It did not appear thus to me—in fact, nothing seemed pleasant or pleasing.

I gave free utterance to my thoughts of the uselessness of my stay in Carlsbad, and one morning said in rather a loud voice to Betti, who never left my side : "It is really a most unwarrantable thing that I should be forced to stay here, when I'm getting yellower and yellower, in place of getting better."—"That's just as it should be," said an old gentleman, who happened to be walking behind us ; "it is very often the case that a complaint gets worse at first, but this is a sure sign that the waters are having effect ; in a week you will speak very differently."—"Indeed !" said I, incredulously.—"You may depend upon what I say, for I have been to Carlsbad regularly for thirty years, and know the waters. My name is Leopold Freund ; I come from Breslau, and I shall be happy to assist you in any way with my advice." I then introduced myself and Betti to him, and we went together to drink the waters. Suddenly Herr Freund said : "Why does your daughter not take the waters, her complexion is rather yellow ?"—"Why not !" I exclaimed, "because the yellow tint you notice comes from the lining of her parasol !"—"Oh ! I see now, of course, it is merely the reflection," said Herr Freund, smiling ; "it is curious how apt one is to fancy people need the waters when one raves about Carlsbad as I do."

As Herr Freund is a living proof of the curative properties of the water, the Carlsbaders look upon him as belonging to the place ; and he is certainly well acquainted with its peculiarities ; this was proved by the effect the waters soon began to have upon me, which became more evident day by day.

The orange colour of my complexion and my irritability began gradually to disappear. My pleasure in life returned, and my eyes were able more and more to enjoy the beauties of nature. Upon first coming to Carlsbad, we had never walked further than to the *Freundschafts-Saal*, or to Pupp's, or the Post-office, but we now gradually began to visit places at a greater distance, and scarcely a day passed without Herr Freund telling us of some new excursion to make. He never accompanied us, as he preferred taking his exercise sitting.

One day he had recommended us to walk across the *Otto's Höhe* and the *Ewige-Leben* as far as the *Berg-Wirthshaus.* We followed his advice, and climbed bravely up the hills. The view was charming and the woods delightful, and we roamed far in amongst its green twilight, till at last we found we had quite lost our way.

"Let us rest here a little, and then we will turn back," said I to Betti; but she replied: "You had better sit down upon this rock, and I'll go and try to find the right path."

What a nice fuss I should have made about this, if it had happened when I first came to Carlsbad, thought I to myself, and kept thinking how marvellous the rock-bouillon was, coming as it did boiling out of the earth, and not only able to clear one's body, but one's spirits too. In a very short time I should be able to fly into Carl's arms a perfectly new creature, as if I had come fresh from Spindler's establishment. Every week there came a letter from Berlin, where things seemed to be going on perfectly smoothly. I found letter-writing somewhat a trouble, which was owing to the waters probably, for they have no effect upon one's mental activity.

Just as I was beginning to fidget about Betti's not coming back, I saw her approaching in the company of an elderly gentleman in a straw hat, with eye-glasses, a white beard, and leaning heavily on his stick in walking. He told us he was suffering from gout, but would be happy to show us our way. We then told him how we had come to be in the woods, where-upon he remarked that there were theoretical as well as practical pedestrians, but that the latter were not worth much when one's potential powers refused to render their services.

Companions in affliction soon strike up an acquaint-ance, and before we had reached the *Berg-Wirthshaus*, he was calling me Mamma Buchholz, and Betti had to call him Papa Michaelsen. He had come to Carls-bad from North Germany to do penance for having indulged too freely in red wine. Upon a remark from me that he shouldn't touch red wine if it disagreed with him, he replied, " Poor Papa Michaelsen couldn't be so cruel as that ! "

" What do you mean ? " I asked. His answer was that if one didn't take pity upon oneself, no one else was likely to do so, and everybody ought to know how much pity they needed. " Are you so much in need of it ? " I asked. " That depends upon circumstances and upon the vintages," was his reply.

We got upon very friendly terms with Herr Michael-sen, for he knew the country about, and became the more willing to join us in our walks the more the waters helped him in his legs.

We all three went one day to the *Hans-Heiling* rocks, which are said to be a wedding party in a state of petrifaction ; also to the Aberg, and on our way there passed the black Madonna which is fixed upon a tree, as a holy image. Poor Papa Michaelsen did not think much of the black Madonna. However, he explained several mineralogical circumstances to us, and the structure of the earth's crust, subjects that Betti understood tolerably well. I made the observation that it was very strange that the waters were supposed to be most effectual when taken in the place itself—as my son-in-law had maintained—and asked him whether he thought scientific men (who seemed able to concoct anything) might not try and open a spring of Carlsbad waters in Berlin? He replied: "There are two kinds of chemists, useless ones and mischievous ones. Both parties have done harm enough already. The one set teach people how to adulterate things, and the others carry out their instructions."

When Papa Michaelsen was not able to join us in our walks, we quite missed him, and the old gentleman thought so much of Betti that he persuaded us to remain a week longer than we had intended. He said his cure would then be at an end, and that we could travel back together. I gave my consent to this the more readily as Herr Freund told me that he considered an after-cure very beneficial in most cases. I do wish now that I had gone home as we had originally proposed doing.

One morning when we were sitting peaceably at Pupp's having our coffee, Betti with hers quite of the wrong sort, more than half milk, we two old people with the right sort as prescribed, with no more cream than sensible folks have ever been in the habit of taking since the days of Adam—all of a sudden up comes a telegraph boy with a message for me; he was accompanied by the maidservant from our lodgings, so as to make sure of finding me. I opened the envelope and read:

" A healthy boy, brown eyes, exactly like his father.
Is to be called Franz.   Mother doing extremely well.
                                                "WRENZCHEN."

This news came most unexpectedly.   Papa Michaelsen congratulated me very heartily, and at once gave
Betti her new title of 'Auntie.   However, I could not
join in any such merriment, for I kept thinking who
there was to superintend matters if I was not there.
A further surprise awaited me, however.   Scarcely
half an hour later a second telegram was put into my
hands, with the words :

" A healthy boy, blue eyes, exactly like his mother,
is to be called Fritz.   The father as well as can be
expected !   WRENZCHEN."

" Herr Michaelsen," said I, " I do not know whether
my reason has been affected by the use of the waters,
or what can have happened.   First I'm told it's a boy
with brown eyes, and now suddenly it's said they're
blue."

" It does sometimes happen that eyes change in
colour," said Papa Michaelsen learnedly ; " and according to Darwin it is a case of atavism, but the short
space of time in which it has occurred in your grand-
son's case renders it a matter of extreme interest.   It
will certainly have to be reported to one of our scientific periodicals."

" But why should the child first be called Franz and
then Fritz?   At first it's said to be like the father, and
then like the mother !   This is surely a human impos-
sibility."

Papa Michaelsen gave me a very sly look across the
top of his spectacles and said : " What if there should
be two ?"

" Two ! " I exclaimed, " when they're only prepared

for one. No, that's nonsense! But I seem to under-stand it now; those words, 'the father is as well as can be expected,' are Uncle Fritz's and nobody else's; all I can say is that such jokes are not very likely to assist my cure."

Next day, however, there came a letter from Carl, an-nouncing the arrival of the twins. He said Uncle Fritz had, no doubt, sent me a telegram, and told me that the children were to be called Franz and Fritz. Dr. Wrenzchen had no time to telegraph himself, and had begged Uncle Fritz to send a message. Emmi was doing very well and was supremely happy.

Franz and Fritz! The names were not at all to my liking. The one might, of course, be called Franz after the Doctor, but would it not have been much better to have called the second Wilhelm, in honour of the Emperor as well as of myself? A nice family ours will become with a number of persons with the same name. It will end in their having all to be called by their full names, else there will be a per-petual confusion. I could perfectly well foresee the muddle there would be in days to come.

Carl's letter had a postscript. "Franz was born during the last hour of the last day in May; Fritz during the first hour of the first day in June. What do you say to that?"

"That, of course, it's natural enough there should be endless stupidity when I'm not by to see to things myself," I exclaimed excitedly. "The poor children! Not a soul will take them to be twins when their birthdays come to be celebrated one in May and the other in June. And then to think of their names, Franz and Fritz. They might as well have been called *Max and Moritz*." *

* The title of a very popular children's story-book, by Wilhelm Busch.

"Herr Michaelsen," said I, "we must be off home at once; I cannot be spared a moment longer from Berlin. If I delay I shouldn't wonder if the Brandenberg Gate were moved from its place, such unheard of things are going on there."

"Is the river Spree on fire then?"

"If it were no more than that! But only think, my son-in-law has absolutely got no one to keep an eye upon him!"

UNCLE FRITZ.

OUR return home was a most joyful one, and when I pressed my first kiss on the little foreheads of my two baby grandsons, truly everything did seem to me perfectly as it should be; for, after all, the two little creatures would not be made responsible for their father, and what is more, too, he will henceforth have to play a subordinate part, as everything naturally will have to turn upon the children. I at once took up my post at the Doctor's house, during the daytime. He objected to this at first, but I asked him: "Do you mean to kill your wife and babes?" That made him give in. And how well he was cared for himself, now that I could look after things in the kitchen without fear of the cook! After a week's time he regularly beamed on me.

Emmi recovered day by day. And under my superintendence she got only what was good for her and strengthened her. If ever there was a Cerberus, it was I, during those days in and out of my daughter's room. One thing that did displease me was that, in place of having cradles, little immovable bedsteads had been ordered. Emmi told me Franz had said that rocking was not considered hygienic, and was apt to make children stupid. "Wasn't he himself brought up in the old fashion," said I, "and he has come to be a doctor! Well, maybe, if it hadn't been for the rocking he got as an infant, he'd long since have been a member of the Medical Council."

Many a time I wished for a cradle, especially for little Franz, who was of a crying disposition, and Grandmamma Buchholz had to carry him about in her arms till he was quiet. I told the Doctor that such fits had never occurred in our family, and that the bad habit must have been transmitted from his side. His reply was: "Dear mother-in-law, it's only external."

Of an evening Carl or Uncle Fritz would come and fetch me, and, at the same time, enquire how things were progressing. On the Thursday evening Dr. Wrenzchen did not go out, much to my surprise. Something did, it is true, seem amiss with him all day long, and as evening approached I could distinctly see how much the usual evening gathering seemed to be upon his mind.

Towards 8 o'clock Dr. Paber called to ask him whether they might expect him at the Medical Society later? I begged Dr. Paber to remain with us to supper, saying that I would send the servant round with a message, and that Dr. Wrenzchen would so enjoy a quiet talk with him here. Dr. Paber agreed to remain, and as there was cold roast veal I prepared an extra good salad of meat with mayonnaise and capers, and decorated it with sliced radishes and not too much gherkin; they thought it delicious. When supper was over I had a large jug of special brew fetched, and my son-in-law thereupon said, "If we could have a

game of *skat* here, I wouldn't change places with a
king !" Dr. Paber looked at me and said kindly:
" How would it be for you to try a hand for once, dear
Frau Buchholz ? "—" What ! I play *skat !* " I exclaimed.
"You must know something about this entertaining
game, from having watched others play it," continued
Dr. Paber. "Come, dear mother-in-law, don't be a
silly," said the Doctor. "I do not think I have any
talent for card-playing," said I. But the Doctor had
already fetched the boards, and the two gentlemen
commenced to teach me the rules with great patience,
without, however, letting me into the secret of some of
the best moves, as I found out afterwards, when Uncle
Fritz appeared and he sat down beside me and helped
me. And actually I won the game. Dr. Paber declared
he had never seen a lady with more natural talent for
the game.

So there I sat with the three gentlemen, who gave
themselves every conceivable trouble to lead another
fellow-creature astray into the vice of card-playing;
and, as I must unfortunately admit, they succeeded
very well, for it was nearly midnight before we had
finished. My gains I divided into two portions, one
for Franz and the other for Fritz. I had become somewhat reconciled to the name Fritz, when Dr. Wrenzchen assured me that their first daughter should be
called Wilhelmine. He knows how fond I am of acting as godmother.

Meanwhile, however, I had a promise as regards
Uncle Fritz to fulfil. All my troubles and my having
to go to Carlsbad had, of course, interfered with my
proposed visit to Lingen. But I had now taken the
necessary steps. I had asked him beforehand, "Fritz,
are you as determined as ever about Erica ?"—"I'm
more wedded than ever," was his reply. "Very well,

then," said I, "we shall see if something doesn't happen now."

And something did happen. The old grandmother wrote and stated that it was her intention to come to Berlin, in order to see whether a person could live in that sinful Babylon without being carried away by the devil. "Wilhelmine, how did you manage to accomplish this?" asked Uncle Fritz. "By means of a very moralising letter," said I. "You told me what a strict hand she kept over the money matters . . . . so I told her how much you made a year, and that there was no need for her to undo her purse-strings. And as to Erica's spiritual welfare, I took the liberty of informing her that we had a dean in our family nearly four hundred years old, and that that was surely a sufficient guarantee for her. She swallowed that." Uncle Fritz seized hold of me and danced me round and round till I was out of breath, exclaiming, "Wilhelmine, you are a regular brick!"

The grandmother had intended to take up her abode at the Krauses, but I considered it wisest to have her at our house; and it was a good thing we managed this, for she was stubborn beyond all conception. She declared that it would be wicked to give her consent to Erica's engagement, without further ado, and to decide upon mere outward appearances. It was not till she had fumbled all through Uncle Fritz's books that she condescended to say that perhaps some day something might come of the engagement. It was a mercy she did not hear Uncle Fritz express his thoughts aloud.

I so constantly drove her into a corner, that at last she hadn't any sort of excuse to make to me, and always wound up with the remark that Berlin was a godless place. "You'd better look a little about Ber-

lin before you judge from mere outward appearances,"
I retorted. She could see from the papers what went
on there. "That's mere chatter."—"Oh, no!" was
her reply.

I made Betti take my place at the Doctor's house,
and determined to plunge into the stream myself. It
was clear the grandmother must be shown something
of Berlin. Uncle Fritz arranged to let us have a carriage from Beskow's whenever we wanted one, and
thereupon we went first to one place and then to another. "People seem to be for ever holding high festival in Berlin," said the old lady one day. "Not at
all," I answered; "the many people you see in the
streets are all going to and fro on some business or
other. They rest when the week comes to an end, and
amuse themselves of a Sunday." The old lady insisted
upon seeing everything that was to be seen, and was,
moreover, so active, one might have fancied she had
been resting all these years, merely in order to begin
trudging all round Berlin now. And I had to go with
her, wherever she went.

She wanted one day to go to the top of the Victory
Column, but was obliged to give up that, for I told
her it was not the correct thing for elderly ladies to
do. To have had to drag myself up there for her ben-
efit was just asking a little too much. And the appetite
all this gave her; the most indigestible things agreed
with her. She would chop away at them on her plate
until she got them all into the smallest morsels. Having to go about with her everywhere was a perfect
penance, for, of course, the object I had in view was
a marriage, and not mere sight-seeing. What did we
care about the rubbish that Schliemann had dug up?
My own cooks have broken me more dishes than the
few fragments he has to show. She wanted to see the

Ruhmes Halle, the Library, the Picture Gallery, in fact, every place she had ever heard or read about, till it got a little too much for us, and we were sick of the perpetual gadding about. No one in Berlin ever thinks of going to such places more than once a year, and not even that sometimes. So when she expressed a wish to see the Egyptian Museum, Uncle Fritz declared that it was shut, as the mummies were being fed. So we got out of that luckily.

It was clear that the old lady was day by day getting to like Berlin better, but her obstinacy about the engagement was not one whit the less, and the day of her departure was already fixed without matters having advanced a step. But she little knew Uncle Fritz.

On the afternoon previous to her departure, we drove out to Potsdam. It was a hot and sultry day; a light haze lay hovering over the water, and before we had reached Babelsberg, there were peals of thunder, and lightnings flashed across the sky, which was rapidly becoming overcast. The wind rose and swept through the tree tops. "We're going to have a bad thunderstorm," said the man at the gates, as we passed into the entrance to the castle. He had prophesied rightly; before long the flashes of lightning and peals of thunder came crashing down together, and the rain poured in torrents. Darkness had come in the daytime, and with the darkness, fear came upon us, and even affected the grandmother. She stuck her fingers into her ears, so as not to hear the thunder, and closed her eyes tightly not to see the dazzling flashes of light; hence she did not see that at the back of the vestibule a pale and terrified girl was clinging to the fearless man beside her, and that he had put his arm round her. And when the sky became a blaze of fire, and the darkened passage was filled with dazzling light, I saw a blissful smile on the man's face. It was Uncle Fritz.

When the storm abated, we were shown over the castle by the keeper. We were allowed to see the Emperor's study and his bedroom. There was no velvet or silk, or any gold ornamentation about those rooms. A narrow camp-bedstead served the Emperor as his resting place at night; but it seemed to me as if some high and holy power had spread its wings over the place, and this called forth a feeling of reverence.

The keeper also showed us a walking-stick which the Emperor, in 1884, had cut from a tree in the park. It is the one he is in the habit of using when wandering out early of a morning among the shady avenues of trees. At those times all the little birds from far and near come flying to him and tell the Emperor many a thing no one else knows. People who are wise and just, understand the language of birds, to them nothing in the world is mean.

The weather had cleared up. The storm was followed by cheerful sunshine—as war is by peace—and woods, water, and meadows lay before us in all their splendour.

We had to proceed on our way, however, and passed the estate of Prince Wilhelm and his consort, the Princess Victoria from sea-encircled Schleswig-Holstein. We saw the children playing in the distance; they were the great-grandchildren of the Emperor, the sweet young buds of the Hohenzollern tree. On Prince Bismarck's birthday the parents and children planted an oak all by themselves. The little ones helped with their little wheelbarrows and spades, and when the tree was planted they watered the earth round it with pure fresh water. When the boys grow to be men, the oak will give them shade.

With Sans Souci the grandmother was enchanted, and she may look far and wide before she sees anything like it again. When entering near the obelisk, and coming in sight of the fountain with its marble gods and goddesses, at the end of a broad wooded walk, the effect is always bewitching, every time one sees it. And then the castle up on the terrace. It was there that old King Frederick lived, and it was there he died. The clock stopped when his heart beat its last, and has never gone since. The old grandmother thought all this wonderfully interesting, and our guide was called upon to answer such endless questions, one might have fancied the man could have but little breath left in his body; we could scarcely get her to come away. She even asked to be allowed to see the kitchens. Of history itself she has no notion whatever. And all the while she would not let Erica leave her side.

With Sans Souci the old lady had indeed been amazed, but she had to open her eyes wider still when she saw Charlottenhof. There the roses grew almost to the top of the Greek House, and the lilies joined the roses in shedding a delicious perfume around. A little further off quantities of light and dark roses were blooming in all their beauty, one more beautiful than the other. Was it to be wondered at that Uncle Fritz went into that garden of roses, and that he drew his white rose to him and kissed her warmly without the grandmother's leave? There was no help for it now. "Are you going to persist in your stubbornness for ever?" I asked.

Had the thunderstorm softened her a little, or was it that she remembered that her own life had once had its day of roses, of which nothing now was left but the prickly thorns? She was silent. I beckoned to the two, and when they came up to us, I gave the old grand-

mother a convenient poke in the back, by way of en-
couragement. And, behold! out she came with "Yes."

As we walked on, we elderly ladies discussed the
practical part of the matter, and I maintained that
there must be no delay about the wedding; this gave
rise to a dispute. "My brother has waited long
enough," I said decisively; "the marriage must take
place in a few weeks' time. What do you say, Fritz?"
—"The sooner the better," he replied. The grandmother demurred, saying it was contrary to all custom.
"That doesn't matter," said I.—"It is necessary to
consider what people will say," she replied. "Have
done with all this talk," said I; "what's decided is
decided."—"It is not," she said.—"It is," said I. For
Fritz's and Erica's sake I gave in; but if those two
hadn't come in between me and the old lady, I do believe we should have ended with *pooh* and *bah!*

Erica all of a sudden stood still, frightened, for shot
after shot was being fired close to us. "What's that?"
she asked in alarm.—"The soldiers are practising
shooting," replied Fritz.—"What for?" she asked.—
"To protect the hearth and home which will one day
be yours and mine, darling," he said kindly; "and no
enemy will ever come to destroy the roses and lilies in
that home of ours." She looked up at him and said in
a whisper, "What should I be without you, dearest?"

In the evening we celebrated the betrothal. Fritz
was inexpressibly merry, and his merriment even affected the old grandmother, who drank "good healths"
with him three times over, and even took more than
was good for her. Next day she had to keep in bed
till midday, and, owing to a severe headache, had to
live upon soda and Juliushall water. When I reproached Uncle Fritz for not having been more careful of her, he said drily, "Wilhelmine, it's no fault of

mine ! It's hard, but just ! Why hasn't she taken more care to accustom herself to spirituous drinks ? "

HOW THEY ALL ARE.

FRANZ and Fritz are daily getting prettier, and although they might perfectly well be baptized now, the Doctor insists upon waiting till Uncle Fritz is back from his wedding trip, for Fritz is to stand godfather to the youngest child, and my Carl is to hold the elder boy.

Emmi is no longer alone when her husband is out upon his rounds, and does not miss him on the Thursday evenings when he is with his friends. And I must confess there is something magnetic about the game of *skat*, for it both attracts and rivets one's interest. When we go to the Wrenzchens of an evening, and Betti and Emmi are sitting on the sofa working (double work being necessary for Franz and Fritz), my husband, the Doctor and I have a game, and it's delightful as long as the twins keep quiet. But scarcely are the words uttered : " Franz is crying," or " Fritz is screaming," than my son-in-law flies off to the bedroom. If he had invested in cradles these disturbances might be less frequent, even though not altogether avoided, and our games would not invariably be interrupted at the most exciting points. Of course, afterwards no one knows whose turn it is to play, and disputes arise.

This coming winter—when we are all together again —I mean to arrange evening meetings for *skat* at our house. Dr. Paber has already consented to be one of the party ; and the Police-lieutenant too, a highly cultivated man, is also a very good player, so there is no fear of our failing from want of forces, especially as we can calculate upon Uncle Fritz too. Herr Kleines also could be invited in case of need ; and it would do him good to have some intercourse with family life.

Uncle Fritz's wedding coat is being made, and he is counting the days when he will be off to Lingen. He intends to go straight from there to the Rhine with his young wife. He has declined my offer for Carl and me to go to Lingen with him. He says that he is afraid that a lot of relatives may merely increase the sentimentality and tearfulness of the day, and that he wants the day to be as merry a one as possible, so he is only going to take his friend Theodor Mann with him as his best man ; for even in the midst of serious matters this friend of his never neglects to give fun its due, and then too his talent for singing and playing brings cheerfulness wherever he goes, and cheerfulness is ever a welcome guest. When Fritz told me that he meant also to invite two or three of the drinking members of his choral society, The Whooping Cough, and the merriest of the lot, I could not help saying : "Fritz, of what good will they be in Lingen?"—"An amusement to the natives merely," said he. I warned him and said, "You surely know the grandmother's character !"—"A veritable old Charybdis !" he exclaimed, laughing, "she revels in water, which is no doubt good for children, and can't be said to harm big people either, and tastes good too."—"Well, my idea is that Erica is not likely to get much fun out of any such arrangement of yours." So he dropped it.

Many changes have taken place in the Weigelts' affairs. Their folly in wishing to appear grander than

they really were, and in running into debt for the sake
of their wealthy connections, was bitterly atoned for.
Emil's sudden death not only altogether upset the
plans they had been weaving for future days, but
showed them, to their horror, that they had calmly
been walking up to the brink of a precipice while
looking up at the clouds instead of down at their feet.

But Augusta did not lose courage ; she again set
about making feather flowers, and was glad to get her
old customers. She also induced her husband to give
up his politics, and managed this more by the example
of her own indomitable industry than by talking.
Fortunately Herr Weigelt had not become riveted to
those political principles of his, and was led back to
the right path. Moreover, old Herr Bergfeldt was no
longer able of an evening to audit the books of tradespeople and others, as he had formerly done ; so Augusta persuaded her husband to undertake this work
and to divide the money with her father. When Weigelt no longer associated with those political criminals
he gradually became ashamed of his former credulity,
and came to see that he hadn't exactly a talent for
governing.

Frau Bergfeldt had taken to letting out her rooms :
hitherto she has been rather unfortunate with the occupants of her furnished apartments. The first of
them made off suddenly with all his goods and chattels,
without having paid for his last month's residence, in
addition to other expenses she had incurred for him
and a couple of crowns he had borrowed. Her present
lodger, she is afraid, may act in a similar way, so she
has run a tape through the keyhole, and fastened the
one end to the young man's box. At night she ties the
other end round her own wrist, so that she may be
sure to wake if he tries to make off on the sly. In

October they are going to move to the Dorotheen
Strasse, where rooms are more easily let, owing to its
being near the university; it is a favourite quarter
with the students, into whose receptive minds the Professors strew the seeds of learning which have then to
be well watered with beer, both morning and evening,
in order to flourish. It did occur to me to recommend
Herr Kleines to them, but luckily, upon second
thoughts, I knew this would not do, as they were not
at all suited to each other. Herr Kleines is much the
same as he was, and Herr Pfeiffer, too, has not become
any steadier.

One day lately I went to see Augusta Weigelt, and
found her dressed in mourning, but busily at work.
She was not, however, manufacturing flowers, but was
stitching away at some very curious-looking material.
" Whatever's that going to be when finished?" I asked.
" A little dress for our boy."—" But tell me, where
ever did you get that extraordinary stuff with its odd
stripes; I never saw any material like it in my life."
Augusta's face coloured up. " Well, why should I not
tell you!" she answered after a little; " it's the covering of those blue silk umbrellas the money-lender
made us take. The things were so peculiar-looking,
we couldn't have used them in the streets. But now
I've got what I wanted," she added, sadly, but smiling
too; " my little ones will both have silk frocks!"

" Better days will come," said I encouragingly.—
" Let us hope so," replied Augusta; " but they won't
come of themselves. So I've taken to using my old
magic words again: 'dalli, dalli,' I keep saying to
myself from morning to.night, and if only we live a
little more sparingly than we actually need to, for a
couple of years, we shall get out of all our difficulties.
Oh, Frau Buchholz, how gladly I would starve, if only

my poor brother were still alive." She began to cry. "You must forget that trouble."—"Never," she replied; "he was such a good, kind fellow."—"But you have got your children, you must live wholly for them now."

"I mean to teach them to work and to be content," said Augusta; "everything else in life is vanity; we have learned that." Thereupon she took up her needle again and stitched away eagerly, as if she had had to make up for lost time.

Suddenly she stopped and listened. "There is father," she said, and hurried to meet old Herr Bergfeldt, who was slowly hobbling up the stairs. He had become quite grey-headed, and looked an old man. "Where is Emil?" he asked, after having bowed to me in an unconscious kind of way.

Augusta went out and fetched little Franz. "There you are, Emil, dear boy!" said the old man in a fondling tone of voice, as the child came climbing up on to his knee. Augusta whispered to me: "He doesn't always remember things properly, and often speaks to our little Franz as if he were Emil. We never take any notice." She had ordered coffee for her old father, for he always came in about this time to play with the boy.

With a trembling hand the old man offered the boy a drink out of his cup, and said: "Do you like it, Emil?" "It's jolly!" replied the boy. That was just what Emil used to say, when he was that age,

Little Franz, after having a little coffee, brought out all his treasures, all sorts of broken rubbish, but the grandfather knew the name of every single piece as well as the boy. They had a headless doll that they called the Princess Vallera, and one remaining ninepin was the gunner Snip Snap; these two lived together in a box that I seemed to recognise. And to be sure it was the little organ. "Is the music all out of it already?" I asked. "It did not last long," was her answer; "it could not stand the inspections made into its interior. I myself am glad that there is now an end to its squeaking, it reminded me too much of my high-flown ideas. For keeping the children's toys in, it is most useful."

In watching the mischievous little pickle carefully, it did seem to me as if he were a little like what Emil had been, especially when brimful of life and spirits; however, the resemblance was not so great for any one to have mistaken them as old Herr Bergfeldt did.

Augusta begged me to take no notice of them, as they were always happier by themselves; this I was the more willing to do as I saw clearly that the old man had himself become a child again. When the boy became more and more uproarious, Augusta called him to come and have his frock tried on. It fitted him very nicely, but the little fellow looked like a blue zebra in it. He did not mind that, however, and stalked about singing:

> "Culture will make us free,
> Strike down the doors for me."

"What in the world is that verse the child has got hold of?" I asked. "It's a stupid old rhyme my husband used to sing when he attended his political club. The words are really: 'Culture will make us free, down with tyranny'—Franz, will you be quiet!" The old man called the boy to him, and I got up to leave. "Do not be discouraged about things," said I, in bidding Augusta good-bye. Her reply was, "I live in hope and trust."

As the Krauses are related to Erica, we unfortunately cannot prevent them becoming a little more intimate with us, but I mean to set up a landmark, to fix the boundary beyond which they shall not be allowed to trespass.

Eduard does really seem to be improving since he left the High School, and is no longer plagued with those dead languages. And, after all, studying may not suit every one ; and perhaps many do not know this till they are in the midst of it, and it is too late to begin a new occupation, either because they're too grown-up, or have become spoiled for other work. In the latter case they will be crippled for life, like Herr Weigelt, and their work will be neither one thing nor another.

If Eduard becomes a sailor, that will be far more rational than for him to be for ever at sixes and sevens with himself and the world; for any one who has been forced to take up some special profession, will have perpetually to act against his own inclination. And yet any other occupations will then rarely be genteel enough; nowadays everybody wants to be at the top of the tree, and to go up by balloon.

Herr Krause has a much greater influence upon the boy than formerly, and told me that if Eduard only keeps as he is, he hopes the boy may yet turn out a useful member of society. This could not but be welcome news to us, owing to our connection with the family; and I do not mean to make any further ado about his once having had to work the treadmill; for I have learned by experience how easily one may be drawn from the quietest of existences into publicity, and have an action brought against one.

What really occurred to make Eduard give up that habit of disobedience which the mother had always encouraged in him, no one here has ever managed to

find out, because old Herr Krause is absolutely silent
on the point. When I asked Frau Krause one day
what Eduard had really been about in Hamburg, she
told me some story about robbers, which she may
believe herself, but can hardly expect other people to believe. She said the boy wanted so much to see the great
ocean, and when he got to Hamburg the captain of
some slave ship got hold of him, and kept him a pris-
oner between the decks for two whole days, probably
intending to carry him off to the South Seas. But his
father fortunately found him in the nick of time.
"That was a great mercy," said I; "for if the ship had
started, Herr Krause would, no doubt, have had to
swim after it."

My goodness! the face she made at that.

Uncle Fritz has furnished his house quite nicely for
the time being. Certain things I did find wanting,
when he came and fetched me to have a look at it; but
he told me that he was looking forward to going about
with his young wife and purchasing, by degrees, all
that they might want. I could not but admit that he was
acting wisely in this, for I remember Carl and I had,
at first, to accommodate ourselves to circumstances.

And we fixed upon our wedding present for them, in
accordance with these arrangements; above all things,
we decided to give no more plated goods, but the genuine article. Dr. Wrenzchen was very generous, and
presented them with an ornamental clock; Betti
worked them a sofa cushion; and Fritz's vocal society,
The Whooping Cough, who knew his tastes, sent him
on the evening before his departure for Lingen a
punch-bowl and two dozen glasses; one dozen for use,
the second as a reserve. I gave him, in addition, a
large packet of bonbons and sweets for Erica's younger
brothers and sisters, in order that the poor little things

mightn't be altogether forgotten. "Fritz," said I, "be
sure and write soon and tell us how things go off."—
"If I have time, and manage to get away without
broken bones."—"Be sure to be attentive to the grandmother."—"Didn't we get on famously the last evening
we spent together?"

The train was moving off. I wanted to call out, as
my last words, "Speed away to your happiness, dear
boy," but he was already too far off.

Uncle Fritz was hurrying away towards Lingen, and
as we did not wish his wedding-day to pass without
any celebration, I proposed to avail ourselves of the
fine weather and have an excursion somewhere. "What
do you say, Betti, to our going out to Tegel again?"—
"Tegel!" she replied in a curious tone of voice,—"oh
yes, if you like."

If I liked! Why, Carl and I had long since settled
our plan, which was now about to be carried out. The
plan was my idea; Carl it was who had to see that it
was carried out properly to the minute.

It was afternoon. We had been sitting in the woods
where there was a view across the lake, and as I had
long since determined some day to have a picnic at
this point, a hamper with good things was provided.
Betti was rather monosyllabic; perhaps she was thinking how happy we had all once been in these woods,
which we were to-day trying to enjoy again.

My husband was rather quiet too, for he knew what
was about to occur within the next quarter of an hour,
and did not feel quite sure how things would go. I,
on the other hand, had no doubts whatever, or why
should I have chosen Tegel? The Present was to be
linked with the Past; what lay between was a winter's
day. Where are frost and snow, when the hawthorn
blooms again? Forgotten!

Carl kept taking out his watch, and looked anxiously out on to the lake; then we both saw a boat leave the opposite shore and steer straight across towards the woods where we were sitting. " I wonder if those people are coming to us?" said I, as if I knew something. " It looks like it," said Carl. " You know," he added, "how much I am in want of a partner; the business requires increased support." The boat was coming nearer. " I have found some one in whom I place full confidence, but I wanted to know whether he pleased you both as well." With this he looked at Betti. " My decision will depend upon your judgment. This was my reason for asking him to join us here to-day. Here he is."

The boat came flying onwards, rowed by powerful arms, and at last shot up on to the beach. Betti had jumped up, and stood immovable; she had recognised the two men in the boat, Felix and Max—the two friends.

With quick and elastic steps Herr Felix hurried up to Betti, stretching out both hands towards her, and she, as if in a dream, laid hers in his. " Ah, ha! it's to be 'Buchholz and Son,' after all," said I in a whisper to Cart. He only smiled.

When we returned through the woods, the lovers in front, Carl carrying the hamper, and Herr Max and I as rear guard, I said to him: " Are you satisfied now?"—" Yes," he answered, "most heartily, for my friend is happy."—" And you deserve to become happy, too; I will help you to find as charming a bride as you could wish."

" You are really very good," he replied, "but unfortunately your offer comes a little late; I have found one already."

" Well, I never—you too!" I said, laughing; "now

remember, Frau Buchholz is dying to be introduced to her."

When Betti's engagement was made known, everybody came to offer their congratulations. The Police-lieutenant's wife seemed very much surprised, and said that she supposed as Herr Felix Schmidt was to become a partner, that the marriage was one of convenience more especially. My reply was that convenience had certainly something to do with it.

Wichmann Leuenfels sent Betti his good wishes in rhyme, which amused us very much, for they were quite idiotic. He is at present writing criticisms on every conceivable subject, especially about things he doesn't understand, and is said to have already succeeded in making people pretty well afraid of him.

· Amanda Kulecke came also. "Child," she said to Betti, " you are really to be envied. You are going to marry the man you love. You look the very picture of a happy bride, and he's good-looking, too, that must be confessed." Betti threw her arms round her friend and kissed her.

"It is time that the sons of our country took a look at me," Amanda continued. "One did present himself the other day, it is true, but he didn't take my fancy; I cannot bear small men, and he had a bald head into the bargain." I could never tell whether she meant to be serious or not, or whether she was having a laugh at herself; this much is certain, any one of the many pale-faced fashionable youths of the day she would rather see starve, than move an arm towards them. She is too repellant, in spite of her really excellent heart. It is a pity for the girl.

A few days afterwards we got our first letter from Uncle Fritz, dated from Rüdesheim. " He has lost his reason," I called out. "Carl, just read this nonsense."

16

—"Dear Wilhelm," he wrote, "here we are at the Rhine. It is considerably larger than the Spree. I do not yet know whether its waters are wet, for I haven't tried them. Yesterday I put Erica right on the top of the Lorelei Rock, where she blew a tune upon a golden comb; I, with Baedeker under my arms, sat in a little boat listening to her. This picture was so exceedingly effective that all the steamers stopped and blocked up the river, and police on horseback had to plunge into the Rhine and make them move on. Wilhelm, won't you come to us; we'll give a repetition of the magic scene, and you shall play the accompaniment on an accordion.—UNCLE FRITZ."

"He must have had a sunstroke," I exclaimed. "Carl, what do you think?"—"Wait, there's something on the other side of the page," said Carl, shaking his head. "What is it, Carl? I really feel quite anxious; he has never shown himself as mad as that." Carl read: "Dear Frau Buchholz, would it be possible for you to come here to the Rhine and pay a visit to two supremely happy children, who wish to show you their gratitude for all your love and kindness to them; they want to tell you over and over again how inexpressibly happy they are. We think of you every day; how highly Fritz speaks of you, and how dearly I shall love you. Do come! Oh, do come! How beautiful this world is. Why cannot we have you with us?—Yours, ERICA."

"Do you know, Carl," said I, "when Fritz wants to express any affection for me, he always does exactly the reverse of what an apothecary does with his pills, he puts his sugary stuff inside, and leaves the bitter stuff outside. This much I can see, however, that if ever two human beings were happy on their wedding trip, it's Fritz and Erica."

I could not leave home, however. The preparations for Betti's wedding in the autumn have to be attended to; the twins, too, have claims upon my time, and experience has taught me that everything is apt to get topsy-turvy when I'm away. The wedding is to be a very quiet one; this is Betti's own wish.

Our house will then be big and empty again, as it was when we first came to it. The children are away; we can no longer hear their steps, or the sound of their voices—they have flown away, like birds out of a nest. It has become silent, and we are again alone, my Carl and I—alone, just as in those first days. My bridal wreath was green then; when the elder-tree blooms again, I shall have my silver wreath.

THE BUCHHOLZ FAMILY.

Sketches of Berlin Life.

By JULIUS STINDE.

OPINIONS OF THE PRESS.

From the DEUTSCHE RUNDSCHAU.

"The social grade personified in this middle-class lady is drawn with such perfect truth to nature that it may pass for a photograph. The author indicates clearly and minutely all that goes to make up her moral and intellectual being, the sources from which she drew her culture, by what means and through what causes she attained her views, on what she formed her opinions, and how she maintained the same. Every phase of Berlin middle-class life is treated with exhaustive thoroughness, and its relation to God and to the world, to the State and Society, to marriage, the family, birth and death, are given so truly and vividly that the reader once for all finds out where he is, and the occasional exaggerations and improbabilities do not come into consideration. . . . Karl and Wilhelmine Buchholz, Wrenzchen and Uncle Fritz, the Krauses, Weigelts, and the Police-lieutenant and his wife, are all people who are equal to their parts, and capable of maintaining their position, and know pretty well that a German exists first of all to fulfil his duty, or—to put it in Berlin fashion—that business comes first and pleasure afterwards."—*June*, 1886.

From BLACKWOOD'S MAGAZINE.

"Our author neither theorizes, nor teaches, nor moralizes. From the dense bewildering throng of human actors in the human drama, he has singled out one tiny group for study of an almost scientific accuracy and thoroughness, and has then fused his observations into such a living picture as only a true artist can create. His sketches are vigorous, realistic, and racy; they sparkle with bright fun and joyousness. . . . The book is somewhat difficult to label or pigeon-hole. It is not a novel. A slender thread of story indeed runs through these semi-detached sketches, and upon it are loosely strung a series of highly diversified scenes and situations; but each chapter is a study almost complete in itself. Light and airy though they be on the surface, a great deal of fine painstaking workmanship has gone into Dr. Stinde's volumes. In their homeliness, their truthfulness, their realism, and their elaborate detail, his pictures are of the Dutch school."—*April*, 1886.

By the Author of "How to be Happy Though Married."

"MANNERS MAKYTH MAN."

One vol., 12mo, cloth, - - - **$1.25.**

CONTENTS:

The author of "How to be Happy Though Married," has written his second work in the same bright and entertaining manner that won for his former book such wholesome praise and so large a circle of readers, and the reception that will be accorded his latest work promises to be no less flattering.

For sale by all booksellers, or sent, post-paid, by the publishers,

CHARLES SCRIBNER'S SONS,

743 & 745 Broadway, New York.

POPULAR BOOKS

In Yellow Paper Covers.

CHARLES SCRIBNER'S SONS, - - - - - - PUBLISHERS

THE MARK OF CAIN.
BY ANDREW LANG.
I vol., 12mo, paper, - - - 25 cents.

In this story Mr. Lang shows us again his remarkable literary dexterity. It is a novel of modern life in London, absorbing, full of spirited and original incidents, exciting to the verge of sensationalism. It is one of those fortunate books which hold the reader's interest to the full from the first page to the last.

25th Thousand.

"Nothing Mr. Stevenson has written yet has so strongly impressed us with the versatility of his very original genius."—*London Times.*

STRANGE CASE OF DR. JEKYLL AND MR. HYDE.
BY ROBERT LOUIS STEVENSON.
I vol., 12mo, paper, - - - 25 cents.

"It is a work of incontestable genius. Nothing, in my judgment, by Edgar Allan Poe, to be generous, is to be compared to it; it has all his weird and eerie power, but combined with a graphic realism that immensely heightens the effect. I read it in a four-wheeled cab the other night, by the help of a reading-lamp, as I traveled through miles of snow-bound streets, quite unconscious of the external circumstances of that melancholy journey. What is worth mentioning, because otherwise a good many people will miss it, is that a noble moral underlies the marvelous tale."—JAMES PAYN *in Independent.*

THE DIAMOND LENS
WITH OTHER STORIES.
BY FITZ-JAMES O'BRIEN.
I vol., 12mo, paper, - - - - - 50 cents.

STORIES:

THE DIAMOND LENS.	THE POT OF TULIPS.
THE WONDERSMITH.	THE GOLDEN INGOT.
TOMMATOO.	MY WIFE'S TEMPTER.
MOTHER OF PEARL.	WHAT WAS IT
THE BOHEMIAN.	DUKE HUMPHREY'S DINNER.
THE LOST ROOM.	MILLY DOVE.
THE DRAGON FANG.	

"The stories are the only things in literature to be compared with Poe's work, and if they do not equal it in workmanship, they certainly do not yield to it in originality."—*Philadelphia Record.*

"Nothing more fascinating in their way, and showing better literary workmanship, has of late come to the front in the shape of short stories."—*Toronto Week*

POPULAR BOOKS

In Yellow Paper Covers.

THE LADY, OR THE TIGER?
AND OTHER STORIES.
By FRANK R. STOCKTON.

CONTENTS:

THE LADY, OR THE TIGER?
THE TRANSFERRED GHOST.
THE SPECTRAL MORTGAGE.
OUR ARCHERY CLUB.
THAT SAME OLD 'COON.
HIS WIFE'S DECEASED SISTER.

OUR STORY.
MR. TOLMAN.
ON THE TRAINING OF PARENTS.
OUR FIRE-SCREEN.
A PIECE OF RED CALICO.
EVERY MAN HIS OWN LETTER-WRITER

"Stockton has the knack, perhaps genius would be a better word, of writing in the easiest of colloquial English without descending to the plane of the vulgar or common-place. The very perfection of his work hinders the reader from perceiving at once how good of its kind it is. . . . With the added charm of a most delicate humor—a real humor, mellow, tender, and informed by a singularly quaint and racy fancy—his stories become irresistibly attractive."—*Philadelphia Times.*

THAT LASS O' LOWRIE'S.
By FRANCES HODGSON BURNETT.

"The publication of a story like 'That Lass o' Lowrie's' is a red-letter day in the world of literature."—*New York Herald.*

"We know of no more powerful work from a woman's hand in the English language, not even excepting the best of George Eliot's."—*Boston Transcript.*

"The best original novel that has appeared in this country for many years."—*Philadelphia Press.*

SAXE HOLM S STORIES.

First Series.

DRAXY MILLER'S DOWRY.
THE ELDER'S WIFE.
WHOSE WIFE WAS SHE?

THE ONE-LEGGED DANCERS.
HOW ONE WOMAN KEPT HER HUSBAND.
ESTHER WYNN'S LOVE-LETTERS.

Second Series.

A FOUR-LEAVED CLOVER.
FARMER BASSETT'S ROMANCE.
SUSAN LAWTON'S ESCAPE.

MY TOURMALINE.
JOE HALE'S RED STOCKINGS.

"Whoever is the author, she is certainly entitled to the high credit of writing stories which charm by their sweetness, impress by their power, and hold attention by their originality."—*Albany Argus.*

"The second series of 'Saxe Holm's Stories' well sustains the interest which has made the name of the author a subject of discussion with literary gossips, and won the admiration of intelligent readers for such attractive specimens of pure and wholesome fiction."—*New York Tribune.*

www.ingramcontent.com/pod-product-compliance
Lightning Source LLC
Chambersburg PA
CBHW030802020726
47499CB00006B/1737